BATTLETECH:

A SPLINTER OF HOPE

BY PHILIP A. LEE

AND

THE ANVIL

BY BLAINE LEE PARDOE

BATTLETECH: A SPLINTER OF HOPE and THE ANVIL
Cover art by Florian Mellies
Design by Matt Heerdt & David Kerber

Published by Catalyst Game Labs,
an imprint of InMediaRes Productions, LLC
113 Cherry Street #93897 • Seattle, Washington 98104-2205

CONTENTS

INTRODUCTION
JOHN HELFERS

Welcome to this edition of two very special *BattleTech* stories. The first ones that break brand-new ground in the *BattleTech* universe in more than a decade. Simply put, this isn't your father's Jihad anymore, but an introduction to the next stage of *BattleTech*, both in fiction and the tabletop game.

Truth be told, *BattleTech* has taken a long, winding road to get here. We thought we were close to getting things back up and running with *Embers of War* (The first original *BattleTech* novel in eight years) back in 2015, then with the wonderful exploration of three-plus centuries of 'Mech combat with the threaded anthology *Legacy* last year. But even though we were producing gripping new fiction, the game itself was still stalled...

Until 2017, when Catalyst's Art Director and *uber*-fan Brent Evans settled into the cockpit as the *BattleTech* Line Developer. The past year hasn't been easy, but with the help of a passionate and talented braintrust (and you know who you are), tremendous strides have been made to shake off the rust and dust and get *BattleTech* moving forward again—into a whole new era.

This book, along with the sourcebook *Shattered Fortress*, is the culmination of that first wave of activity, with much more to come on both the fiction and game sides. When Brent first revealed that he was taking over the *BattleTech* line, I was ecstatic, because I knew both of us would do whatever it took to get it back on track again. And a key component of that shared vision would be to have the fiction begin driving the game storyline again, like it had done years ago.

With that goal firmly in mind, I'm very proud to present two very different stories that herald the arrival of this long-awaited new era. "*A Splinter of Hope*" by long-time *BattleTech* editor and writer Philip A. Lee, picks up with the leader of the beleaguered Federated Suns, Prince Julian Davion, embarking on a bold and risky campaign to strike at an age-old enemy for personal and political vengeance. But the Capellans will not relinquish their prize without a fight, and Julian soon finds himself embroiled in intrigue both on and off the battlefield.

The second story is "*The Anvil*" by stalwart *BattleTech* author Blaine Lee Pardoe, a bestselling historical writer in his own right. Blaine brings his understanding of history and military experience to bear on this story of Stephanie Chistu, galaxy commander of the Jade Falcons, and one of the holdouts under Khan Malvina Hazen's brutal Mongol Doctrine. When Chistu is handed a nearly-impossible assignment—not only liberate Coventry from the Lyran Commonwealth, but make the planet an example to those who would attempt to resist the Jade Falcons at all—she must find a way to win with honor. But General of the Armies Roderick Steiner and General Jasek Kelwsa-Steiner intend to make the Falcons pay very dearly for their invasion into Lyran space, and in the end, there can be only one victor.

Two great *BattleTech* stories that set the stage for the machinations, plots and campaigns to come, written by two of the many authors both that will be telling the stories of this new era in *BattleTech*'s future history.

So climb into your cockpit, fire up your fusion reactor, take the safety off your weapons, and charge into the fray right alongside us as we enter a new period of *BattleTech*, where as always, life is cheap...but BattleMechs aren't.

—John Helfers
CGL Fiction Director
July 2018

A SPLINTER OF HOPE

PHILIP A. LEE

PART ONE

While the summit's attendees gathered, First Prince Julian Davion watched a recorded scene on the small screen in front of him: the keen edge of a *dao* sword glinted in the air, high above the neck of a kneeling elderly woman he knew all too well.

Julian hadn't set foot on New Syrtis, the Capellan March capital, in quite some time, but even the minor cosmetic changes in this footage imbued the scene with a surreal air. Though the date stamp on the footage was more than two years ago, he could ill conceive that this was the same Saso Square he had visited many, many times before.

Instead of Federated Suns BattleMechs flanking the path leading from the FedCom Civil War Monument to the Saso Statehouse, he saw Capellan Confederation 'Mechs stand sentinel while others patrolled nearby streets in search of insurrectionists. Instead of the round sword-and-sunburst iconography of House Davion gracing the Statehouse's facade in the backdrop of the footage, an all-too-familiar triangular emblem of House Liao replaced the original. Inside the stark-green Confederation insignia, an upraised arm held a curved scimitar, the blade's tip breaking out from the triangular border with hostile intent.

Below the Capellan emblem, the masked soldier held his *dao* aloft in perfect mimicry of the House Liao sigil. Below the blade, Duchess Amanda Hasek knelt in her finest courtly attire, her hands bound to either side of a block of wood. Despite the Damocles sword of a hated foe more than a meter above her neck, she struck Julian as surprisingly calm, a sinner who knows she is ultimately responsible for her own crimes.

Few members of House Davion agreed with her politics, with her rabid, outspoken loathing of the Capellan Confederation. Her decision more than forty years ago to instigate the disastrous Victoria War without then First Prince Harrison Davion's approval had sealed her fate, and the Confederation's long-awaited reprisal against the Hasek family's homeworld was her well-deserved recompense. But this was too far.

Julian had never initially been destined to lead the Federated Suns, but the duchess had seen great potential in him and groomed him to be a contender for the throne. He owed this woman—his surrogate mother, his mentor—a good many things, including his current position as leader of the Federated Suns.

A man royal in bearing and military in garb—Daoshen Liao, Chancellor of the Capellan Confederation—rose to the platform and addressed both the accused and the crowd assembled before the square. Though Julian kept the sound muted for courtesy while waiting for the rest of the attendees to arrive, he could have quoted the Capellan's speech verbatim.

"For war crimes perpetrated against the celestial sovereignty of the Capellan Confederation," Daoshen mouthed with a smug smirk, *"I find you guilty as charged on all counts.*

"The sentence is death."

With a slow nod, the Chancellor signaled to the executioner. The *dao* descended as a curtain of silvery light reflecting off the blade. Blink, and Julian would miss it.

Something twisted inside Julian's chest, as though some part of him died along with her every time he watched the gory, decapitated form of his mother figure slump gracelessly to the platform.

He paused the playback on the Chancellor's satisfied grin, the look of a fox strutting out of a henhouse with feathers stuck between his teeth.

This was the reason for what he was about to do. For what *needed* to be done. *Revenge* was such a pedestrian word. This feeling in the First Prince's breast went far beyond mere vengeance. This was a matter of putting things right, resetting the equilibrium between the Suns and the Confederation.

But he could not make this decision lightly. Only last September had he and Daoshen's envoy—the Chancellor's younger sister, *Sangshao* Danai Liao-Centrella—brokered an armistice between their two nations. The truce had justified itself at the time: the Confederation was cowering under the phantom threat posed by the Republic of the Sphere, while the Draconis Combine continued conquering world after Federated Suns world, including the Draconis March capital of Robinson. Soldiers of the Armed Forces of the Federated Suns retreating from New Avalon meant the Draconis Combine had captured House Davion's capital and two march capitals. The nation had spiraled into deep recession, and according to this summit of his top political and military advisors, the best economic stimulus was to retake one of the capital worlds. Like deer ticks, the Dracs were hooked too deep into New Avalon and Robinson, which left New Syrtis the easiest nut to crack. All he needed do was approve the proposed campaign. Loath as he was to break his ceasefire with the Capellan Confederation, Julian saw a certain amount of wisdom in the action. However, every time he considered the long-term implications of breaking a pact signed by his own hand, the thought sat heavy in his guts, as though he'd swallowed a Gauss-rifle slug whole.

Julian looked out across the assembly hall. All the necessary personnel were now present. The Prince's Champion, Erik Sandoval. The Prince's Intelligence Advisor, Jennifer Dawes. MIIO Director Gary Harding. Field Marshal Anastasia Zibler. Colonels Sortek and Rhys. Everyone of consequence from the Suns' government-in-exile, the AFFS, and the intelligence arms. Satisfied, he deactivated the hand-held screen and called the summit to order.

"Friends and family, colleagues and brothers and sisters-in-arms," he began, "I have decided the time has come to start rebuilding our great nation. Since my coronation as First Prince of the Federated Suns, many of you have compelled me to see virtue in an attempt to retake one of our lost capitals, to rekindle the faith and spirit of our people into a blazing pulsar for the whole galaxy to see. As a man of conscience, I have wrestled long with the matter of breaking truce with our Capellan neighbors. However, circumstances being what they are, if we are to do right by our people, now is the time to seize the initiative and restore freedom to those worlds that the Capellan Confederation snatched away from us in their bid for dominance.

"The time has come to execute a campaign for New Syrtis."

He paused to gauge reactions across the assembly. Expressions ran the gamut between unabashed patriotism to quiet condemnation. Among them, he imagined Amanda Hasek standing in cool approval of his proclamation.

This is what I would have done, he could hear her apparition say, *had I control of the Federated Suns.*

"As First Prince," he continued, "the armistice with the Capellan Confederation is mine to break. Because of this, I have decided to lead this assault personally. No one else should bear culpability for my actions."

Julian activated a podium control, and a breakdown of his invasion plan projected onto the wall screen behind him. "Ladies and gentlemen, I present Operation CERBERUS. This campaign calls for three task forces, code named Chimera, Orthus, and Hydra. The objective of Phase One is the envelopment and isolation of New Syrtis from the rest of the Confederation. Phase Two entails the assault on the march capital itself.

"Now, let's poke some holes in this, and see where we can patch them."

Julian acknowledged Harding's upraised hand, and the MIIO director rose to speak. "Your Grace, is this invasion the best allocation of our military resources? We have a standing truce with Daoshen Liao, and MI6 agents on Sian report that he spends more time jumping at Republic shadows than trying to wage further war against us. Would it not be more prudent to focus our military efforts on the Draconis Combine instead? Snatching back Robinson or New Avalon from the Dragon's clutches would strike a deeper moral victory for our people."

Julian shared a knowing glance with his champion, Erik Sandoval, before answering. "Director, we are already at war with the Combine. Coordinator Yori Kurita knows this. The Combine's warriors know this. Even now, they sit in entrenched and fortified positions, expecting—no, *daring* us to fight them. They are more than ready for us. The Confederation is not, and we can no longer squander the advantage of surprise. If we can ever hope to stand against the Combine in the future, liberating New Syrtis *now* is the key."

CERBERUS RALLY STATION
NEW DAMASCUS
CHIRIKOF OPERATIONAL AREA
CRUCIS MARCH, FEDERATED SUNS
19 SEPTEMBER 3147

From across the bargaining table inside the canvas tent, Captain Malerie Faulkner was unimpressed with this new Federated Suns liaison. It took a lot to impress soldiers of distant Clan pedigrees. This scrawny lackey, sent straight from First Prince Julian Davion himself, had to be a pencil pusher, a desk rider, not an actual warrior worthy of the title. Mal knew soldiers, and this sorry excuse for a uniform probably had a law degree, not a diploma from some MechWarrior academy or other.

She disliked lawyers. Such a dishonest, two-faced profession. She would much rather have solved negotiations the way her Clan ancestors did: put up your dukes, and the winner dictates the terms. Don't like the terms? Win the rematch. So much simpler than listening to sales pitch after sales pitch.

Thankfully her boss, Major Tallula Zheng, seemed to pay more attention. As executive officer of Tally's Talons, Mal could voice concerns about a contract, but the decision to accept terms was ultimately in Tally's court. Tally, the battalion's golden-haired matron, gave the Davion lackey a glare that would've withered a lesser man. Mal frown-smiled to herself, slightly impressed at his resilience. But only slightly.

"No, no, no," Tally said, knifing her hands in an x in protest. "Our contract expired on the seventeenth. Under the terms we negotiated with your office, the Talons are now free agents, able to pursue whatever course of action we desire."

Lackey tapped his sheaf of papers atop the table to align them and straightened the sleeves of his olive-drab uniform jacket. "We understand that, Major. However, your presence here on New Damascus puts us in a precarious position. Your participation to this point required you to possess partial operational knowledge of our movements—"

"—and," Tally cut in, "our contract doesn't include a non-compete clause." She waved a hardcopy of the contract at him. "I never sign one that does. Non-competes put a serious damper on future mercenary employment."

"Be that as it may, we are offering to extend your current contract plus an additional ten percent." With a hopeful curl to the corner of his mouth, Lackey slid a paper across the desk.

Tally shared a knowing glance with Mal. They'd acted out this charade often enough that they could do it in the middle of the night after being roused by a proximity alarm. "Faulkner, what do you think of this?" She gestured her jaw toward the new draft. "Does it look good, or should we hit up the Chancellor, see if he'll give us a better deal?"

Mal echoed her CO's nonchalant posture and made a good show of pretending to read the new contract. All the legalese was bound to be the same as the last contract: a self-righteous prick like Julian Davion lacked the necessary guile to pull off any kind of deception. People like him were known for keeping their word, even to a fault.

Mal crossed her arms and shook her head. "Twenty. We want twenty percent, or we walk."

Tally hooked a thumb Mal's way. "What she said. If you want me to take our business to the Capellans, then say so. No pay, no play."

An exasperated huff escaped Lackey's throat. He gathered up his papers and stood. "Uh, if you'll excuse me for a moment..." Without waiting for an answer, he slid a perscomm from his uniform pocket and stepped out through the tent flap.

Mal leaned closer to the tent flap as though that might help her eavesdrop on the call Lackey was obviously making out of their earshot. She caught the indecipherable muffle of Lackey's end of the conversation, but much to her irritation, that was all.

Only the Feddie's upper half reappeared through the tent flap. "My humblest of apologies, but I have something to attend to. I will return shortly."

Tally frowned once Lackey departed. "Ah, he won't be back. Shall I see if the Cappies are actually hiring these days? Or would you rather strike out to the Free Worlds League, hit up a province or two? The Clan Protectorate would probably hire us."

Moments later, the tent flap parted, and in strode three uniformed soldiers, the foremost a man Mal had only ever seen in photos and vids. Throughout her mercenary career, she had dealt with the occasional dignitary, noble, and celebrity. Every time she came across someone even remotely famous, the same thought struck her: these people the galaxy placed up on pedestals were mundane, ordinary folk just like her. Sans makeup or image retouching. Rough around the edges. Fame and celebrity—the mortal equivalent of godhood—were nothing but manufactured concepts.

But this man—

Mal's stomach seized upon seeing his countenance in person. Her brain knew he was mere flesh-and-blood, but this man, with short golden hair, arresting blue eyes, an honest, clean-shaven face, and an aura of regality—he filled the tent with a kind of palpable majesty she had never before witnessed, as though his otherwise average build dwarfed the roomy space. Something about him suggested—no, *de-manded*—respect, but quietly rather than by bluster.

Now *this* was a true warrior.

"Captain Sharma tells me you are considering not re-upping," First Prince Julian Davion said. Even the timbre of his voice was real and honest, unmodulated by the reverb and resonance typically saturating stately speeches given by monarchs and other interstellar politicians. "I would respectfully wish to know why."

The accusing tremble in his eyes sent a wave of guilt through Mal. "Our...our contract has expired, Your Highness. We are...merely exploring our options."

The First Prince approached the table and rapped knuckles in thought atop its fiberplast surface. "Thus far, your battalion has performed admirably as part of Task Force Hydra. My House troops are familiar with you, and you have worked well with them during combat exercises. You form a solid, cohesive force, one I will need for the days ahead."

Boots on the tabletop, Tally tipped her chair back on two legs, far enough Mal worried she'd fall backward. "Frankly, Your Highness, it's not a matter of what you need. It's a matter of payment. Are you prepared to pay us what we're worth?"

"At the risk of sounding desperate," said the First Prince, "I don't have time to scour the Inner Sphere for competent mercenary battalions on such short notice. Name your price."

Mal broke her gaze from Julian Davion long enough to wordlessly confer with her CO, then turned her attention back to the First Prince. "Twenty-five percent above our original contract," she said. "Plus combat bonus."

His throat contracted almost imperceptibly. Twenty-five meant a substantial amount of money, and even Mal knew the Federated Suns' coffers were running on fumes.

"Done," he said with a definitive nod. He extended a hand—bare skin, ungloved—and Tally shook it, firm and businesslike.

Mal narrowed her eyes just enough to not reveal her jealousy.

CYLLENE FOREST
TAYGETA
SIAN COMMONALITY
CAPELLAN CONFEDERATION
25 NOVEMBER 3147

The planet was lost. This much *Sang-shao* Eliza Zhao knew without a doubt, long before she'd had occasion to fire a single one of her *Tian-Zong*'s weapons.

Both hands clenched around her 'Mech's controls, she squinted against the actinic blue flare of an incoming PPC bolt her optics couldn't quite compensate against. The approaching black-and-gold *Prefect* wasn't aiming at her 'Mech, but the resolute steps of its defiant advance alarmed her.

Not two days before, the Enemy had come screaming down from the sky like *yaoguai* demons, combat-dropping on prepared positions in strategic places across the planet. Government buildings, spaceports, maglev transport hubs, supply depots—anything at all that could put her command off its game.

In retrospect, multiple factors had doomed their defense from the start. After the successful drive toward New Syrtis two years ago during Operation CELESTIAL REWARD, Chancellor Daoshen Liao had ordered Zhao's Dynasty Guard regiment to Taygeta for a period of refit. Rumors of an incoming Federated Suns invasion force within the Confederation's borders goaded Zhao to put her troops on high alert, but the refit wasn't entirely complete yet. To worsen matters, the Dynasty Guard represented the best offensive regiment among the entire Capellan Hussars brigade. Her command could fight defensive battles when absolutely necessary, but to truly shine, they needed to go on the attack.

The advancing Republic of the Sphere troops never even gave the Guard a chance to rally and spearhead an assault into the invaders' lines. Their sheer mass forced her to make the hard choice between letting her command get pulverized between the hammer of these so-called Dawn Guards and the regiment-plus anvil of unmarked, primer-gray mercenary BattleMechs.

What in the Chancellor's name did the *Republic* care about a relatively unimportant former Feddie world so far away from the Republic's impenetrable Fortress-wall border?

She snap-fired her own light PPCs at the target of opportunity and continued backpedaling into a stand of trees along with the rest of her augmented lance. More Dawn 'Mechs crested the rise ahead, their torsos tracking in her direction. Two flights of Schracks in Republic colors shotgunned across the angry sunset in search of easy fodder along the Dynasty Guard's line of withdrawal. Two platoons of Behemoth II tanks rumbled up into view, turrets traversing for targets. Three squads of Republic-painted Taranis battlesuits emerged from beside the Behemoths.

The array of Republic troops before her only confirmed her suspicions about this invasion's outcome. Now it was merely a matter of how to conduct this defeat. It would come from no real fault of her own, but the Celestial Wisdom would not see it that way if she ordered her soldiers to pull out and head for another planet. Her duty was to ensure she and her regiment gave as good an account of themselves as possible, leaving full, off-planet retreat as the very last contingency.

In the old days of the Succession Wars, the desperation of the Capellan Confederation Armed Forces often saw units embrace "hopeless battle syndrome" and fight to the death, even in the face of insurmountable odds and guaranteed destruction. Daoshen Liao and his predecessor were far less frivolous with Capellan lives, but retreating now, when so many of her regiment and the enemy still remained operational, would be viewed as a dereliction of duty.

Though the Chancellor harbored a near-pathological fear of the Republic—an understandable sentiment, given the disaster of the Capellan Crusades nearly four decades ago—Zhao did not. Republic troops were no different than any other. With all due respect to the Celestial Wisdom, no military was truly invincible. No army lacked a weakness. As commander of a prestigious Capellan Hussars regiment, she was not about to kowtow to these invaders, not yet.

She would tear them apart, limb from limb, before ever deserting her station. For all she knew, the Strategios, CCAF High Command, could already have reinforcements en route, and abandoning her post now would doom her relief. In a fleeting moment of whimsy, Zhao imagined the familiar silhouette of *Yen-Lo-Wang* descending from orbit and landing in a cloud right before the terrified Republic troops. But Danai Liao-Centrella, Zhao's longtime friend and owner of the legendary Centurion BattleMech, was currently on Sian, trying to make some sense of the tactical disaster on Marlette that had claimed the lives of countless CCAF troops.

Amusing as it would be to witness incoming Republic forces cower at the sight of a single BattleMech, Zhao knew she had to damage her enemy's war-making capacity as much as possible before she could justify retreat. The Celestial Wisdom would expect no less from her.

She adjusted her aim on the nearest target downrange, a battered Scapha hovertank, and the *Tian-Zong*'s frame shook from the tremor of a Gauss rifle discharge. Faster than a snap of the fingers, an obscenely sized hole plowed through the Scapha's glacis armor. The tank stilled.

She was about to order a strategic fighting withdrawal when a voice from her regimental command channel piped up into her neurohelmet's earpiece.

"Sheng One, this is Two," *Zhong-shao* Bogdanovich, Zhao's executive officer, transmitted from his sixty-five-ton *Vandal* nearby, just out of her sight line. *"We have received a priority-one message."*

One of the dead tank's companions replied with a rotary autocannon blast. Zhao's cockpit bucked from explosive shells impacting across her 'Mech's torso. "A little busy here, Two."

"It's from Sian, sir."

Zhao's fingers loosened on her controls. The Confederation capital meant two things: orders either from CCAF High Command—or from the Celestial Wisdom himself.

Neither possibility appealed to her.

Another flight of Schracks tore across the rapidly darkening sky. "Give me the short version."

Bogdanovich transmitted the official verigraphed communiqué, which displayed on Zhao's command readout. The orders came straight from the Chancellor himself:

Sang-shao, you are hereby ordered to disengage and report to New Syrtis ASAP.

Zhao clenched her jaw and fired off another salvo of Gauss-rifle fire along the encroaching tank platoon. One nickel-ferrous slug cratered the ground, kicking up a cloud of dirt clods. The other instantaneously transformed a large, majestic tree into a sawed-off stump.

The planet was already lost, but the relief a retreat order should have elicited did not come. A profound sense of hollowness inside made her feel as though obeying the Chancellor's order would still be betraying his trust in her command ability.

"All right," she replied, her voice hesitant. "Give the orders for a full fighting withdrawal from the planet."

PART TWO

OVERLORD-CLASS DROPSHIP *KINGSMAN*
ZENITH JUMP POINT, TAYGETA
TAYGETA OPERATIONAL THEATER
CAPELLAN MARCH, FEDERATED SUNS
4 DECEMBER 3147

The briefing room hushed as Julian took his place among the assembled officers. All eyes turned in his direction; some with pride, some with concern, others with an air of curiosity. The mixture of pride and concern, he understood—what military operation could occur without some measure of patriotism tempered by a healthy amount of trepidation?—but he doubted he would ever get used to people regarding him with a sense of awe.

You've been behind the wall of Fortress Republic, he could almost sense them thinking. *You know what's on the other side. You know what's coming.* Such sentiments elevated him, the first person to gain access to the closed-off Republic since the JumpShip-impenetrable walls went up in 3135, to an almost mythical status throughout the Federated Suns. No one knew how he had gained entry—in truth, Julian wasn't entirely certain himself—which only added to his mystique.

But all of their unspoken accusations were right. He *did* know what lay beyond Fortress Republic's wall; he *did* know what was coming. All the more reason to prosecute this campaign now, while there was still time to consolidate the Suns' gains.

Without wasting time or mincing words, he outlined the approved invasion plan for the commanders and staff officers of the regiments that composed Task Force Styx. Questions were asked and answered, concerns were raised and addressed, all per standard protocol.

A quiet descended on the meeting before Colonel Siobhan Sortek, Commander of the First Davion Auxiliary and Julian's XO for the operation, spoke up.

"Your Highness, where will you be in all of this?" Siobhan already knew the answer, but she wanted the others to know as well.

"I will go in alongside the other troops," Julian said. "No special bodyguard detail this time. The last thing we need is the Maskirovka easily figuring out where I am in our formations."

"And if bad luck were to strike?" asked Admiral Ryan Davion-Coles III of the Fifth Crucis Lancers.

"Then that is the price I must pay for breaking this peace." He scanned the room and saw no further questions or objections. "All right, you all have your assignments. Task Force Styx is set to jump in six hours.

"Godspeed to you all."

DROPSHIP *KINGSMAN*
LUNAR ORBIT NEW SYRTIS
SIAN COMMONALITY
CAPELLAN CONFEDERATION
4 DECEMBER 3147

Through the viewport on the *Kingsman*'s bridge, Julian marveled at the vista arrayed before him. At the screen's edge, a bright-orange K5IV star blazed in space. A tiny black dot on the orange dwarf's face indicated the transit of one of the system's planets, but he only had eyes for the fourth planet in the system.

A sunlit, bluish-white ball hung in the blackness. At this distance, New Syrtis resembled an icy marble with an equatorial strand of tans, greens, and the occasional black scar. Even from lunar orbit, wounds inflicted during the Word of Blake Jihad seven decades ago were still visible, and here he was, coming to inflict more.

At the edge of the planet's predominantly white disk hovered the cratered lump of New Syrtis's solitary moon, Varnay's Star. The satellite's gravity-neutral L2 Lagrangian point had served as a pirate point for half of Task Force Styx's in-system jump. So much rock also obscured most of four regiments' worth of JumpShips from aerospace patrols, but even that only bought them enough time to uncouple the DropShips and make a hard burn planetside.

At the peripheries of the scene, he witnessed other JumpShips disgorging their payloads. Spheroid DropShips bearing the sword-and-sunburst emblem of the Federated Suns peeled off from the elongated interstellar vessels like pearls from a broken necklace, and they rotated and maneuvered in a kind of quiet, slow ballet Julian always found fascinating.

Somewhere out in the dark, at the planet's own L2 point, three other regiments were debarking from their JumpShips. Not only did they serve as a distraction from the rest of Task Force Styx, but they also represented Julian's insistence that the invasion force be split in two, in the event one front turned horrendously wrong. During previous campaigns, his most ardent critics had accused him of holding too many AFFS troops in reserve, leading to the wholesale slaughter of under-supported mercenary units, so it pained him that those three regiments exposed in New Syrtis space were irregulars. The decision ultimately boiled down to logistical matters, but his critics would never see it that way, no matter what justification he or his staff gave.

"Begin decoupling," the *Kingsman's* captain ordered. The distant *clunk* of the docking-collar release resounded throughout the whole ship. Bulkheads trembled. Seconds later, before Julian had a chance to strap himself in for planetary insertion maneuvers, a battery of alarms and warning lights filled the bridge.

"Incoming contacts!" the sensor technician reported. "Multiple bogies approaching on an intercept course! I'm reading two assault DropShips with fighter escort."

Damn. Julian shook his head. The Capellans had taken the wrong bait.

Captain Chastain strapped into the command chair. "Evasive maneuvers!"

The *Kingsman's* hull shook like a rung bell around them. Julian scrabbled around for a handhold to keep from floating off in microgravity. "Anything I can do, Captain?"

Chastain ground his teeth. "With all due respect, Your Highness, I advise you to get the hell off my bridge and into your 'Mech. If those Cappies have more friends on the way, we may need to perform an orbital drop to get you planetside in one piece."

Explosions and laser fire bathed the bridge with blinding brilliance. Julian squinted away the scintillating light and braced himself against the bulkhead until the *Kingsman* stopped shaking.

"Go, sir!" Chastain chided.

Julian ducked into the corridor and didn't stop until he reached the cargo bay and slid into the command couch of Arthur, his *Templar III*. He sat in the cockpit and prayed Chastain and the *Kingsman's* crew could make it through the Capellan aerospace storm.

UNION-CLASS DROPSHIP MAXILLA
PLANETARY ORBIT, NEW SYRTIS
SIAN COMMONALITY
CAPELLAN CONFEDERATION
4 DECEMBER 3147

In the claustrophobic darkness of her sealed cockpit, a shudder worked down Malerie Faulkner's spine. An armored reentry shell obscured her forward view, reducing the entirety of her world to the soft illumination emanating from her OmniMech's control panels. Trapped in an orbital shell, sensor blind, and with spotty communication—this was the part of a combat op Malerie hated the most. On the ground, she would feel confident enough behind the armor and maneuverability of her seventy-ton *Flamberge* to approach all but the heaviest of enemy units, but up here her fate remained at the fickle mercy of the Maxilla's crew and the Fortune Charlie regiment's combat aerospace patrol.

How did her fearless geneparents deal with it? They didn't have to—mostly. The average combat trial for a Clan MechWarrior usually occurred on terra firma, within a clearly delineated Circle of Equals. Rare were the times Clan warriors needed to make orbital drops, but they did perform them, and they did so with a kind of grace Mal lacked.

She wasn't quite Clan, though. Much as she wanted to emulate their honor and quest for battlefield glory, distant genes from someone of the Folkner Bloodline and the beat-up, refurbished OmniMech she had purchased represented the only tenuous links to her heritage.

The shell trembled around her, hard enough to yank her stomach around. From what radio chatter she could make out, the Maxilla had engaged braking thrusters to maneuver into low New Syrtis orbit. Any moment now—

The Maxilla's drop controller piped into her slim neurohelmet. *"All Talons units, brace for drop! Dropping in five...four...three–"*

Mal yelped. Her cockpit and insides lurched as she—drop pod, OmniMech, and all—disgorged from the Maxilla a second earlier than announced. Her world spun uncontrollably, end over end over end.

Radio chatter exploded into pandemonium. Something had gone wrong. Dead wrong. And her pod was tumbling toward the planet. She swore.

Hyperventilation steamed up her neurohelmet's faceplate faster than its defoggers could compensate. Her temples pounded. Bright, pulsating spots danced before her eyes until she couldn't tell spots from control-panel lights.

A single strong but distorted voice cut through the noise. "Talon Two!"

Tally...

"You still with me?"

Relief flooded Mal's senses, but even hearing her friend and commander's voice couldn't stall gravity or negate physics. *"Aff,"* she croaked.

"Maxilla was hit."

"Figured..." Mal managed between ragged breaths. "Uh, still tumbling blind here...."

If she didn't do anything soon, she would careen into the planet with the force of a meteorite. Trapped in this coffin, unable to witness her own impending death, then instant vaporization. Not a glorious way to go, Clan descendant or otherwise.

Heat—blistering, unquenchable heat—and the stink of hot metal filtered into her shaking cockpit. On the outside, the hurtling drop-pod shell had to be blazing from reentry friction.

Tally said something over the comm, but the roar of reentry, the static of radio blackout, and the drumbeat of her heart swallowed her words.

Mal knew if she ditched the shell too early, reentry would melt her to slag. Too late, and she'd have no time to reorient herself before—

Seconds ticked by while she envisioned herself as little more than a smoking black streak plowing through a layer of continental ice.

No time...no time.... She had to do something, or the next few moments would be her last.

"Freebirth...."

She clenched her eyes shut and shook her head to alleviate disorientation. Somewhere in that moment, everything quieted away until she could hear nothing but her own heartbeat in the blast-furnace heat.

The temperature fell just a few degrees, but her brain still jumbled around in the pod's spin. In a fit of desperation, she braced herself to be flash fried and then engaged the manual pod release. A white line of daylight split down the center of her canopy, banishing the darkness as the shell panes obscuring her view blasted away and spiraled into the atmosphere like sheet-metal slabs shot from a cannon. The ground whirled below her, then became sky, then ground again—

—sky—

—ground—

—sky—

—ground—

Mal wanted to throw up, but there was no time. Her stomach could wait until they were on the ground.

She fought her control sticks and attempted to use her sense of balance to twist the seventy-ton meteor out of its spin. The 'Mech was too heavy, and its pseudo-wing assembly was not designed for actual atmospheric flight.

She pulled back on her controls and screamed to force the *Flamberge*'s right foot forward. Then she slammed down on the corresponding foot pedal hard enough to feel the gears working beneath the cockpit floor. The whole 'Mech shook and pitched backward as the jump jet ignited. Mal felt like a Hell's horse had bucked her in the chest, but at least she had finally stopped spinning.

Now all she needed to do was land the damn thing. Some of the other Talons had already made safe landings in the snow, so she stabilized her descent with the left-foot jump jet and used the pseudo wing's lackluster aerodynamics to steady herself. All she had to do was survive this landing.

She sucked in a deep breath, and her unsteady world snapped into razor focus. Muscle memory replaced fear. The warrior within took over as she screamed her angry resolve toward the swiftly approaching ground.

**MAWREDDOG DRIFTS
NEW SYRTIS
SIAN COMMONALITY
CAPELLAN CONFEDERATION
4 DECEMBER 3147**

All things considered, some battered leg armor and a knee-actuator malfunction was a fair price for Mal's survival, but the resultant limp kept her from ranging too far ahead of Tally's damaged *Shrike*. The feed mechanisms of the ninety-five-ton 'Mech's paired Ultra-class autocannons had suffered damage during the drop, and Tally was not happy about that, not one bit.

"This wouldn't have happened if His Highness hadn't dangled us out as bait," she confided over a private channel as they advanced toward the rendezvous point.

"Tacnet says the AFFS contingent got hit hard too," Mal offered.

"Convenient, wouldn't you say? Did they actually get hit, or is this another case of 'Let's not get attacked but say we did'?" The major drew a deep breath. "I won't believe anything until I see their official repair assessment forms."

Magnetic resonance sensors picked out a column approaching through the swirling whiteout conditions— friendlies, according to IFF transponder codes. As the Talons' command lance approached, Mal zoomed in her view and recognized AFFS colors.

A good many of them already bore blackened scars of heat and smoke. One among them, an eighty-five-ton *Templar* III bearing arctic camo and Davion livery, had somehow managed to make it through the landing relatively unscathed.

Mal narrowed her eyes, unsure what to believe.

Eliza Zhao had long suspected Chancellor Daoshen Liao was a divine manifestation, but not until she looked up and watched hundreds of invading troops dropping from the skies did she confirm it. No matter that she loathed falling back while most of her command remained operational; the Celestial Wisdom had been downright prescient in his insight that the Enemy would strike here on New Syrtis, and that the Dynasty Guard's seemingly premature relocation from Taygeta was the best use of her regiment's preserved strength.

From her *Tian-Zong*'s cockpit, Zhao gazed up through the swirling snow at the last of the descending BattleMechs and smiled. Two triples of maroon *Transit* aerofighters knifed across the blue expanse as easy as lines drawn across a page. Together their lasers scythed through a pair of falling 'Mechs—a pod shell that had not yet jettisoned despite its altitude and some heavy 'Mech she couldn't ID at this range. The pod fractured and burst apart into a roaring fireball in midair. The heavy went limp and tumbled head over legs before impacting in what she imagined was a satisfying crunch and explosion at the crash site. Smooth as could be, the blocky *Transit*s arced around for another pass on the beachhead the invaders sought to establish.

A small wave of triumph coursed through her shoulders. Her troops had executed their orders beautifully thus far. Good muster and response times, mercifully few casualties. Even the other on-planet forces, the Home Guard, the Warrior Houses, they had all deferred to her leadership.

It was all textbook, which meant something would go wrong. Disaster was long overdue.

Ovoid and spherical DropShips, more than she could easily count, descended to the rolling, icy plains on columns of superheated-plasma thrust. The sun-and-sword insignia of House Davion was emblazoned larger than life on each one of these vessels. Carbon scoring and craters pitted a good many of the emblems—a tangible result of the Chancellor's mandate to step up aerospace patrols—which she took as a good omen. But vigilance was still the order of the day: divine insight and good omens alone did not win battles.

As Zhao understood it, the Celestial Wisdom's divine insight captured the broad strokes of history, and she could hardly believe a consciousness spanning thousands of worlds could be expected to zero in on the minutiae of a roiling battlefield. Such a feat was beneath him. That was why he surrounded himself with competent and able military leaders like her, like Danai, like Strategic Military Director Sang-jiang-jun Isabelle Fisk or Warrior House Grand Master Gangshiao-zhang Jiang Hui—all commanders who could translate his will and forge it into victories.

"Sheng One," Bogdanovich transmitted on the command frequency, "scout elements report contact with the Enemy."

The encroaching blizzard peppered her tactical radar display with noise, but she could still see the shape of the conflict. The sensation demonstrated her understanding of the Celestial Wisdom's insight: small details coalesced into larger ones until she could no longer discern the discrete elements of Third Battalion's recon company.

Time to leverage her regiment's specialty on these presumptuous Davion swine.

"Pull them back and move in the heavier elements of Second Battalion," she ordered. "Let's go on the attack. Formation Tiger-Six."

There were too many invaders to make a truly effective assault run against the Enemy's LZ with the forces currently under her command, but every piece of hardware she could deny the Fedrats now would mean one less they could unleash later. She knew why the Enemy was here: they wished revenge for their former march capital, for the beheading of that warmonger, Duchess Amanda Hasek. Theirs was a campaign of blind retribution led by a young truce-breaker, and it would not succeed.

The command frequency clicked on again. "Sheng One, this is Barduc Three-One." *Sao-shao* Kenzer from Third Battalion. "The Enemy plowed through our pickets on a flanking maneuver. You have a heavy column heading your way."

Zhao studied her radar and swore. The noise had obscured the Enemy's approach, and her troops would be forced on the defensive yet again. "All Sheng units, prepare for incoming." She kept her voice as level and emotionless as possible to avoid undue panic. "Left flank. Engage and withdraw to favorable position."

Yellow-starburst muzzle flashes from distant autocannon fire cut through the swirling snow haze. Emerald and ruby beams from unseen attackers stabbed in her direction. Visual sensors couldn't quite pick out the incoming 'Mechs from the blizzard, but the marching machines positively glowed on infrared and mag-res.

"Here they come!" Bogdanovich announced.

Zhao eased up her throttle lever and cut the seventy-five-ton 'Mech to the left, out of the immediate fire lane as more laser beams whined nearby.

On radar, she couldn't help noting a small cluster of Davion 'Mechs hanging slightly farther back from the flanking vanguard's foremost brawlers. They seemed to be watching the battle evolve, rather than actively engaging First Battalion and her command company. While on the move, she ratcheted up her *Tian-Zong*'s visual sensors to magnify the knot of heavy and assault 'Mechs. There, out in the haze of blowing snow, lumbered a *Templar* III painted in the grays, whites, and blues of arctic camouflage.

This was a relatively new model, a rare sight on recent battlefields. Intel indicated that mid- to high-level commanders favored this chassis, which meant she was likely looking straight down her sights at a person of import in this invasion force.

According to Maskirovka reports, the First Prince, damn his soul, was personally leading this attack on Capellan sovereignty. Other reports claimed Devlin Stone, former exarch of the Republic of the Sphere, had personally gifted Julian Davion with one of these eighty-five-ton machines. So if this was all true...

It was an impossible shot, but she lined up her reticule with the distant cockpit and fired one of the *Tian-Zong*'s shoulder-mounted Gauss rifles regardless. Her 'Mech bucked from the recoil.

A gust of snow obscured Zhao's optics. When it cleared, the *Templar* no longer appeared on her scopes. Like a specter, the First Prince and his entourage had vanished into the blizzard.

PART THREE

Though the worst of the blizzard conditions had lifted, wind still howled outside the mobile HQ—a ghostly reminder of the people they had already lost during planetfall and while securing the LZ from Capellan hostiles. Extreme temperatures would make the going harder from here on, but Julian had planned for such possibilities.

For the final time before the task force disseminated, he had gathered the leadership to review the plan and work out any final challenges caused during planetfall. The mishmash regiment of various smaller merc commands, code name Fortune Charlie, had lost a pair of vital DropShips, which hamstrung Charlie's mobility enough to necessitate target reassignment. As luck would have it, Julian's revised plan also assuaged some of his guilt regarding the unintended segregation of his troops during the in-system jump. Now most of Styx's objectives belonged to a good, even mixture of mercs and AFFS regulars.

Julian called the meeting to order and brought up a topographical map of the Mawreddog continent in the HQ's holotank. "All right, here's the game plan. At oh-six-hundred hours, we'll begin staggered deployments to our respective targets.

"First up is the ducal mansion." A red triangle flashed with a dotted-line route between the task force's LZ and the estate grounds that were once the ancestral home of the Hasek family. Julian zoomed in the map to show a wireframe representation of the manse and its grounds. Though a squad of Death Commandos had collapsed the estate during the abduction of Amanda Hasek, the command center beneath it remained intact and thus represented an important military objective. According to intel, the occupiers had since rebuilt much of the structure in Capellan-style architecture.

"Admiral Davion-Coles and Colonel Sortek will lead the Fifth Crucis Lancers and the First Auxiliary, respectively," Julian continued. "This is where preliminary intel places a good number of Capellan nobles and dignitaries—including the new governor of New Syrtis, *Shonso* Balian Armando—so I would expect stiff resistance from the Dynasty Guard, and possibly one of the Warrior Houses.

"Our next target is Saso Spaceport." The holomap panned over to the outskirts of New Syrtis's capital city. Abstracted representations of Confederation-marked DropShips dominated the locale. "Control of outbound space travel is paramount to prevent Capellan troops from easily refueling their DropShips or fleeing to summon reinforcements. Colonel Rhys will be taking the Second Auxiliary, and the Illician Lancers' Fifty Ninth Striker will be accompanying them.

"Colonels Rhys and Bradley, this will be a tough fight, but it is absolutely vital that we maintain a tight grip to prevent information from leaving this planet. If Daoshen can commit sufficient reinforcements before we are ready to face them, then that might jeopardize this whole campaign. Understood?"

The two regimental commanders gave silent nods, and Julian continued.

"Following right on their heels will be the Twelfth Vegan Rangers. Colonel al-Nahib, you will be in charge of securing the Saso Statehouse."

He paused a moment at the holomap's representation of Saso and pictured the Statehouse in his mind, just off the square where the duchess had been beheaded after her kangaroo-court trial. More than once he'd imagined himself leading the charge to the center of the capital, his *Templar III*'s lasers and particle projector cannons shredding every single Capellan defender present into mangled wrecks.

That was why Julian had assigned the objective to someone else. He never considered himself a wrathful, vindictive man, but tempting fate would be the first step down that long and counterproductive road. The injustice done to Amanda Hasek had partially goaded him here to New Syrtis, and that was more than enough.

Julian drew a deep breath before proceeding. "We do not foresee heavy resistance, as the Capellans will likely occupy themselves defending targets of far more military significance, but to truly reclaim the Capellan March capital, we must take and hold the Statehouse."

Della al-Nahib nodded. "Understood, sir."

"That leaves the final objective, the target of the utmost importance to the successful prosecution of this campaign." Julian zoomed the holomap out to a seemingly empty area on the Mawreddog continent before descending below the topographical surface. A subterranean network of caverns terminated in a massive underground military installation. "The First Davion Guards will spearhead our assault on the Cave, and Fortune Charlie will accompany them. Also, I will personally lead this attack from the field."

He glanced around the room at General Edward Nanava of the First Davion Guards, then at the major leadership of Fortune Charlie. "The Cave is not just a command-and-control facility. It also provides the Capellan leadership an easily defensible redoubt to withdraw into should our campaign be successful. Because of this, we must take the Cave as soon as possible, to not only deprive CCAF leadership of the ability to easily coordinate their defense, but also to leave them no easy place to run and hide.

"If we can secure all of these positions, New Syrtis will return to the Suns' fold. Now, any questions?"

Major Zheng from Fortune Charlie raised a hand to shoulder height. "Will Charlie be taking point for the Cave assault, sir? We lost a lot of good people on the way down, and I'd prefer not to be first course into the meat grinder this go-around."

Julian had expected some pushback to Charlie's last-minute reassignment. Charlie would make good scouts in the cave network, but the Tally's Talons commander raised a good point: there was zero reliable intel on what Capellan defenses the vanguard would be walking into. The more he was seen to value AFFS troops over irregulars, the less apt mercs would be to sign on with the Federated Suns in the future. And with the state of the AFFS as it was across the whole nation, Julian *needed* reliable irregular troops to cover gaping strategic holes. Much as he wished otherwise, he needed to make a concession, at least this once.

"The First Guards will lead the charge," he explained. "Charlie is assigned to rearguard and mop-up duties unless complications arise."

Zheng nodded her approval, as did all of the other Charlie commanders.

After the strategy meeting broke, Colonel Sortek pulled him aside for some privacy. "Your Highness, before you go, we should we talk about what happened out in the Drifts."

Julian scoffed. "There's nothing to talk about, Siobhan. A Capellan shot at me. Nothing to concern ourselves over."

She shook her head, and worry sank into her furrowed brow. "The problem is that whoever it was only took a shot at *you* before we lost them."

"Then you're saying I need to be a little more discreet? My cousin Victor once piloted an OmniMech known Sphere-wide, and he never shied away from combat. Why should I do anything different? I'm not about to cower and hide, not from this. This is my invasion, my truce to break. My enemies have a right to know whose resolve they face."

Siobhan swallowed, and her expression softened as she touched him on the shoulder in a platonic display of longtime camaraderie. "Highness, I understand. We *all* have great things to live up to. I am just...advising that you take a more prudent position on the battle-field, that's all. We cannot afford to lose you."

Julian nodded. "I will keep it under advisement. Now go see to your troops. Dismissed."

MAWREDDOG DRIFTS
NEW SYRTIS
SIAN COMMONALITY
CAPELLAN CONFEDERATION
5 DECEMBER 3147

Her 'Mech marching through ankle-deep snow, Malerie had to dial down the volume of the command channel in her neurohelmet to keep from rupturing her eardrums.

"Where in the actual *hell* does he get off?!" Tally shrieked from her nearby *Shrike*. "I mean, who does he think he is?"

Mal thought to respond with some quip about who died and made Julian king, but thought better of it and held her tongue. Tally didn't appreciate humor from *anyone* when she was off on a tear like this. Better to let her blow off steam now than let it build and explode under pressure later on, so Mal contented herself with the pleasant monotony of the march, the trance of traversing a vast, snowy land-scape. The rolling white hills lay completely untouched except for the 'Mech footprints of the Fifth Crucis Lancers, who were trailblazing a path for other task force regiments whose objectives lay in the same line of advance. Despite the tirade blatting in her ear, she found the scene almost peaceful, the rhythmic *thud, thud, thud* of her *Flamberge*'s footsteps hypnotic.

"You *know* that bastard was going to assign us to point before I said anything," Tally went on. "You *know* it. And knowing Cappies, they probably have those tunnels mined all the way to their final chokepoint. I don't mind a fair, honest fight, but Cappies aren't above dirty pool. They'll bring down that whole damn cave before they let a Davion have it."

"So he extends us a carrot," Mal said, shrugging despite the snugness of her cooling vest. "What's the big deal?"

"'What's the *big deal?!*'"

Stravag. Mal should've kept her mouth shut.

"I'll tell you what the big deal is. The First Prince doesn't want to hire actual professional soldiers. He wants cannon fodder. Forlorn hopes. Sacrificial lambs to buy his own precious troops a higher survival rate. But make no mistake: mercs don't get paid to *die*. We get paid to *fight*. If he wants people who'll throw their own lives away on the cheap, I know plenty of Capellan citizens who aren't doing anything useful with theirs."

"Looking on the bright side, at least we're not in the van this time, *aff*?"

"*Aff*, this time. But next time?"

"And we qualify for the combat bonus—"

Tally snorted. "All the combat bonuses in the world don't matter a single damn if you never live long enough to spend them."

Mal sighed. Her friend and commander wasn't wrong, but of the pair, Tally always worried about the money; Mal just wanted to fight. If she hadn't crossed paths with Tally after the Blackout, Mal probably would've ended up fighting arena duels on Solaris VII, as much as the thought disgusted her. Something about winning while the whole Inner Sphere watched seemed to ruin the integrity of the contest. Having integrity, as was once explained to her as a child, meant doing the right thing even when no one was watching. *Especially* when no one was watching. Of *course* people on camera would do everything they could to win. True glory and honor lay in the purity of the act, not in how spectacularly it was performed. So Mal preferred honest battlefield combat, where eyewitness anecdotes and after-action reports, not broadcast spectacles, shaped her reputation as a MechWarrior.

Mal twisted her OmniMech's torso away from the advancing column and leaned her cockpit upward a few degrees to watch a dazzling aurora ripple like a ribbon in the ionized atmosphere. "What do you suggest we do?"

The line quieted for a moment. *Too* long, Mal figured.

"I'll think of something," Tally said at length. "I just...I just need to stew for a bit."

The channel closed. A pang of guilt stung her, as though this were all her fault.

Less than five minutes of rhythmic, soporific marching later, the command frequency shared by all task force regiments still on this continent squawked to life: *"All units, all units, enemy contact at grid zero-three-niner-five-niner. Watch your flanks."*

Mal shook off her reverie and snapped into combat mode. A quick cross reference of her radar and tactical maps showed contact all across the column's northern flank—the nearest falling dangerously close to Charlie's position.

She traversed her *Flamberge*'s torso toward their exposed flank only seconds before the silhouettes of a reinforced Capellan lance stormed down over a nearby embankment. A quartet of light and medium 'Mechs and a pair of Regulator hovertanks popped up into view and scattered before she could get a solid bead on them. Targeting analysis of the insignia marked the harriers as the Fourth McCarron's Armored Cavalry— masters of mobile warfare, Mal recalled from reviewing the intel brief.

The harassers loosed a coordinated missile salvo and swept a barrage of coruscating laser fire across the Talons' flank. Instinct took over, and Mal stomped her foot pedals. The *Flamberge* arced skyward on jump-jet plumes, leaving her stomach somewhere back in the snow. She adjusted her trajectory to land right in front of a twenty-ton *Locust* careening her way too fast to change course. Mal unleashed two dozen missiles at point-blank range. Only wreckage emerged from the resulting bouquet of fireballs. The *Flamberge* shuddered as jangling bits of still-moving *Locust* collided and bounced off its shins before coming to rest in the snow.

"Negative, negative, Charlie," an insistent voice protested over the radio. Comms IDed it as one of the Fifth Crucis Lancers battalion commanders. "All Charlie units are to disengage and continue on to target."

Mal backpedaled closer to the avian outline of Tally's *Shrike*, which had traded shots with one of the attacking *Assassins*. "Say again, Cross Three-One?"

"We've got you covered, ma'am," the Suns major responded. "Disengage and continue on to target. We aim to get you to your destination in one piece."

"Acknowledged, Three-One." Mal withdrew from the next incoming light lance until more Crucis Lancers 'Mechs spilled in to cover the gap in their lines.

The First Prince might not care about preserving mercenary lives, but his troops certainly did.

DUCAL MANSE ENVIRONS
NEW SYRTIS
SIAN COMMONALITY
CAPELLAN CONFEDERATION
5 DECEMBER 3147

Following her command lance, Eliza Zhao threw her *Tian-Zong* into a hard run to duck behind cover as a pair of *Chippewas* in Davion colors tore through her skies. The desert air stilled during the long seconds after the fighters' payload dropped free of their hardpoints and succumbed to the planet's gravity. Then the world became fire and damnation: a curtain of flame launched skyward and rippled outward as the cluster bombs devoured everything in their path.

Chips of shale hailed down on Zhao's canopy before clattering and tumbling out of sight. She growled and shot a recklessly aimed Gauss slug at the lead fighter, then cursed the waste of ammunition when the shot vanished into the stratosphere. The aerofighters were circling around for another pass, and she could not afford to squander any more of her limited ammo reserves.

"Status report," she radioed.

Her three lancemates responded with minor damage, but the Enemy deserved complete annihilation for blasting even one Capellan armor panel out of place.

During the *Chippewas'* initial flyby, she had assumed the Fifth Crucis Lancers' air support was targeting the ducal mansion her regiment had been ordered to defend. Since the CCAF liberated the planet from the Federated Suns almost four years ago, the Chancellor-appointed governor had appropriated the ruins of House Hasek's ancestral mansion and rebuilt it as his own private estate. Hours ago, *Shonso* Armando and his entourage had fled to the estate's military-grade command bunker in hopes of weathering the Davion attack. If the Enemy wanted to deal a deep blow to the planet's administration, they could do so by bombing the entire mansion into dust, but these last few runs demonstrated that the invaders aimed to hurt Zhao's troops, not the mansion. They wanted the estate for themselves.

Zhao chinned her helmet mic and radioed the *sang-wei* of her fire-support company directly. "Get me AA fire on those Davion birds, *now!*"

A few moments later, orange muzzle-flash plumes from a distant Partisan platoon's autocannon arrays stabbed the sky. One of the banking *Chippewas* wobbled in flight as though pummeled by an invisible pugilist. Just when the fighter seemed it might right itself, a gout of flame burst up and through its fuselage in a spray of spinning armor plates. Thrusters winked out, and the aircraft twisted silently in flight. Zhao knew it was doomed, so she turned her attention to more important matters.

The Fifth Crucis Lancers and an unmarked Davion regiment—the First Davion Auxiliary, according to intel—were hammering her lone regiment all along their line of engagement. She was no stranger to being outnumbered—inferior numbers only demanded more creative employment of her assets—but her skin simply crawled at being forced on the defensive yet again.

My kingdom for an offensive engagement.

A quick study of her tactical displays showed lance and company commanders reporting points of failure across several places in her battle line. Pickets were being overrun. Aerospace runs were plowing holes large enough for Davion brawlers to exploit.

Zhao ground her teeth. "Sheng Two, what's our status at the Igloo?"

"Everything reports secure, Sheng One," Bogdanovich responded.

She scanned the radar readout one more time and made a judgment call. Perhaps the Celestial Wisdom would find it in his heart to forgive her.

"Give immediate evac orders to all VIPs from the Igloo. Get them loaded up and ship them to nav point *Ài*."

"Sir...?"

"Just do it."

"Yes, sir. Relaying evac orders now."

Zhao sank back into her command couch and watched three squads of Fa Shih battle-armored infantrymen on guard disappear inside the majestic wood-and-marble mansion. Then she turned her attention back to the battlefield.

Matters had worsened. Limping Dynasty Guard 'Mechs fell back toward Zhao's position, until she could see their incoming Davion pursuers with visual sensors. The incoming 'Mechs carried heavy firepower toward the ducal mansion. Hovertanks powered across the sandy landscape with relative ease. Grenadier battlesuits dismounted from their OmniMech rides.

Maintaining range, Zhao fired at random targets of opportunity as she fell back toward the relative safety of the main manor house. A lucky light-PPC shot tore open a Davion Fulcrum's skirts, robbing it of mobility. Paired Gauss slugs struck a charging *Centurion* at center mass and flung the 'Mech flat onto its back. Another PPC lance vaporized a Grenadier trooper on the spot.

Amid the chaos of controlled fallback, a new blip appeared on radar. Sound dampening in the *Tian-Zong*'s cockpit ensured she saw rather than heard the pair of Karnovs swooping in toward the estate grounds. The rotorcrafts' gray camo blended well with the clouded sky. Like phantoms, they descended out of harm's way, their downdraft destroying a beautifully landscaped garden of hardy native vegetation.

Zhao kept one eye on the VTOLs in her rearview while offering the Enemy as much resistance as she and her command company could offer. Less than thirty seconds after touchdown, she caught sight of a dozen or more dignitaries hustle across the ruined garden and into the Karnovs' cargo bays, and the three Fa Shih squads followed. Both boarding ramps buttoned up, and the aircraft took to the skies.

"Igloo evacuation complete, sir," Bogdanovich reported.

"I see them. Initiate fighting withdrawal to our rendezvous point." She switched comm channels and said, "*Dàngong* One, fire mission at the following coordinates." She rattled off a string of numbers to the distant artillery team. "Fire for effect on my mark."

"That's danger close, sir," *Dàngong* replied. "Are those the correct coordinates?"

"Affirmative. Just do your job, soldier."

She did not have long to wait. Less than a minute after beginning her withdrawal, apocalypse whistled down atop the Hasek ducal mansion. A series of blinding fireballs replaced the majestic angles of its regal Capellan architecture. When the fire died down, little remained standing, only a few blocks that looked like a series of broken teeth in the jaw of a servitor begging in the street.

"*Dàngong*, again. Full spread."

"Sir?"

"Bring it down, *Sang-wei*. Bring it *all* down."

Zhao and her command lance withdrew from the site of carnage, snap-firing weapons at every moving target that came within range. In her head, she counted off the seconds since giving the order, knowing how efficient the distant artillery teams would be in serving their Chancellor on the battlefield. She knew how long it would take them to reload, how long the shells' flight times would be, and by the Celestial Wisdom, they would be prompt.

Every second bought Zhao's troops more time to fall back, more opportunity to goad the pursuing Enemy into the kill zone....

Right on time, hellfire whistled from the sky, catching pursuing hovertanks and battle armor unfortunate enough to be caught in the blast radius centered on the mansion's remains. Everything burned to cinders, until not a single brick or marble slab remained standing. And if the ordnance had done its job, the military bunker beneath the estate had been buried beneath so much rubble the Enemy would likely spend months excavating to reach it.

Despite the strategic retreat, Zhao allowed herself a smile. The imagined howls of Davion commanders were more than a satisfying trade.

PART FOUR

Julian saw the Cave, code name Root Cellar, on Arthur's scanners long before he and his First Davion Guards reached the outer approaches. The average aerial observer would have difficulty finding the subterranean stronghold's cliff-side entrance, especially amid the glacial landscape, but Julian knew its location well. However, the latest recon flyovers showed that the planet's current owners had undertaken some creative renovations since AFFS troops last controlled the base. Instead of seeing a virtually invisible entrance that called no attention to itself, he noted that the Capellans had dug in to the snow and ice like a tick on a beefalo. A series of trenches and revetments paired with heavy gun emplacements radiated out from the only access to the underground complex. In aerial imagery, the long, sweeping arcs of the layered defenses reminded Julian of stylistic radio waves emitting from a broadcast dish formed by the cliff.

In centuries past, the Haseks had relied on New Syrtis's relative distance from the Capellan Confederation border to provide security for the Cave. Now that New Syrtis sat on the Confederation's front lines, the CCAF had decided to beef up the installation's defenses, which made Julian's job all that much harder. Given a long enough timetable, slicing through these exterior defenses would be a foregone conclusion, but if they failed to take the Cave before Capellan reinforcements showed up, they would have to abandon the mission and defend themselves. Everything hinged on this outcome. Even if they could break through the outer defenses, Julian imagined the nightmares the Capellans no doubt had waiting for them in the underground tunnels. Artillery or an airstrike would've cleared out all but the worst of the conventional troops awaiting Julian's arrival, but necessity shot down that plan. A misfire could potentially collapse the cavern leading into the side of the cliff. The base itself could endure siege tactics for months, but if heavy ordnance caved in the entrance, his troops would be forced to spend precious time digging their way inside.

Brilliant flashes of laser fire and autocannon discharge in the distance testified that the real battle for New Syrtis had finally begun.

"Scepter One," General Nanava broadcast in Julian's neurohelmet radio, "This is Scepter One-Two. Forward lances report contact with the enemy at objective Root Cellar. As we expected, we're up against elements of the Fourth McCarron's Armored Cavalry. Conventional forces are reported as elements of the fledgling New Syrtis Home Guard."

Julian mentally paged through what he recalled of the DMI brief on the defending forces. Commander of the Fourth MAC, *Sang-shao* Lindsey Baxter, was a young graduate of Capella War College and the granddaughter of Capellan war hero Marcus Baxter. Her tactics favored mobile warfare, which meant the Fourth wouldn't wage a stand-and-fight defense. Baxter's youth and her likely desire to live up to a tall legacy meant she might try something reckless to prove her worth to the Strategios. All of these were weaknesses a shrewd battlefield commander could exploit.

Ahead, the Guards' recon lances swept in to flay entrenched infantry and defiladed tanks, then retreated behind friendly lines while relief lances of heavier BattleMechs provided them covering fire. At this distance, the return fire from Capellan field guns resembled nothing but an ineffectual light show of low-caliber tracer rounds. In stark contrast, heavier weapon cupolas buried into the cliff wall on either side of the Cave entrance blasted autocannon fire indiscriminately at any AFFS units that dared come within range. Julian saw at least one light 'Mech, a thirty-ton *Javelin*, take a fusillade of explosive shells to the torso and pirouette into the snow with smoking craters in its front armor.

Far ahead, the main thrust of the battle raged on. Davion and Capellan 'Mechs collided amid LRM smoke trails and autocannon barrages from Po tanks, and machine gun fire from Ying Long infantry.

What had not long ago stood as a serene example of order now descended into unbridled chaos. But after several minutes of intense fighting, the Capellans were starting to fall back. Julian zoomed his visual magnification and caught a few Fourth MAC BattleMechs performing a fighting retreat into the underground complex.

"We've got incoming!" someone shouted on the regimental frequency. "Arty, up on the ridge! All units, evasive action!"

Plumes of fire ballooned up from the ground, close enough that Julian felt the ground quake even in the relative safety of his 'Mech's command couch. More shells screamed down from the sky. Some burst in midair, turning the frozen snowscape into the very vision of hell itself. One exploded less than a dozen meters in front of Julian's advance, but he continued through the wall of flame as it engulfed his visual sensors for a moment before dissipating in the frigid clime.

The armor-damage wireframe readout in his instrument panel barely showed scratches on Arthur's paint, but that mattered little. Out there, in the middle of the battle, in a well-armored BattleMech and surrounded by a full command company of his most trusted First Guards officers, the First Prince of the Federated Suns had never felt so utterly exposed in the face of an enemy.

He had told himself every day since approving Operation CERBERUS that if he died during this campaign, such was his fate. This assault was meant to be his crucible, to prove once and for all his worthiness to lead and revitalize a nation quickly sliding toward the brink of oblivion. He told himself his presence on the front lines was needed for morale, to inspire his troops. If he died, the fate of the Federated Suns would fall to another. But if he triumphed...

He barely heard the radio over the tumultuous noise inside his head. "Scepter One, this is One-Two. We've got a problem here. A *huge* problem."

Julian swallowed and gripped his BattleMech's controls. "Go ahead, One-Two."

Nanava didn't need to respond. Through the dissipating smoke, he could see what the general meant.

An entire squadron of dark-green *Transgressor* heavy aerofighters careened overhead, each one laden with a full payload of ordnance.

Those bastards were going to collapse the entrance to the Cave.

Several hours into the tedious march toward Fortune Charlie's objective, Malerie began regretting her battalion's assignment. Fighting for sure footing against the uneven, snow-covered terrain was bad enough, but she started believing the Talons would never see true combat during this campaign. Sitting in the cockpit of an incredible war machine such as this for so long and *not* shooting at anything massing more than a handful of tons seemed to betray her heritage. Her Clan ancestors were bred specifically for combat, each one honed from birth to be a living weapon capable of fighting any battle, regardless of the situation or venue or handicap. She had half a mind to try contacting the First Prince himself and demanding that the Charlie battalions be rotated to the vanguard just so she could once more feel that life-or-death connection with her forebears. *You don't put your finger on the trigger unless you intend to fire*, she fantasized telling him. She'd learned that lesson early in her own training. Right then, her *Flamberge* was the pistol, she the trigger. And unless something hostile wandered into her scopes soon, she felt liable to accidentally subject her lancemates to friendly fire.

Enemy. Friend. *Some*one. The target no longer mattered. She lifted and balled her left fist, and shook it, imagining herself looking like a stim addict with an itch she couldn't quite scratch.

Transmissions from the First Davion Guards filled her ears. In their distant, partially garbled communications, the sweet song of battle called to her. Explosions, whooshes, shouts, squeals of tortured metal—all combined into the din Mal lived for. *She* should be the one out there beating on the Capellans, not the Davion Guards.

From amid the consternation on the task force channel, she picked out a desperate transmission: *"All Root Cellar units! All Root Cellar units! Incoming enemy aerospace on bombing vector to primary target! Priority-one target. Engage at will! Repeat: Priority-one target! Engage at will!"*

Combat instinct kicked in, and Mal's eyes dove into the tactical map illuminating one corner of her instrument panel. IFF transponders tagged a squadron of *Transgressor*s arcing in from the outermost fringes of her map's range. Resolution of their line of attack crossed both Charlie's and the Fifth's lines. In precious seconds, the squadron would be right over Able Company—prime pickings for her restless trigger finger.

At that moment she wished the Cappie birds were within range of the RFL-8D *Rifleman* from Baker Company, but the Talons companies were spread out to hell on this march.

"All Charlie Three-One units," she radioed her company, "This is Three-One actual. Target incoming birds at three o'clock! Fire at will!"

A rush of glee filled her as she steadied her 'Mech and primed her medium lasers and SRM launchers. With practiced skill, she raised her 'Mech's clawed arms and zeroed her rangefinder and reticule on the lead *Transgressor*. Magnification showed its wings and fuselage pregnant with the rounded profile of high-yield ordnance. Altitude was good. Range was good. She led the target to get good tone, flicked up the safety catch over her firing stud, and—

"Belay that, Three-One," Tally's voice cut in over the channel. "Hold your fire!"

But it was too late. The primal took over, and Mal crushed the trigger to silence the tone lock, her teeth grinding in bloodlust.

A quartet of emerald beams stabbed heavenward, punching straight through armor. Enough missiles caught the fuselage, and after an eerily silent moment, the fighter vanished in a spectacular midair fireball when the payload detonated.

She wasn't alone in flouting orders though. A half dozen other Able Company laser beams in varying hues coursed upward through the snowy sky like memorial tributes of past tragedies. Some caught the remaining *Transgressors*, but the rest of the Capellan birds soared by unscathed. Within seconds, the survivors had already diminished into little more than specks on her horizon. In the distance a concentrated torrent of lasers and autocannon tracer rounds tore the rest of the bombers from the air.

"*What the* hell, *Mal?*" Tally screeched at her over their private frequency. Her *Shrike* trundled over beside the *Flamberge* and shouldered into Mal's side, hard enough for the ninety-five-ton 'Mech to jostle her seventy-ton machine slightly off balance, but restrained enough to not stove in armor panels they'd have to pay to replace later.

Mal recovered, using control sticks and her own balance via neurohelmet feedback to steady the *Flamberge*'s gait. "My finger slipped," she said. "And maybe I was bored."

"If we were an actual Feddie outfit, I'd have to write you up for that."

Mal didn't care what Feddies did. She had another official kill on her record and had lent the Talons' employers support for a critical objective. A reprimand from someone who would never fire her was the least of her concerns. "Good thing we're not Feddies then. Or Cappies, for that matter. Anyway, we all make mistakes. It's a fact of warfare."

"Riiiight," Tally replied. "*But things like this are the reason* I'm *the major and you aren't.*" The line quieted again for a few seconds too long. "Those birds were loaded for bear. What if that had come down right on top of us, with its ordnance still armed?"

But it hadn't, Mal wanted to say. *You* know *I'm a better shot than that.*

"Pull another stunt like that, Captain, and I'm docking your pay. Got it?"

"Ma'am, yes ma'am," Mal mocked with practiced military precision.

She closed the channel and grunted. Tally could dock her pay all she wanted. Money was inconsequential, a fringe benefit. All Mal really wanted to do was fight. Her geneparents would've wanted that. And she could see the real action flaring far, far afield from Charlie's current area of operations.

At least shooting down that now-burning column of smoke in the distance silenced the itch again—for the moment.

GOVERNMENT QUARTER
SASO, NEW SYRTIS
SIAN COMMONALITY
CAPELLAN CONFEDERATION
7 DECEMBER 3147

The clogged streets of Saso were utterly crawling with Fedrat mercenary troops.

Everywhere Eliza Zhao turned, more of the Enemy filled her *Tian-
Zong*'s scopes. Down one street, a Davion foot infantry platoon traded
laser-rifle fire with Fa Shih battlesuits from Warrior House Hiritsu's infantry battalion. The opposite direction, a jungle-camo *Wasp* bearing
the insignia of the Twelfth Vegan Rangers touched off its jump jets
and sailed out of sight.

Directly along the boulevard in front of her, a grumbling platoon
of Patton tanks in a similar camouflage crept into view from behind
a reflective blue-glass skyscraper. Their turrets traversed Zhao's direction—an immediately hostile gesture—but their chattering autocannon fire was not meant for her. A pair of *Warhammer*s from her
command company ran in ahead of her and opened fire. The Pattons'
concentrated barrage barely dented the lead *Warhammer*'s armor,
and the cowardly drivers hiked in reverse to avoid PPC retribution.

Cretins, all of them. These Fedrat mercenaries had no grasp of
basic military doctrine. Their green-andbrown jungle camo just made
them easier targets to spot among the Government Quarter's predi-
lection toward light-colored structures.

As if to confirm her unspoken critique, the *Wasp* she spied a moment earlier landed in the center of the boulevard, crushing a well-
manicured median under its feet. The two *Warhammer*s ahead of her
twisted their torsos and unleashed enough short-range missiles to
tear the light 'Mech into smoking pieces.

Somewhere deeper in the Government Quarter, the main body of
Warrior House Hiritsu's BattleMech battalion was fighting a doomed
holding action against a full regiment of these wretched Davion mercenaries seeking control of the Statehouse.

After the fiasco at *Shonso* Armando's manse, Zhao's Dynasty
Guard had seen to evacuating the *shonso* to a more secure location.
She would have preferred a redoubt like the Cave, but aerospace
recon and the tacnet reported that at least two full regiments of
Fedrats and their mercenaries had steamrolled their way through the
Home Guard and into the subterranean complex. In coordinating
the planet's defense, Armando had assigned Zhao to relief efforts in
Saso, and from the look of things, she had finally caught up with the
Twelfth's rearguard elements. Now all that remained was to relieve
some pressure on House Hiritsu by lancing this mercenary boil.

"Janshi Prime," Zhao transmitted over a heavily encoded frequency relayed through Armando's temporary mobile HQ, "this is Sheng One. What is your disposition, over?"

"Sheng One, this is Janshi Prime," replied the wise and patient voice of *Shiao-zhang* Xun Kuang, his voice heavily distorted from the encryption. "Our southern flank along Statehouse Boulevard is under heavy fire and in danger of faltering. Please advise."

"It seems these Davion dogs are unfamiliar with the fearsome reputation of our Warrior Houses," Zhao replied, unable to suppress a smirk. "We must remedy this deficiency." A quick survey of her tactical map showed an estimated distribution of forces across the Government Quarter, and she quickly formulated a plan. "Stand firm, Janshi Prime. Reinforcements are en route. I'm uploading you our path of advance. Do what you can to meet us at map coordinate *Ài Lè*, and we can catch the bulk of their battalion between us."

"Acknowledged, Sheng One. Who shall be the hammer in this plan, and who shall be the anvil?"

Zhao chuckled. "Why not both of us be hammers?"

"Understood. May the Celestial Wisdom guide your hand. Janshi Prime out."

A moment of reflection on Kuang's words reminded her of the Chancellor's divine prescience. Had he not the forethought to pull the Dynasty Guard from Taygeta's defense, then the intact ducal mansion would be back in the Enemy's hands, and Warrior House Hiritsu would have waged this battle alone, a battle they might not survive otherwise.

More infantry fire from the periphery distracted her attention from the road ahead, but only for a moment. Ballistic rifles pinged harmlessly on her *Tian-Zong*'s armored skin, and she marched forward one seventy-five-ton footfall at a time, ignoring the mute, openmouthed protests of Enemy soldiers that couldn't sprint out of her path fast enough. Together, she and her command lance pressed down the main thoroughfare leading through the Government Quarter. At the terminus of this artery, the rotunda of Saso Statehouse waited, slightly hazed from both distance and smoke.

She clenched fingers around her controls and ensured all the weapon safeties were disengaged. Then she keyed the regimental channel so she could address the entire Dynasty Guard at once. "All Sheng group battalions, this is Sheng One. Coordinate full aggressive push toward coordinate *Ài Lè*. Give no quarter, no mercy. We must cleanse this Davion taint from our hardwon soil and ensure no weeds remain."

All across the line, Dynasty Guard BattleMechs surged forward, Zhao right in the middle of them. Her lancemates softened up an Enemy *Griffin* foolish enough to wander into range down the boulevard, and her paired Gauss rifles and light PPCs finished the job.

Supersonic slugs tore the Enemy 'Mech's right arm off at the elbow, and beams of charged particles shredded the remaining torso armor. Sparks and a plume of gray smoke billowed out from the hole in the *Griffin*'s chest. The Enemy 'Mech fell hard. Even from the relative safety of her cockpit, Zhao felt the ground tremble the moment all fifty-five tons of *Griffin* struck pavement.

Another Enemy joined the dance, a *Vulture Mk. IV*, followed by a *Thunderbolt*. Neither of them would stand a chance.

Zhao designated the first target, the *Thunderbolt*, by firing her PPCs and blasting two deep furrows in its forward armor. Her lancemates closed the distance, as much as the street and abandoned cars would allow, and opened fire in a bright display of lasers and detonating missiles. Within seconds, the *Thunderbolt* went down to the pavement with a *thump*, cut off at the knees. Its partner suffered a similar fate as Zhao's lance dismembered the Enemy 'Mech with ruthless efficiency.

Her lance operated as a disciplined, well-oiled machine. They needed no radio chatter to coordinate their attacks. Subtle, practiced movements and sports-style playbooks told the rest of her unit what their next action should be without wasting precious time and distraction with radio contact unless absolutely necessary. The complete lack of radio chatter also tended to unnerve the Enemy, and anything that set them ill at ease was a weapon for her arsenal. None of these cowards deserved mercy. Their very presence on this planet was a personal affront to the Celestial Wisdom's sovereignty, and Zhao and her troops saw to it that every Enemy 'Mech charging down along the boulevard fell to the onslaught of Capellan guns.

Upon reaching the foot of the Statehouse, Zhao caught sight of a quartet of battered and abused 'Mechs limping into view before them. Caught up in the hyper-focus of battle, she raised her 'Mech's arms to fire before her instruments blatted confirmation of friendlies. Her fingers relaxed. The armor of the sixty-five-ton *Shen Yi* in her sights had been so badly damaged she could just barely see hints of metallic green and black— House Hiritsu's colors—left in the 'Mech's paint.

"Looks like the Enemy is in retreat," *Shiao-zhang* Kuang radioed from his *Shen Yi*.

"Indeed." Zhao glanced at her 360-degree vision strip to gauge the scope of devastation behind her. Smashed and broken bits of 'Mechs, burned-out husks of tanks and IFVs, mangled battle armor shells, and the paste of crushed foot soldiers littered their wake.

It was not enough to ensure victory for control of this planet. Not nearly enough.

"Now," she said at length, "we must hunt them all down."

PART FIVE

THE CAVE
NEW SYRTIS
SIAN COMMONALITY
CAPELLAN CONFEDERATION
7 DECEMBER 3147

Deep underground, Julian felt the whole chassis of his 'Mech shudder through his seat. A cloud of dust shook loose from the cavern ceiling, and pebbles of bedrock rained down against his canopy. He winced, not from the suddenness of the sensation, but what it represented. He could already imagine the report that would inevitably trickle down through the command chain: another explosive surprise laid by the Capellans, another 'Mech down—the sixth one in the past hour.

This vast network of underground tunnels represented the Cave's greatest defensive strength. The honeycombed bedrock formed a virtual warren able to confuse even the most relentless of attackers. Without an accurate map, it was easy for an assault force to get hopelessly lost while defenders harried from all directions, picking off the enemy one at a time. During his enrollment at the New Avalon Military Academy, Julian had participated in theoretical tactics simulations just like this, including one based on the Cave itself; however, that project had focused solely on defense and used a purposefully fanciful model of the cavern system's layout rather than an accurate representation, for reasons of operational security.

"Scepter One," General Nanava radioed from his *Stalker*, "this is One-Two. Forward elements of Scepter Two report another plug. We're plotting another route around it."

Julian had expected minefields, 'Mech traps, and other surprises, but just as dangerous were the unexpected number of tunnels the Capellan combat engineers had flooded with ferrocrete to block passage. These plugs changed the whole architecture of the cave system by turning parallel tunnels into a single chokepoint, or creating other such dangers that rendered unit coherency damn near impossible. Given enough time, a lance of 'Mechs could break through a blocked tunnel, but time was not on their side. Julian's tac maps were constantly updating based on reconnaissance data—if they updated at all. Down here, communication relied on data relays passing from 'Mech to 'Mech, like an old-fashioned game of telephone. "Understood. Any word on that last explosion?"

"Yes, sir. A leftenant from Two Batt, Baker Company. Broke her arm in the fall. Medic says she'll have to wait for medevac to an aid station until we sort this place out."

Julian screwed his eyes closed and shook his head, neurohelmet and all. "Acknowledged. Mark the minefield and continue on forward."

As a matter of habit, he checked his six in his vision strip. In infrared, he saw the command company of Charlie Three picking up the First Guards' slack. Tactical and safety considerations placed the command elements of both units near the middle of the combined formation, to better thwart headhunter units looking for easy prey.

Major Tallula Zheng's dark-gray *Shrike* and her XO's *Flamberge* brought up his rear. The *Shrike*'s paired autocannon hung limp from the birdlike 'Mech's left arm, their ammo feeders in tatters. The *Flamberge* progressed with a noticeable limp, and one of the vestigial wings atop the 'Mech's shoulders had bent just enough off true to be noticeable at a glance.

The other two members of the Charlie Three command lance bore similar yet largely cosmetic scars. All of this represented damage sustained during the initial drop, not combat, and the operation's timetable could not afford a stop for repairs until the Cave was secured. Zheng had expressed her disapproval, but the needs of the op took precedence over the desires of one mercenary commander.

"Charlie Three Actual," he radioed, "What's your status? How are we looking back there?"

"All quiet on the home front, sir," Zheng replied after a beat of silence. "Too quiet, in my professional opinion."

"The van is quiet, too." Julian overlaid his current tunnel map over the archived map and noted places where, in the unaltered layout, enemy units might be able to trickle through the outermost parts of the network and prepare a flanking maneuver. In his NAMA project, he'd had considerable success with such a tactic. "All right, I want you to probe the coordinates I'm transmitting. Spread out and keep your eyes open. Could be they're trying to circle around us, catch us in a pincer."

Before Zheng could respond, Nanava's voice cut into the transmission. "Sir, we've got contact at multiple points. Fourth MAC with House Kamata support."

"Stick together and hold position. Don't chase after them. That's what they want." Julian flicked back to the Charlie frequency. "Charlie Three, acknowledge receipt of last transmission?"

Charlie's line deadened with static.

"Charlie Three, this is Scepter One. Please respond." The tunnels could easily bounce signals, but Julian had a direct line of sight to the recipient. He glanced at the rearview of his vision strip to witness the *Shrike* dart forward into a lumbering run. In a frigid rush of horror and instinct, he twisted Arthur's torso and stomped foot pedals to wheel around...

But not fast enough. Twin ruby beams of laser light blotted out his rearview vision long enough to deliver untold megajoules of heat to the eighty-five-ton 'Mech's vulnerable rear armor. Whooshing plumes of gray smoke announced the imminent arrival of a long-range missile salvo. Each warhead impact rattled him in the seat and jostled the 'Mech forward.

Alarms echoed throughout his cockpit as he fought the controls and his own sense of balance to keep the *Templar III* on its blocky feet. He swung around as fast as the gargantuan war machine's physics allowed and confronted the traitor.

The incendiary fire of anger and the cold sting of betrayal mingled in his heart. As he took in the line of his would-be killers, it dawned on him anew that the *Shrike*, the *Flamberge*—all of the Charlie Three 'Mechs in immediate sensor range—bore no scars from battle with the Capellans. All their damage had occurred during the initial drop.

"You misunderstand, Your Highness," said the garbled voice of the *Shrike*'s pilot. "The pincer has already caught you."

Malerie couldn't believe the words coming out of her earpiece.

During the march beneath the bowels of the Mawreddog continent's massive ice shelf, Tally had hopped onto their private channel and casually said: "We have a contract to take out the First Prince."

Mal blinked, nonplussed, certain she was experiencing communications failure or the beginnings of some kind of battlefield fugue. She felt as though the nearby *Shrike* had reached out with its taloned right hand and wrenched her guts out through her abdomen.

"Here's the deal," Tally said when no response was forthcoming. "That 'combat bonus' you've been seeing since New Damascus? It's from a Capellan contract I negotiated to secure the future of this unit.

"Look, you *know* the Suns don't give two flying figs about us. We're just warm bodies to them, meat shields. And their behavior during this campaign so far has convinced me I made the right choice. This isn't Operation Cerberus. It's Operation Get Behind the Mercs."

Mal's throat contracted. Ahead, she could see the steadily marching form of the First Prince's *Templar III*, its back exposed to this person hired to kill him. Stomach acid burned the back of her throat. Beyond his dashing looks, Mal didn't really trust the First Prince, not completely, but that was immaterial.

Such a dagger-in-the-back move was a direct breach of contract. It was dishonorable.

UnClan-like.

Chatter of incoming Capellan forces filled the task force channel. It all mutated into so much noise as steam and rage built up inside her. Because of Tally, her supposed friend, Malerie Faulkner would be branded a traitor to the contract they had signed with the Federated Suns. The Mercenary Review and Bonding Commission would black-list the Talons, and no other reputable employer would ever hire them after this.

But even worse, the Confederation hadn't truly hired mercs in almost a decade. By trying to cheat the Davions, all Tally had done was ensure the entire regiment would become indentured slaves in the Capellan military. Tally had mortgaged their future for a lifetime of servitude to a totalitarian regime ruled by a deluded dictator.

Mal heard the command to attack, but her brain refused to comply, as though some connection had broken inside. The surreal image of the *Shrike* discharging its large lasers and missiles into the *Templar III*'s rear seemed torn straight from a dream. Armor vaporized and blasted away from the First Prince's slowly turning 'Mech as the rest of the Talons turned their weapons toward Julian Davion's entourage.

Such a dishonorable, *dezgra* action would have sent her ancestors into a raging fury.

The First Prince and his command company returned fire, but Mal only had eyes for the *Shrike*'s winged, avian silhouette.

In any other terrain, she would've launched skyward on jump jets to gain superior position, but the low height of the cavern would spell suicide—which meant the *Shrike* was also earthbound.

Instead, she throttled up and lifted both of her *Flamberge*'s arms. The barrels above and below each taloned hand screeched with lasers that raked welts across the *Shrike*'s flank. A full two-dozen missiles with varying warhead types arced away from the shoulder- and wing-mounted launchers. New craters appeared in the assault 'Mech's hide.

"Traitor!" Tally squealed.

Mal ground her teeth at the irony. "*Dezgra stravag!*" She redlined her throttle to close the range, cursing the actuator limp that slowed her.

The *Shrike*'s weapons turned on Mal, the *Templar* all but forgotten amid the swirling melee. But Tally was too late to fire. Mal angled all seventy tons of her war machine toward this backstabbing coward who had ruined her—had ruined all of them—and braced for impact.

In a deafening *clank*, the two 'Mechs collided, *Flamberge* shoulder to *Shrike* chest. The heavier *Shrike* reeled back on its heels but stood firm. Mal threw her throttle in reverse to line up another salvo, but the claws on the *Shrike*'s right arm snatched the left-hand flange of her pseudo-wing assembly.

Whiplash jerked the *Flamberge* to a halt. Mal fought her joysticks to wrench away, but Tally's myomer-fueled grip was far too strong. The squeal of crushing, tortured metal filled her cockpit. Through her canopy she saw the beaklike projection of the *Shrike*'s head, of neurohelmeted Tallula Zheng sitting in her own command couch. Their eyes met for the merest of moments, but in the other woman's gaze Mal witnessed the blind fury driving her traitorous desperation.

Claws extended, Mal bashed her 'Mech's right arm into the *Shrike*'s head. Its beak crumpled. Her claws clamped down with incredible force until she felt something snap deep within the *Shrike*'s chassis. She withdrew the arm, leaving a hole surrounded by mangled metal and cracked ferroglass. The *Shrike* went limp. Its still-clenched claws nearly tore off the *Flamberge*'s pseudo-wing before letting go and crumpling face first to the cavern floor.

Mal backed up, with no time to reflect on what her battle lust had accomplished. All around her, the Guards and Talons traded fire in desperation and confusion. No matter which side she fired on, the other would brand her a traitor.

The coruscating particle beam from a Talons *Griffin* staggered the *Flamberge* and wrenched Mal back into the moment. She turned to reply in kind, but missiles from another direction exploded across her torso. Lasers sublimated armor. Autocannon shells blasted ceramic-steel armor fragments into the air. Within seconds, Mal felt reduced to a speed bag, pummeled from every quarter, thrown about her cockpit over and over again until physics and gravity won their battles.

The remains of the *Flamberge*'s left leg exploded away from the chassis, and Mal went down to the dirt, hard. Her neurohelmet smashed into a bulkhead, and white exploded across her vision. Next thing she knew, her whole existence lay sideways, her cockpit positioned to stare right into the gaping, twisted hole betraying where the fallen *Shrike*'s head once was. Mal's warrior instinct and the bloodlust pulsing through her veins urged her to try standing the 'Mech up on its remaining leg, but a groggy glance through her cracked canopy showed the Talons running distracted around her.

An unfamiliar, static-laced voice emerged over the comm to confirm her suspicions: "Task Force Root Cellar, this is Cross One, en route to your position. Figured you could use the help."

The Fifth Crucis Lancers were out there somewhere in the caves, pulling the heat off the trapped First Davion Guards.

Mal aimed her prone 'Mech's right arm at the distracted *Griffin*. Her paired pulse lasers stabbed her target and tore a gaping hole in its weaker rear armor. Tactical missiles from her torso launchers struck armor, but a few tunneled through the gap and detonated inside her target's exposed structural supports. The *Griffin* bent backward as though struck in the spine by a massive club, and it hit the ground hard enough for Mal to feel the tremor through her seat.

Her body shook again, this time from the icy chill of adrenaline fading from her blood.

What have I done? What have I done?

She'd killed one of her oldest friends for breaking their code of honor. She'd shot down another Talon in self-defense. But the Davions would mark her a traitor, regardless.

The battle swiftly shifted and moved away from her prone position, forcing her to follow the progression from her crippled 'Mech via radio chatter. The First Davion Guards and Fifth Crucis Lancers had trapped what remained of the Talons and Fortune Charlie between them, and any Charlie 'Mech that refused a stand-down order was cut down with prejudice.

With a missing leg, Mal had no choice but to crawl— away from the battle, past the broken husk of Tally's headless *Shrike*. But which way to go? Capellans ahead, Davions behind. Escape was impossible. She was doomed no matter how the cards fell.

Within ten minutes of clawing her way across cavernous ground, three First Davion Guards 'Mechs approached, their every barrel and missile tube pointing her way.

The middle 'Mech: a *Templar III*.

Julian Davion. The one who'd gotten her into this mess in the first place.

Warrior reflex lifted her *Flamberge*'s arm toward the trio of 'Mechs.

"Charlie Three-One," the First Prince himself spoke into her helmet's headset. "Stand down. Repeat, stand down. That is a direct order. Comply or be fired on."

Warrior blood pulsed hot in her veins, but she knew better than to pointlessly throw her life away on a moment like this. A true warrior remained prepared to fight any battle at any moment, but the smart ones knew when to fight and when to stand down.

Mal knew which category she fell into.

The *Flamberge*'s arm lowered.

RUINS OF JOHNSTON INDUSTRIES
CILITREN HAZARD ZONE, NEW SYRTIS
SIAN COMMONALITY
CAPELLAN CONFEDERATION
21 DECEMBER 3147

All of it, the whole planetary defense, was coming apart like so much crumbling foundation.

Eliza Zhao matched her *Tian-Zong*'s pace with the rest of her command company, but traversing the cratered, irradiated remains of an old Jihad battlefield along the equator proved more difficult than anticipated. Demolished buildings and other unidentifiable rubble lay hidden beneath a thin layer of windswept dust in blackened, seventy-one-year-old nuclear blast craters. On the positive side, the worst areas of radiation levels had thankfully faded decades ago, and the craters themselves provided excellent defilade positions for what few armor companies remained of the Dynasty Guard Calvary regiment, but Zhao found little else to celebrate as she fell in alongside Bogdanovich's *Vandal*.

Two weeks ago, the Cave, their primary stronghold after the ducal manse's destruction, fell to the Enemy, and the headhunting attempt on the First Prince himself had failed spectacularly. Trapped in the tunnels, most of the mercenary headhunters had been pulverized between the First Davion Guards and the Fifth Crucis Lancers. Together, the First and Fifth had forced the Cave's beleaguered defenders to retreat through a hidden egress tunnel.

Three days ago, House Hiritsu, still recovering from the devastating assault on Saso's Government Quarter, abandoned the Statehouse in the face of a renewed attack by Davion auxiliaries. The loss of Saso stung, but with Shonso Armando and other important dignitaries evacuated to safer locations, all was not yet lost.

However, the final straw had come just before dawn, when an urgent communiqué from the *shonso* woke her with word that his mobile HQ was under attack. The detached Dynasty Guard 'Mech company and accompanying infantry platoons were facing one of the Davion auxiliary units. Before Zhao could even get properly dressed and mount her 'Mech to give her troops aid, the enemy had overrun the HQ position, and Armando was reported missing and presumed dead. Of the company and its support elements, only four heavy 'Mechs and three squads of Fa Shih battlesuits managed to limp back to the Dynasty Guard's cantonment.

Other regiments fared no better. The fledgling New Syrtis Home Guard had largely been wiped out during the battle for the Cave and the defense of Saso. The Fourth MAC had suffered difficult losses during their retreat. House Hiritsu had already gone to ground. House Kamata had returned to Sian under orders from the Chancellor himself. Of all the planetary defenders, only the First MAC remained in favorable condition, and they were too far afield to offer Zhao meaningful assistance.

The cratered ridge where she and the remnants of her regiment had gathered was proof that the Davionistas could be hurt. In 3076, Taurian Concordat forces had bombarded the equatorial regions, leveling countless major cities. What better place to make a last stand than the monument to one of the Enemy's most bitter defeats?

She held few illusions about their chances, but one chance in a thousand was more favorable odds than no chance at all. Better to try and fail than to never try. And try they had, several times.

If only she had held the line back on Taygeta. If only she'd made that shot on the First Prince's 'Mech. If only they had repelled the Fifth Crucis Lancers at the Hasek manse.

If only. If only. If only...

The Confederation was on the verge of losing its most important conquest in centuries, and she knew that burden lay squarely on her own shoulders.

Danai, she thought, *what would you have done differently were you here?*

But Danai, many light years away on Sian, could not answer her.

A spume of black dust on the gray horizon announced the imminent arrival of Enemy tank platoons kicking up irradiated dirt. Seismic sensors warned of an indeterminate number of approaching BattleMechs. The sky remained clear of Davion birds solely due to the residual radiation interfering with fragile aerospace avionics.

Zhao crested the crater's lip and came to a halt; Bogdanovich's 'Mech stood shoulder to shoulder with her.

"*Sheng One,*" her XO radioed, "forward scouts confirm elements of the Second Davion Auxiliary on attack maneuver."

Zhao ground her teeth. History often represented last stands as defensive engagements: a vastly outnumbered ragtag group attempting to stand their ground against an unstoppable military juggernaut. She was tired of constantly being forced on the defensive during this campaign. The Second Auxiliary would expect the Guard to either stand firm or withdraw.

As more and more olive-drab 'Mechs and armor fanned out around the craters, she flexed both control sticks in white-knuckled fury. There would be no preemptive retreat order this time, not from the Celestial Wisdom, not from her, not while she still drew breath.

If she indeed had only one chance in a thousand, she would be that one chance amid countless thousands. She would take every asset at her disposal and make these Davion fools realize the gross error they had committed in crossing swords with her.

This was her destiny. This was why the Chancellor had placed such trust in her command here. If she could not win on New Syrtis, then no one could. This battle *belonged* to her. It was already written in the stars.

Zhao inhaled deeply through her nose and straightened her spine with pride. "Formation Tiger-Six," she dictated. *"Now."*

"Sir—"

"Do it!"

As one, her *Tian-Zong* and the other Dynasty Guard 'Mechs dashed down from the crater's lip, weapons lighting up the dull sky. But the Enemy came through the ruined wasteland like a storm, like the wrathful fist of an angry god.

Gray trails from countless defiladed LRM launchers streaked over Zhao's head and blasted holes in the Davion lines. Hidden artillery rained down death.

Each Enemy 'Mech or tank that fell to Capellan rage counted as another small victory. Enough small victories, and they would carry the day.

Zhao punched a single Gauss-rifle slug through a twenty-five-ton *Osiris* she suspected was spotting for Enemy artillery. A precision PPC shot gored through the tracks of a Rommel tank trying to get a bead on her, and she crushed a lone battle-armored trooper beneath a clawed foot. At her flank, Bogdanovich's *Vandal* scored devastating hits on a wounded *Blackjack*, which toppled to one side from a shattered knee.

Amid her regiment's charge, the well-oiled machine of Zhao's command lance made every shot count. The artillery bombardment and LRM salvoes had done the job well, softening up the opposition just enough for her charge to take maximum advantage. All they had to do was make that advantage last.

If she won this engagement, she could fight on to win the rest of the battle. If she won today's battle, she could press onward to win the entire campaign. One engagement at a time. That was all she needed...

"Sheng One," Bogdanovich's transmission crackled in Zhao's ear, "we have incoming."

Zhao toggled to magnetic-anomaly sensors, which showed the outlines of several 'Mechs ascending the other side of the crater slope.

Large 'Mechs.

Scouting reports hadn't expected them to arrive so soon. Somehow, they had outmaneuvered her.

A 100-ton *Devastator* bristling with Gauss rifles and PPCs appeared at the top of the rise, and sensors showed three more heavy or assault 'Mechs on its heels. All of the *Devastator*'s arm- and torso-mounted weapons traversed toward her—

Zhao didn't give the brick house of a 'Mech time to react: she already had shots lined up on it while maintaining her forward momentum. All of her *Tian-Zong*'s weaponry opened fire. PPC bolts scorched the *Devastator's* untouched hide. Both of her Gauss-rifle shots left visible dents in her target's torso armor and forced the 'Mech to pivot drunkenly in mid-stride to fight the tug of gravity...

"*Fall*, you Davion bastard..." she hissed, just above a whisper. "*Fall...*"

But the Enemy held firm as its lancemates crested the rise to join it.

Zhao caught an argentine flash—

—She woke in a bleary panic to an alarm-filled cockpit, dark except for a soft control-panel glow. Her inner ear told her the *Tian-Zong* had landed face first, burying her entire canopy in the blackened, irradiated soil, obscuring the calamitous action going on around her.

Her five-point safety harness secured her in her seat while dangling her above the command console like a marionette. She lamely reached out to do something, *anything*, on her control board, but everything seemed too far away.

A dark circle plopped right in the middle of her tac map. Smaller dots followed.

Plip. Plip. Plip.

Zhao looked down the length of her torso, saw the shrapnel poking out of her ribs.

Fingers twitched. Vision blurred. Cold.

So cold.

So—

PART SIX

AFFS Leftenant Malerie Faulkner adjusted her *Flamberge*'s scopes to zoom in on the reported disturbance, but too many skyscrapers blocked her view. For all intents and purposes, Saso's Government Quarter seemed no different than on any other day. Pedestrians filled sidewalks, and street traffic pulled out of her lance's way as though the quartet of 'Mechs were emergency vehicles with wailing sirens, but nothing out of the ordinary caught her eye. Apart from the occasional blown-out storefront or partially collapsed building—all unrepaired scars from last December's battle over the Saso Statehouse—the downtown atmosphere seemed like a typical lazy Sunday morning.

Mal wandered toward Statehouse Square, shaking her head at the slight limp in her 'Mech's gait. Even months after repairs, she still felt a slight hitch in its stride, most notably on the left side. The damage was something not even a prince's ransom could fix, apparently, since one of the necessary parts had proved difficult to come by this far beyond the Clan Jade Falcon Occupation Zone. Had she accepted the offer to join Julian Davion's personal entourage, Julian's quartermaster might've been able to pull some strings, but being that close to the First Prince meant she'd probably die of boredom before ever seeing true, frontline combat ever again. Rare exceptions like the Cave betrayal aside, nobles seldom got shot at, so the closer her proximity to the First Prince, the further away from battlefield action she would likely be. And if she wasn't on the front lines, why bother being a MechWarrior in the first place? She wasn't born to just sit on a garrison somewhere; she and Tally took offensive-combat contracts more often than anything else for that very reason. Someday she might accept promotion to command her own battalion, but for now she focused on earning her way through the AFFS ranks the hard way and remaining a field officer for as long as she could.

"You see anything, L-T?" Sergeant Hitchens radioed from his *Caesar.*

"*Neg*, Sergeant." As soon as Mal rounded the corner onto Statehouse Boulevard, she didn't need optical magnification to confirm why Captain Witherspoon had called them in.

In the shadow of the sword-shaped Civil War Monument, a multitude numbering in the hundreds, or possibly even thousands, clogged the quad across Statehouse Square. Law enforcement in riot-control gear hemmed in the protesters as best they could, but with so few versus so many, the higher-ups had reason to believe the situation could escalate faster than a lit match dropped into a black-powder keg. The picketers, as free citizens of the Federated Suns, had every legal right to protest, but Captain Witherspoon felt sending a few BattleMechs to put the fear of God into them would be both productive and fun. All they had to do was shake the ground a little, rattle the sabers, and make sure no one did anything stupid.

Zooming in her view of the crowd revealed a number of placards bearing a varied array of witticisms and amusing anti-Davion sentiments:

You can't spell D-a-v-i-o-n without N-o

Julian Caesar: Davion Megalomaniac

Bring Back the Celestial Wisdom

"Confederated" not "Federated"

Mal didn't believe for a second that these were actual longtime citizens of New Syrtis legitimately dissatisfied with the planet's recent change of ownership. No one would put it past Daoshen Liao to recruit fake protesters just to grind the AFFS garrison's gears.

"Sergeant," Mal broadcast to her lance, "you want the honors, *quiaff?*"

"*Neg*, L-T," Hitchens replied, chuckling at his own mimicry of her quaint Clan affectation. "You can have first crack at it."

Didn't matter to Mal one way or another, but the sooner this was done, the better. She took pole position, and the rest of her lance fanned out behind her along the boulevard to maximize their physical presence and present a wall of steel that would steamroll anyone who did anything outside legal bounds.

Mal lifted the *Flamberge*'s clawed arms just enough to leave the impression that their mounted pulse lasers could easily pick off targets if pushed too far. She triggered her external speakers and keyed up her neurohelmet mic. "Attention citizens of—"

A brilliant fireball consumed Statehouse Square in mid-sentence. The entire Civil War Monument disintegrated with enough concussive force to rock the *Flamberge* on its heels and tremble nearby build-ings in the shockwave of a deep thunderclap Mal felt in her bones. For a single instant, the mushrooming incendiary cloud dominated her vision and sucked horrified air from her lungs. Then just as quickly, the incandescence dissipated, leaving a haunting afterimage despite the 'Mech's flare compensation filters.

She counted herself lucky that the purple specter she couldn't blink away hid the worst of the carnage from sight. There had to be hundreds, thousands of incinerated bodies down there, both civilians and police alike, strewn about her 'Mech's feet—but she couldn't see them, didn't want to see them.

That wasn't all. The smoke left behind was *wrong* somehow, like someone had futzed with the tint of her visual sensors.

"What the devil...?" Hitchens radioed in disbelief.

Mal switched into fight-or-flight mode, but there was nothing to run from, no one to fight. A quick scan of the quad showed nothing but soot-blackened paving stones, a multitude of the dead, and the skeletal remnants of the Civil War Monument sticking upward like a rude gesture.

She dialed up her magnification and swept back and forth across screaming, fleeing survivors. The Guards occasionally trained for disaster relief, but this went far beyond such a limited scope. She lin-gered on one fleeing couple, and the man crumpled, spat up blood. His companion turned, crimson pouring from her eye sockets. Within seconds, their bodies stilled.

All around them, others met similar fates.

Mal choked down stomach acid. She knew her 'Mech's envi-ronmental sealing would protect her and her lance, but all of these people—

And then the wind picked up. Snatched up the smoke. Tossed it adrift into the atmosphere to rain over the rest of the Government Quarter, over the whole *stravag* city.

She stared dumbfounded at the smoke, paralyzed and helpless—unable to run, unable to solve anything with customary 'Mech-on-'Mech violence.

The wind kicked up again, carrying more of the lethal plumes with it. Beyond the smoke, far in the distance, a shape took form, the recognizable silhouette of a *Cataphract* painted in black with crimson trim.

More smoke blew in over the shadow, and just like that, it van-ished from visual sensors, leaving Mal wondering whether she'd imagined it.

Magnetic anomaly sensors confirmed her sanity: a faint signa-ture rippled at the very edge of maximum detection range. Whoever this pilot was, it wanted to be seen.

"Talon Two and Three," she radioed to her lance, "scout for hostiles at the coordinates I'm uploading. Talon Four, contact emergency services. Some of those civvies might still be alive."

Seconds stretched into minutes, long minutes with no activity save the commotion of rescue vehicles choking through the gaseous smoke. Mal craved a normal stand-up fight, but no attack came from any quarter.

The radio chirped through the somber, aggravating silence. "Talon One, this is Three. I've got no readings. Whoever you saw out here must've gone to ground and powered off."

Mal ground her teeth. "That's what I was afraid of. Just keep looking. We're going to find whoever was responsible for this and bring them to justice."

THE CAVE
NEW SYRTIS
TAYGETA OPERATIONAL AREA
CAPELLAN MARCH, FEDERATED SUNS
3 AUGUST 3148

Not five minutes off the DropShip all the way from Remagen, Julian stormed into the Cave's command center and demanded answers based on the reports he had received upon arriving in-system. New Syrtis had been declared secure back in February, and in his absence, matters had devolved from decent to bad to worse. Now, a more personal touch was needed. The recovery of the Capellan March capital was the first vital step toward economic and military recovery, and for all those who had bled and died on this planet, he was not about to let the situation fall apart so soon.

General Nanava, Admiral Davion-Coles, and a number of aides and attachés had joined Julian in the conference room to review the situation in depth.

"We've had further developments since you've been in transit, Your Highness," Nanava said. "Here's what we know."

He activated a wall screen and paged through several disturbing holoimages of the devastation that had rocked Saso almost two weeks ago. "On the eighteenth of July, a bomb in Statehouse Square destroyed large portions of the Statehouse, claiming the life of Governor Bakema and several thousand protesters gathered nearby. The bomb released a potent nerve agent into the atmosphere, and the estimated death toll is upwards of two hundred thousand."

The holo changed to a silhouetted BattleMech partially obscured by smoke. "This still is from Leftenant Faulkner's battleROM footage, captured moments after the attack. Remind you of anything, Highness?"

Julian's stomach churned. The flat black paint that seemed to suck in light brought to mind field manual images of Death Commandos, the *crème de la crème* of the CCAF. Instead of being trimmed in customary Liao green, however, the 'Mech sported lines of stark scarlet.

"Since then," the general continued, "The Guards have encountered these 'Mechs in the field on at least a dozen occasions. We're not quite sure how or when these Death Commandos—or whoever these jokers are—got on-planet, but one thing's for sure. They're *good*. I've lost a lot of good folks trying to take out these bastards, and all they do is rile up the populace. Problem is, there's never very many of them, so it's like trying to swat a gnat with a fishing net. Damn things give us the slip almost every time. The few we have managed to take down, though..."

"Let me guess," Julian said, grinding his jaw. "False tooth cyanide capsules, and equipment with no identifying markers."

"Affirmative. Classic Maskirovka tactics. But the admiral has a different theory."

Admiral Davion-Coles smoothed the front of his uniform and paged through a few other holo slides. Julian recognized the images: Confederation 'Mechs locked in combat with opponents bearing the seal of the now-conquered St. Ives Compact. The devastating Capellan-St. Ives war, fought between 3061 and 3063. One of the holopics centered on an explosion with a profile and coloration similar to the Saso blast.

"Analysis of the nerve agent indicates a chemical similarity to the agent used in the Black May attacks in 3062," Davion-Coles said. "Those attacks were associated with a dangerous Thuggee cult led by the Chancellor's now-deceased aunt, Kali Liao. Though the cult was allegedly destroyed during the Jihad, it is my belief that its remnants are now operating in our midst."

Julian frowned. "Do we have any evidence to support this?"

The admiral brought up another series of images. Julian was no stranger to the horrors of war, but this—this turned his stomach. A whole street filled with civilians of all ages, each one brutally murdered until the gutters ran with blood.

"Sir, this is from the town of Ross. Residents woke up to find hundreds of their neighbors dead in the streets, each one showing signs of ritual mutilation. There were no messages, no apparent motive, no witnesses."

A second holopic came into focus: a similarly grisly scene, only in a smaller, snowier, more rustic locale. "This was just a few days ago, when someone stumbled into this no-name shantytown out in the mining belt. Maybe two hundred transients, all dead to a man. Same MO as before."

Julian avoided staring at the images for as long as he could get away with. "So we're either looking at copycats, the real McCoys, or Capellan PSYOPs tactics."

"Far as I'm concerned, Highness," said General Nanava, "I don't care what they are. These aren't just your run-of-the-mill guerrillas. They've got the populace running scared, thinking their community might be the next victims, which just makes our job all that much harder. There's been riots, suicide bombs, the works. Got so bad that Leftenant Governor Ralston had to declare martial law just to keep the peace. And that's when you come in."

Julian regarded his commanders. "Then we deploy to the field, draw them out."

Admiral Davion-Coles shook his head. "Highness, if it were only that simple—"

"You misunderstand me, Admiral," Julian cut in. "I've not come all the way from the Crucis March just to hide in a command center. Make it known that I am here, deployed along with the First, and I am certain our mysterious friends will come calling within hours."

General Nanava's eyebrows lifted. "Sir?"

"It's *done*, General. See to the preparations. We fought hard to retake this planet, and I'm not about to let some death cult terrorize the very people we just liberated."

"I only fear there is more to this than random acts of terrorism and sabotage. We need to follow these cultists—or whoever they are—back to their nest and eliminate—"

"Apologies, Admiral," interrupted a mortified, out-of-breath leftenant as she charged into the room. "Colonel Brody's on the horn. First Battalion's barracks are under attack."

Julian and his commanders all exchanged glances. "Opposition?" asked Davion-Coles.

"It's those same bandits we've been tracking, sir." "Force strength?"

"Unknown, but they're out in droves. More companies than ever reported. Seems like they've all come out of the woodwork this time."

Julian nodded at her. "Thank you, Leftenant. Tell the colonel to stand firm. We're on our way." After she scurried out, he said, "It seems news of my arrival has certainly traveled fast."

Nanava offered a grim smile. "Looks like you got your wish, Highness."

Before Julian could respond, the same leftenant barged back in, even more breathless than before. "Sirs, we've got incoming from a pirate point. Force estimate of at least two regiments."

Julian closed his eyes a moment. "How long do we have?"

"Twelve hours until their DropShips reach combat-drop altitude."

Not nearly enough time to prepare proper defenses, as far as Julian was concerned.

His fists clenched.

There was *never* enough time.

APPROACH TO AFFS CANTONMENT
SASO, NEW SYRTIS
TAYGETA OPERATIONAL AREA
CAPELLAN MARCH, FEDERATED SUNS
3 AUGUST 3148

The blocky feet of *Yen-Lo-Wang* touched down on the snows of New Syrtis, heralding the arrival of *Sang-shao* Danai Liao-Centrella from orbit. She braced for impact, allowing temporary jump-jet pods and the 'Mech's leg shocks do their job. The moment her stomach settled and firm ground jostled her command couch, she jettisoned the jets and leaned forward into a run. The fifty-ton *Centurion* loped forward into the fray as though the storied 'Mech owned the space around it. Even her nearby troops seemed to give her a wider berth than when on noncombat maneuvers.

Fear was a powerful ally in battle, and she always used it to her advantage. To many, this galloping *Centurion*, serial number FS1010-031X, was the purest symbol of Capellan pride and tenacity in the face of overwhelming odds. Three generations of Solaris VII arena fighters had piloted the 'Mech, and its previous owner, her cousin Kai Allard-Liao, was still considered among the greatest MechWarriors in history, thirty-five years after his death. Even the greenest of recruits recognized the power and presence of *Yen-Lo-Wang*, the Chinese god of death, king of the nine hells, and Danai perpetuated the legend.

"Forward!" Danai commanded. "Tear them to ribbons!"

Through a hail of laser fire and missiles, the command company of the Second McCarron's Armored Cavalry formed up around her and pressed their advance down the slope leading toward the growing fray, firing long-range weapons downrange at targets of opportunity. Seemingly all around them in the sky overhead, spherical *Union* DropShips bearing the Capellan Confederation emblem descended on columns of plasma thrust.

In the distance, arctic-camo 'Mechs engaged black 'Mechs trimmed in red. The Fifth Crucis Lancers were faltering under the onslaught, and the newly arrived First Davion Guards balked in the face of three Capellan 'Mech regiments. By the look of how the battle was progressing, the Death Commandos that had hidden near the radiation belt had done their job well.

Her longtime friend Eliza Zhao had been the one to suggest hiding elite partisans on the planet in case the defense crumbled, but it was Danai who had brought it to the attention of her elder brother, the Chancellor. Daoshen embraced the idea with glee. Two years prior, Julian Davion had made the CCAF look the fool on the Crucis March world of Marlette, and Danai herself had met with the novice First Prince on Daoshen's behalf to broker the armistice between their two nations. Now the Enemy had fallen victim to Daoshen's own "Marlette Deception," but in miniature.

The trap sprung, Danai had no trouble justifying her decision to deploy the Second MAC to New Syrtis. She would've come even without support. For her, this campaign meant more than simple revenge. The Enemy had racked up a balance—for the Marlette Deception, for breaking their truce, for the death of Eliza Zhao— and she aimed to collect, with interest.

Some of the Enemy 'Mechs turned to greet her and the other newcomers, which was exactly what she wanted—to draw off their fire while the Dynasty Guard battalions circled in from behind Danai's screen and attacked the Fifth Crucis Lancers' cantonment itself as the McCarron's Armored Mosquitos executed a bombing run. MechWarriors could spend extended periods in their 'Mechs if necessary, but rob them of a place to barrack, and watch morale crumble. The best way to defeat an army was to attack its heart—or at the very least, to stab them as close to the heart as possible. Until the First Prince lifted his head high enough to be seen, this was the most devastating option. A victory here would not win back the planet, but it would be a start.

By the look of Enemy 'Mechs faltering across the line, the surprise maneuver had worked very well. The Dynasty Guard's charge on the Fifth's rear pulled enough attention away that the Second MAC could storm in with relative ease.

With little consideration for her safety, Danai barreled straight down the slope. She raised *Yen-Lo-Wang*'s tall, curved *scutum* shield and charged down the hillside along with her lancemates, hatchet raised high. Others called her methods foolhardy, but she delivered results. Even the weapons of overconfident MechWarriors seemed to miss her when she approached. Few pilots expected an opponent to drive straight toward them, guns blazing, no holds barred. Such a maneuver was usually suicide, which was why it worked so effectively for her. When a freight train is coming your way, you get off the tracks or get hit. Only the most foolish chose to stand and fight, and those that did rarely lived to tell the tale.

Danai painted her first target in her HUD, a daring twenty-five-ton *Gunsmith* that darted across the battlefield to take potshots at her from short range. She felt *Yen-Lo-Wang* shudder from recoil as twenty long-range missiles ripple-fired from their launch tubes. A split second before the smoke tendrils reached their target, she triggered her Clan-made heavy large laser, gouging a blackened hole dead center on the *Gunsmith*'s side armor. Enough warheads found their way through the melted breach to detonate inside. The Enemy 'Mech's limbs locked, and the dead machine plowed face first into the snow as though it had suffered a cataleptic episode.

Adrenaline from the kill coursed through her like a double jolt of espresso. Without slowing or hesitating or even wasting time to gloat, she traversed her torso in search of another target while her lancemates sought out their own.

A forty-five-ton 7S *Hatchetman* unleashed its nine-tube multi-missile launcher in her direction. Not bothering to raise her shield, Danai shrugged off the hull-rattling short-range warheads and replied with a long-range salvo of her own. The *Hatchetman* staggered in mid-step. Clearing smoke revealed the blast had torn off one of the lateral fins from the 'Mech's head. Danai growled and juked in the Enemy's direction.

But the Enemy pilot hesitated in the face of Death.

And, like so many others, that was his undoing.

With open-mouthed rage, Danai swung *Yen-Lo-Wang*'s hatchet full force as she passed, cleaving straight through the *Hatchetman*'s ruined fin. The 'Mech's head crumpled and tore free, and the god of death rushed on to its next target.

New Syrtis would be theirs again, she vowed, even if she had to destroy every one of these Davionistas with her own two hands.

PART SEVEN

Malerie didn't relish the prospect of marching through an irradiated wasteland. All craters and pits, the ruins of a city stripped bare by nuclear fires decades ago. During the march to attempt a counterfeint against the Capellans, she occasionally needed to sidestep her *Flamberge* around the twisted wreckage of a BattleMech. Most of these wrecks bore Confederation insignia—casualties from last year's fighting.

"Baker Company," Captain Witherspoon broadcast to Mal's unit, "We're approaching enemy lines. Stay sharp. Just remember that the Second Auxiliary beat the Cappies here once before. And if an auxiliary regiment can beat them, then we sure as hell can too."

Mal stepped around another wreck—a blackened and melted *Tian-Zong* ground facedown into the soil—and took her place in line with the rest of her lance. She rotated her 'Mech's torso to scan the battlefield. Far to the northern flank, she spotted a familiar 'Mech amid the others: a lone *Templar III* painted in dark-gray camouflage like the rest of the regiment. Her experience in the Cave last December had burned that 'Mech into her memory, so there was no question who had accompanied them to the battlefield.

In her estimation, the First Prince was not the shrewdest of military strategists, but even she had to admit the planet's defense would have faltered long ago had he remained back on Remagen. Julian Davion acted as a potent morale booster, something the remaining Davion troops sorely needed for this battle.

"Here they come!" Witherspoon warned. "Attack pattern alpha-three. Good hunting!"

Like revenants returned from shallow graves, the enemy 'Mechs cresting the rise of a distant crater seemed to rise up from the ground. So many of them approached that Mal had to let her sensors identify and designate targets. Many lesser MechWarriors would have buckled under such an assault, but Mal had war in her blood. Her hands never wavered on the controls.

"Falchion Three and Four," she radioed her lance, "take down that *Sha Yu*! Two, you're with me on the *Victor*!"

A chorus of acknowledgements replied. Laser and PPC discharge flared downrange toward the forty-ton *Sha Yu*. Missiles and autocannon savaged the eighty-ton *Victor*'s armor. Laser flashes from near-misses whined past her cockpit, but Mal drove on, almost unaware of that *stravag* hitch still in her left leg.

Between shots, her attention would occasionally flit over to the distant *Templar III* just long enough to ensure it remained in the fight. As the old saying went, if you saved someone's life, you were responsible for them from that moment onward. Her ingrained sense of honor found that hard to shake, even in a pitched battle like this.

"Taking fire!" Hitchens shouted, transmission crackling with interference.

Large-bore autocannon rounds drilled straight through the sergeant's cockpit, leaving behind a fragmented, smoky mess of support beams.

Mal gritted her teeth, but refused to waver in the face of the incoming *Victor*.

From Arthur's cockpit, Julian zeroed in on another target of opportunity and mashed the triggers. The 'Mech bucked as recoil from his paired Clan-tech PPCs blasted charged particles downfield to pulverize armor plating on a distant *Vindicator*. He braced for return fire, but none came. The melee had already devolved into such chaos that the *Vindicator* pilot probably couldn't tell which 'Mech had fired the shot. Julian hung back and let his lancemates finish off his target, which afforded him a moment to gauge the fight's prognosis.

Even before this battle had begun General Nanava, Admiral Davion-Coles, and he all knew the offensive was ultimately doomed, but that was no reason to quit, not just yet. For nearly two weeks, the First Davion Guards, Fifth Crucis Lancers, and a smattering of hastily trained militia had held out against three Capellan line regiments and nearly three companies of Death Commandos, despite the loss of important support facilities and supply depots. Recent thrusts across this no man's land had resulted in a stalemate, and this final push was meant to break Capellan morale while holding out long enough for off-planet reinforcements to arrive.

If the SOS he'd sent had managed to get out, that was. Without a working hyperpulse generator on New Syrtis, he had no guarantee the message had even gone beyond this system. His troops could be holding out for nothing, and Julian knew it. The regimental COs knew it. Deep down, he believed even the lowliest grunts knew it. But still they fought on—because of his presence among them. This resolve was why he'd refused to hole up in the Cave's warrens and fight a losing war of attrition.

Better to take to the field with even a splinter of hope than let that hope shrivel up and die.

With little warning, a ninety-ton *Yu Huang* manifested at the top of the rise. Julian swallowed. Its large-bore autocannon posed a hazard for even an assault 'Mech like his. Before Julian's lancemates could head off the threat, the *Yu Huang* stampeded in his direction, with eyes only for him.

Julian triggered every weapon at his disposal, but the *Templar III*'s lasers, PPCs, and missiles that struck seemed to leave little more than dents and carbon scoring across the sunburst design worked into *Yu Huang*'s sturdy torso. Julian backed up to create range while waiting for his lasers to recharge and missiles to reload. The *Yu Huang* pressed forward and unleashed its large-bore autocannon square into Arthur's chest.

Julian reeled from the hit and prepared to answer in kind—

Something caught the corner of his eye—a tiny orange glow in the dull gray skies overhead, a point of light like a firefly. It elongated and flared in brightness and intensity like a meteor hurtling earthward.

This was no meteor, however.

A blur descended, and the *Yu Huang* vanished in a quake that rocked Julian's 'Mech. From the steaming impact crater rose the blocky silhouette of a ninety-five-ton *Peacekeeper*, looking for all the world like a god reborn in its white-and-orange livery.

Julian smiled.

The Dawn Guards had arrived.

Despite the armored shell of *Yen-Lo-Wang* projecting a confident aura of victory around her, Danai was quickly losing grasp of her battle-field patience.

As the Chancellor's sister, she had claimed authority of this oper-ation and commanded the might of three full BattleMech regiments, yet somehow these Davion swine insisted on waging their losing battle. And unless the First Prince had turned coward and hid in some bolthole, he would be out here in this cratered wasteland, trying to prove to his troops he wasn't above fighting alongside them. She only needed to remove him from the equation, like the general in a game of *xiangqi*. Take out the head, and his troops would surely break.

But then the Enemy's reinforcements had arrived. Their unit insignias matched those Eliza Zhao had reported fighting back on Taygeta, but this time they bore Davion colors, not RAF.

It was no matter. These new troops could not stop her from carrying out her brother's wishes. They would fall just the same.

From her position on a cliff above the blackened ruins of Cilitren, she observed the lay of battle against her tactical map. Aerospace reconnaissance supplied what data she could not glean from visual sensors. Once she found where the First Prince was hiding and eliminated him, she would join the fray and erase from existence any Davions who graced *Yen-Lo-Wang*'s gun sights.

"Come out, come out, wherever you are..." she singsonged under her breath to the map.

As if in response, her command channel clicked on with an incoming transmission. *"Sang-shao,"* her XO radioed, *"Sao-shao* Vogel reports spotters have IDed the potential location of primary target. Transmitting coordinates now. Please advise."

Danai focused on the blinking crimson x on her tac map. She traversed *Yen-Lo-Wang*'s torso to face the marker and dialed up her zoom until she could see into the distance below. Her view danced across the writhing orgy of destruction and chaos until she caught sight of a blocky assault 'Mech whose arms bristled with laser and PPC barrels: a *Templar III* with a gaping hole blown in its right side.

She keyed her mic. "Current status of air support?"

"Mosquito Squadron is on station and awaiting orders."

Danai mapped the aerospace squadron's prospective flight plan in her map. "All right, keep Vogel's spotters on the target, and coordinate fire mission with Mosquito Squadron and the Gypsies ASAP."

"Acknowledged."

She clapped her hands together and stared daggers at the zoomed-in *Templar*, the source of so many of her nation's problems. "I have you now," she whispered to the distant 'Mech.

She monitored background chatter on the regimental frequency as her XO called in the air strike. All of the *xiangqi* pieces were moving into place. Now, only one piece remained—the god of death.

Danai throttled *Yen-Lo-Wang* in reverse, away from the cliff and back down the incline. Above, the skies roared with the coarse thunder of incoming fighters. She smiled, hefted the *Centurion*'s hatchet, and advanced down toward the city ruins to collect her prize.

Like winged demons of apocalyptic prophecy, a half-dozen *Měngqín* aerofighters swarmed across Mal's view, temporarily distracting focus away from her opponent. These *Měngqín*s, no mere interceptors or superiority fighters, were laden with heavy ordnance. Since both sides' support bases and aid stations lay far from the battlefield, the only remaining targets of military significance within bombing range were BattleMechs.

And the *First Prince* piloted one of those BattleMechs.

Mal shifted her focus toward the *Templar III*, which fought alongside the newly arrived Dawn Guards. She angled her *Flamberge* upward to get tone on the lead *Měngqín*, but was too late.

The aerofighters' bullet-shaped payload unhooked and dropped in slow motion.

On instinct, Mal stomped a foot pedal and leaned into a hairpin turn. In the back of her mind, she knew she'd never beat a bomb in a footrace, but that only spurred her on faster. If she could only reach the First Prince soon enough to shield him, push him away from the worst of the blast—

The *Flamberge* stumbled in midstep—that damn hitch in the left leg! She felt something slip and give out in her hip actuator, and seventy tons of OmniMech plowed into the dirt, shoulder first. Before the dust could settle, she looked up from her cockeyed position to see the *Templar* running hard, too slow to avoid what was coming.

The world exploded into blinding fury and heat Mal could feel even from inside her cockpit.

When the fire dissipated, the brutalized *Templar* sank back onto its haunches, but it remained upright amid a fresh graveyard of Davion 'Mechs wrecked by the blast.

Through the pulsating afterimage, she caught something out of the corner of her sideways canopy: a hatchet-wielding *Centurion* bearing the Second MAC's colors.

Yen-Lo-Wang.

The god of death was coming for them both.

Mal struggled to rise, to fight back, but the hip couldn't confidently support the weight.

Instead of charging in to finish them off, the *Centurion* held its position among the cratered landscape, as though waiting for something.

Moments later, the ground around the *Templar III* erupted in fiery plumes of artillery bombardment. The smoke cleared, leaving the First Prince's 'Mech slumped back, crumpled, pitted, unmoving.

Mal slammed her fist on the dashboard hard enough to feel a bone break in her hand. Even if she had been able to react a few seconds earlier, it wouldn't have mattered. The artillery would have just killed them both.

Awareness came to Julian in flashes of dream.

—broken cockpit glass—

—a curtain of eclipsing flames—

—sparks and flashes, heat and pressure—

—the cacophony of a tortured battlefield—

Through a floating delirium, his right leg tingled as though waking from paresthesia. He tried to move it in his command couch.

Gazed down.

Saw the endo-steel beam that had erupted from his left shin, the bar large enough to obscure the rest of his leg from view.

He reached out to touch the beam, to separate dream from reality—

A blackened char covered his extended hand. At least two fingers were partially missing. Burned, cauterized stumps remained.

But despite the ashes, he felt no heat.

Everything went cold—then blackness stole him away.

Beyond the spidery crack in Mal's canopy, through a veil of smoke, the menacing silhouette of *Yen-Lo-Wang* approached the fallen *Templar III*. Mal didn't need a malicious imagination to know that the enemy MechWarrior planned to either ensure the First Prince's death or otherwise desecrate his body. Capellans did not believe in half measures.

Some small spark within her wanted to believe Julian Davion had survived, despite the devastating barrage his 'Mech had suffered. If even a shred of life remained in that blackened shell of a 'Mech...

But *Yen-Lo-Wang* and its executioner's ax raced closer to the *Templar*'s crateous ruin with each passing second.

Once more she fought her controls to stand, wincing at the broken bone in her right hand. All seventy tons groaned upright, but she knew from the *Flamberge*'s drunken motions she would be unable to keep it upright for long.

She stomped both foot pedals hard enough to feel them strain and wiggle beneath her boots. The 'Mech shot skyward on tongues of plasma, and Mal steered in mid-jump to train all of her weapons to bear on the Capellan champion below. The bent pseudo-wing ruined her intended trajectory, but she corrected in midair as best she could.

"Falchion Lance," she radioed, "follow my lead! Protect Scepter One at all costs!"

Mal touched down with the force of an earthquake—right along *Yen-Lo-Wang*'s path. Right before the incoming maw of the god of death.

Though she outmassed the *Centurion* by twenty tons, this close *Yen-Lo-Wang* seemingly dwarfed her *Flamberge*. In the stretched seconds after landing, a shudder shot up her spine. How many opponents had this 'Mech destroyed in its long history? How many total MechWarriors had its famed pilots killed in combat? Hundreds? Thousands?

Honed warrior instinct beat down this fear like a sledgehammer.

Mal raised her 'Mech's arms and lit off all of her still-functioning pulse lasers and tactical missiles, heedless of the lancing fire in her broken hand as she squeezed the trigger over and over, regardless of whether the weapons had finished cycling or reloading. *Yen-Lo-Wang*'s *scutum* shield caught most of the blinding explosions and pulsating strobes of laser light, but a few beams and warheads scored and pitted armor on the advancing *Centurion*'s arm—

The same arm swinging back its massive hatchet, in prelude to a strike.

Yen-Lo-Wang's weapon descended with the frightening precision of a Solaris VII champion.

Mal instinctively moved both mechanical arms to shield her cockpit–

A great and terrible *clang* resonated throughout her entire body.

She must have blacked out for a split second, because the god of death was already yanking the embedded blade from the wound in the *Flamberge*'s torso, just below her cockpit. Fragments of armor and internal structure tore away, tumbling to the irradiated ground. Sparks showered through her cockpit. Internal smoke dimmed the cockpit and clogged her lungs.

Neg! She would not go down like this, not until she knew the First Prince was safe.

Like her Jade Falcon ancestors had done, Mal screeched through the searing agony in her broken hand to clench her triggers and fire every available weapon at point-blank range. High-yield tactical missiles erupted from the *Flamberge*'s torso and struck hard enough to stagger Death itself.

Yen-Lo-Wang took a single step backward to put some distance between them. The mangled wreck of its hatchet hung limp from a ruined hand, and a blackened missile-blast crater marred the *Centurion*'s otherwise pristine head.

Mal's warrior blood urged her to pursue her backpedaling foe all the way through the nine hells, but unexpected missile tone shrieked in her ears. A score of hot-loaded long-range missiles ballooned out from *Yen-Lo-Wang*'s torso. Explosions rattled across every quadrant of the *Flamberge*.

A surge of lightheadedness smeared and tunneled Mal's vision. Radio chatter filled her ears, but she couldn't make out the words.

Warmth spread across her chest. She chanced a look down. Shrapnel had punched through her cooling vest. Green fluid mixed with red and pooled in her lap. A chilled wave of nausea struck her.

The *Flamberge* stumbled two steps forward in pursuit, but the hip actuator gave out entirely. The 'Mech fell to one knee. Mal struggled to stay upright, but the damage to her 'Mech—no, to herself—was too great for even a Falcon descendant to overcome.

Like the rumble of a conquered beast striking the earth, seventy tons of metal collapsed with teeth-rattling force, never to rise again.

Through smoke and blood haze clouding her vision, Mal's lancemates advanced past her fallen wreck, in fast pursuit of the king of the nine hells. Scintillating laser beams and autocannon shells drilled furrows at *Yen-Lo-Wang*'s feet, none scoring hits. Seemingly from nowhere, a wall of Capellan steel swarmed in before the legendary 'Mech, intercepting Mal's lance and covering *Yen-Lo-Wang*'s withdrawal down a nearby slope. Two Capellan 'Mechs, four, eight. No matter how hard her lancemates fought, the screen proved impenetrable.

She winced and smiled, blood dribbling down her chin. Didn't matter whether Julian Davion still lived. Malerie Faulkner, proud descendant of Clan Jade Falcon, had retained her honor by forcing the Capellans' champion into retreat, away from the First Prince's downed 'Mech.

She closed her eyes. *I've done my duty. Now Julian must do his.*

And if Julian was indeed gone, like her twisting gut warned, she could imagine worse company in whatever afterlife awaited warriors like her.

Mal clenched both fists around her *Flamberge*'s control sticks and let the encroaching coldness claim her.

Julian awoke on a gurney in a darkened room, an IV drip nearby.

A shadowed figure waited for him.

"Ah, Highness." The voice of General Nanava echoed as though distant and underwater. "It is good to see you back with us. We were afraid we had lost you."

Julian tried to sit up, but a wave of nausea killed that idea. "How... how bad...?" he managed to croak between dry, cracked lips.

Nanava sighed. "I won't lie to you. The surgeons... ah...had to take the leg from just below the knee. Your physicians will go over all of that with you in time."

The leg—the one he'd dreamed about the beam impaling—it still tingled like it begged to be woken up, like it was still attached to his knee. He tried to sit up to see the extent of the injury, but the drugs made everything too liquid and syrupy to comprehend, and he lapsed back into unconsciousness.

GOVERNMENT QUARTER
SASO, NEW SYRTIS
TAYGETA OPERATIONAL AREA
CAPELLAN MARCH, FEDERATED SUNS
30 AUGUST 3148

A fitting place for a summit, Danai thought as she strode into the conference room with her entourage of regimental staff and Death Commando bodyguards. She had adjusted her officer's cap to better conceal the bandage on her forehead, but not even a CCAF infantry-style cape could hide the sling holding her broken arm close to her torso.

For this conference, Julian Davion had chosen a site within view of the nerve agent attack. Through the bulletproof transpex of the extravagant room's large bay window, Danai could look out onto the still-chaotic ruins of Statehouse Square, centered on what remained of the FedCom Civil War Monument—now a memorial site for another unspeakable tragedy.

Her lips thinned into a grim line as she surveyed the scene. She had possessed no operational foreknowledge of the Death Commandos' role in the terror attacks on the populace, but she would have a stern talk with her brother over this matter. There were many ways to win wars, and the wanton murder of civilians—some of whom had doubtless been loyal Capellan folk!—was unconscionable. She knew Julian planned to use this vista to gain her sympathy vote, but she would have none of it.

A Davion general guided in a wheelchair bearing the First Prince—what was left of him, at least—and sat him at one end of the rich mahogany table dominating the center of the room. Danai had met with Julian Davion before, in the wake of the disastrous Marlette Deception, but this blonde, blue-eyed figure seated before her in plain AFFS fatigues and days of untouched stubble was a different man than the one she had once treated with: a shadow, but a strong and resolute one. Her attack on the Cilitren battlefield had not killed him, but instead it had done quite the opposite: this man was very much alive, despite his wounds.

"So, Your Highness," she said, "here we are again, negotiating yet *another* ceasefire." She cocked her head to one side and narrowed her eyes with accusative curiosity. "Tell me, have you finally lost your taste for conquest? Or do you plan to break this new truce less than two years after we forge it? Assuming we do reach an agreement to suspend hostilities here, that is."

Julian adjusted in his wheelchair, and a twinge of pain visibly stung his eyes—whether from battlefield injury or her pointed, truthful barbs, she could not be certain. "You are well within your rights to be angry, *Sang-shao* Liao-Centrella. But I will not apologize for my actions. This invasion was undertaken to secure my nation's future in the face of unremitting war against the Draconis Combine.

"But let us not belabor the point. True, your regiments had us on the ropes before we agreed to meet, but you know as well as I that you agreed to temporary armistice because you cannot hold this planet with the forces at your disposal. Your brother has focused the lion's share of his military attention on the Republic, in anticipation of the Fortress wall coming down and Republic troops swarming the Confederation. Therefore, unless I have grossly misjudged the Chancellor's state of affairs, he has denied your request for reinforcements. Also, the people of this planet who, for countless generations have been free citizens of the Federated Suns, have also taken it on themselves to rise up against your troops in any way they can."

He fell silent for a beat and took a breath that seemed to pain him. "So tell me, *Sang-shao*. Tell me my assessment of this situation is wrong."

Danai swallowed down her first retort to his accusation. He was right on all counts, but she would not openly admit as such. Her upbringing in the courts of Sian had taught her this political dance all too well. *If only all matters of state could be solved at the controls of a BattleMech,* she lamented. "As an official spokesperson for the Celestial Wisdom, Chancellor Daoshen Liao is prepared to hear your proposal for a temporary ceasefire."

Julian sighed, but his pale demeanor remained firm. "Very well. For now, the Federated Suns will retain control of New Syrtis and all of the planets my troops have occupied in advance of the New Syrtis invasion."

He activated a holomap showing the Davion-occupied territory surrounding the planet, with several planets marked in Federated Suns yellow amid the sea of Capellan Confederation green. "I will allow you and your regiments to depart safely to Capellan space, where you can bring my formal proposal for a truce to Sian."

Danai considered him with a level stare. She had expected a proposal of this sort, but was it wise to accept? Since breaking the truce, Julian had claimed a small handful of Sian Commonality worlds in addition to New Syrtis—but what was the loss of this planet compared to the looming threat of Republic invasion? If she fought to hold on to New Syrtis, would spending her troops here, without hope of reinforcement or resupply, ultimately risk the Confederation losing Liao, Tikonov, or other major worlds to the inevitable Republic invasion?

The First Prince inhaled and exhaled slowly before continuing. "You and I both know the Chancellor needs this ceasefire just as much as I do. I have other wars to fight, *Sang-shao*, as does your brother, and us continuing to tear each other apart now will only make both of us easier targets for our enemies down the road. Remind him of that when next you see him."

Danai nodded. She buzzed with delight, but refused to let it reach her eyes. Brokering this peace, however temporary it might inevitably be, would further elevate her star in her brother's eyes, and among the Capellan nobility and the CCAF High Command.

"Then we are in accord," she said at length. "I will speak with the Chancellor on your behalf. In the meantime, I suggest you discover what this truce will ultimately cost you."

A faraway look haunted the First Prince's unblinking eyes. "Believe me, *Sang-shao*, I already know."

THE ANVIL

BLAINE LEE PARDOE

DEDICATION

To Victor Milán, fellow author and the architect of Malvina Hazen's rise to power. I only met Vic once, but his passing leaves a hole in our ranks. He created awesome characters and neat units. His 'Mech stomped the ground, and it quaked every time he produced a new book. *Seyla*, Vic! May the warriors of Valhalla tremble as you walk their halls.

I have built my words on the shoulder of a giant. I only hope I did him honor in moving the Jade Falcon storyline forward.

To Philip A. Lee, who originally plotted this battle out for the *Shattered Fortress* sourcebook. Phil put up a lot with my shenanigans on our weekly creative calls.

To Ray Arrastia, who kept me honest with his sage advice.

And to Brent Evans, who convinced me I could take this idea and make it cool. I hope I didn't let him or the readers down. I've never tackled the Jade Falcons before, but it was much more fun than I ever imagined. Brent, buddy, the foundation has been laid...

ACKNOWLEDGMENTS

BattleTech is about to enter a new era, and being a part of that is exciting. I thought it would be best to not go into this new era alone. Truly great warriors surround themselves with other greater warriors. That is where legends are born.

I tapped the *BattleTech* fan community on Facebook, and have taken the liberty to include some of them in this novella. *BattleTech* is all about the fans, so I grant these brave souls placement in the universe we all love.

Honors, hut!

Moses Obadiah
Nicholas Tockert
David DiFranco
Eric Belcher
Clifford McKinney
Jeff Sockwell
Daryl Noonan
Jonathon Scott Schofield
Cord Awtry
Ryan James Broadhead
Ben Myers
Troy Lee Cowell
Krzysztof Krecislaw
Chad Parish
Jack Lafreniere

Joshua Bressel
Marcus Odekirk
Robert Ostrowski
Mark Havener
George Tholburn
Erik Helgeson
Winter Guite
Jukka-Emil Vanaja
Christopher Turco
Juan Ochoa Jr.
Steven Molen
Broccán Mac Rónáin
Kenyon Burguess
Dave Alsager

Trueborn Warriors all.

CHAPTER 1

Khan Malvina Hazen of Clan Jade Falcon leaned back in the tall brown leather chair in her office and narrowed her gaze at newly appointed Galaxy Commander Matthias Pryde of Gamma Galaxy. She looked down on him despite his taller height—courtesy of her seat being elevated and his being lowered. Matthias was uneasy, she could see that in his face. She had summoned him without any pretext. His nervousness fed her, forcing her to suppress the smile she wanted to show. *Fear is what makes the Jade Falcons powerful. Even fear of ourselves makes us stronger.*

People had good reason to fear her. She was not just a Khan, she was a visionary. Her adoption of the Mongol Doctrine made her dangerous in the eyes of her fellow Clans. The lower castes and the civilians of captured worlds were not human in her thinking. They were mere chattel, just resources for her to use or crush as she saw fit. Crushing them instilled the fear that she knew made her Warrior Caste strong again, stronger than it had ever been. *For years we allowed the Traditionalists to rule and under them we became just one of many. Now we stand to crush the Lyran Commonwealth. Shattering one of the Great Houses, grinding it under my heel, will cause others to submit. Those that do not would simply be killed. Any form of resistance will be eradicated, burned, and their ashes scattered into nothingness.*

"Take a seat, Matthias." She gestured to the smaller, hard wooden chair opposite of her desk. "I can have Cynthy get you something to drink if you want. She likes catering to my guests."

His eyes darted to Cynthy, the young girl Malvina had taken under as her prisoner and personal toy. Cynthy wisely averted her sunken eyes from both of them. *I trained her well.* Matthias's gaze on her clearly made him more uncomfortable. He slowly turned back to look at her as Cynthy bowed her head and backed out of the office, closing the door slowly, quietly, as she had been trained to do.

"That is not necessary my Khan." He managed to gain more composure. "May I ask why you needed to see me?"

"Matthias, let me ask you. What is the greatest threat that the Jade Falcons face?" Her question was bait, and both of them knew that.

"The Lyran Commonwealth is less of a threat than another Clan, especially the Wolves."

"*Neg,*" she replied coolly. "That is pedestrian thinking. The Wolves are an annoyance, persistent, but too soft to be a true menace. When we become the ilClan by conquering Terra, they will be the first to feel my wrath. No, Matthias, the greatest threat to our people is that they will drift into their old ways of thinking. The doctrine that I have ushered into our culture is one that will lead us to endless victories—to Terra, then to the rest of the Inner Sphere. That can all be undone by the knee-weak Traditionalists. Their very presence creates a threat to our future, a drift back to misguided ideals of what constitutes honor."

"The majority of our people follow your vision."

"I agree. At the same time, there are those that refuse to commit fully to our doctrine. Tell me Matthias, who do you think is the most staunch Traditionalist?"

He paused in thought for a tedious moment. "There are several that come to mind. The one I would worry about the most is Galaxy Commander Stephanie Chistu of Delta."

Malvina leaned forward, resting her elbows on the obsidian desk top and steepling her fingers. *I agree, but I want to see what he thinks.* "Tell me why."

Pryde's face tightened, careful of the words he chose. "She says nothing against our Mongol Doctrine, not publicly. She simply does not follow it. When presented with opportunities to impose herself over lesser castes, she does not. Chistu does not have to *say* anything. Her actions are a beacon to others. They see her, and realize she can resist your will with no consequences. In some respects, she is teaching them *how* to resist the doctrine. Her example is a threat because others watch it and seek to emulate it. And her extracurricular activities are, dare I say, unbecoming a warrior."

"Exactly!" Malvina replied, pounding her black bionic fist on the desktop. "I have not crushed her because she would only serve as a martyr to the other Traditionalists. At the same time, she must be dealt with."

"What do you have in mind, my Khan?"

Malvina reclined in her chair again, locking her gaze with Pryde. "Do you know the worst thing you can do to someone that refuses to follow the path you lead them on?"

"*Neg.*"

"You make them take that path on their own accord. Stephanie Chistu loathes the Mongol Doctrine. I intend to force her to follow that doctrine of her own accord. I will make her become the very kind of leader she holds in disregard. I will make her walk a path of *my* choosing, by *her* own decisions. If this is done, those that look to her will see what she has become. Their precious beacon will be snuffed out."

"It can be done, *quiaff?*"

"It can and will be done. That, or she will perish in battle. Either way, I will get what I want. Moreover, I have the perfect place to make it happen."

Galaxy Commander Stephanie Chistu stood before the anvil and hit the glowing hot metal bar with the hammer. The metallic ringing from each impact was so strong that it made the metal glow brighter for a moment. She rode the recoil and let the hammer drop again and again, pulling the metal on the anvil and changing its shape slightly with each hit. The key was to let the weight of the hammer do most of the work. Sweat stung the corners of her eyes and she adjusted the soaked hat that covered her cropped black hair.

She paused and looked at the metal, studying its new shape for a few seconds, then slid it into the coals of the forge. This forge, which the local artisans had graciously offered to her, was different than ones she had used before. It was much easier than hauling such gear with her from post to post. Stephanie did not mind the smell of coke or the roaring heat of the forge that soaked her body.

Making knives and swords was not the typical hobby for a warrior, but she considered herself a bit of a different kind of warrior. Working with the metal, giving it shape and form, was strangely satisfying and relaxing—despite the upper body workout. It was hard to explain to her peers, how it gave her solace and allowed her to think. Some scoffed at her choice of relaxation. Chistu ignored them. *What I do off duty is my concern.*

This blade was not exceptional in its artistry, but there was something about it that appealed to her. It was nearly ready to quench, sharpen, and polish. It was eloquent, not a hunting blade, but more than capable of killing. *It takes two things to make a knife special. One is its creation, the other is what is done with it. There is something about this blade that tells me it has a particular role to fill, something special.*

Using the tongs, she pulled the metal out and swung it back to the anvil, hammering furiously at it again until it eventually cooled to a dull gray color. Each blow rang not just in the air, but in her body as well. Each strike gave her incredible focus and concentration. Working with scalding hot metal forced discipline. She had earned her burn scars early on from the process.

This blade was taking a long time, but it would be worth it in the end. *I am not a destroyer like others of my caste—I am a creator.*

After three minutes of carefully placed hammer blows, she turned to put the metal into the forge, and saw Khan Malvina Hazen standing there, arms crossed. Behind her stood her "pet" Cynthy. Stephanie placed her project on a cooling rack.

Malvina was not an imposing figure like many warriors. This meant that she and Stephanie looked each other eye to eye. Hazen's hair was ash-blond, almost silver in color, worn long, with a single braid draped over the shoulder of her black uniform. That uniform, the black dress attire, was one of the ways to identify those that followed her Mongol Doctrine. It was meant to intimidate, but on Chistu it was wasted.

Cynthy looked like a broken child—Stephanie could see it in her dark-rimmed eyes and shrunken cheeks. *Perhaps "broken" is the wrong word. "Abused" may be more fitting.* Malvina gloated at how badly she treated her. She embodied what the Inner Sphere would be like under Hazen's rule. Seeing Cynthy there, two paces behind her Khan, almost quaking in fear, only tempered Stephanie's ire. *She uses her as a living symbol of what she plans for the Inner Sphere...a symbol of fear.*

Khan Hazen sneered. "Look at you. Working at a blacksmith's forge like a common bellycrawler. This is not a true Jade Falcon warrior pursuit. Your time might better be served attending one of my doctrine sessions. I wonder at times if you have the heart of the Falcon in your chest." Malvina's words dripped with contempt.

Do not react to her tone. I will not be taken in by her bait. "I find that the forge gives me time to think. It works my upper body and at the same time it gives me mental focus. Do not mistake my time here as anything other than a means to relax. I am every bit a warrior."

"It is beneath a warrior to have such hobbies. You set a poor example for others in my eyes."

Her doctrine blinds her. It oozes from her pores. There is more in life than battle. "Warriors are more than actors on the battlefield, my Khan. Almost all have some sort of hobby. When it comes to mine, I would suggest that you lack an understanding of the process. The combination of the heat, the hammer, the anvil, and what they can create. Working in unison, dull metal becomes something of use—be it an implement of war or a decoration."

Malvina reached for the new knife blade with her bionic hand, but was stopped when Stephanie lightly tugged at her sleeve. "My Khan, the metal is hot."

"It is not glowing."

"It does not glow until it reaches four hundred sixty degrees centigrade. While it does not look hot, it would burn through your hand in a matter of seconds."

Hazen slowly retracted her hand. "You know a great deal about the ways of a blacksmith for one that was reared as a warrior."

"I pride myself on mastering new things. This hobby constantly challenges me and forces me to learn new forms and techniques."

"What kind of blade are you making?" she asked, clearly feigning interest.

I will play along. It is best to do so when combating another's ego. "I do not know for sure, my Khan. Each blade takes on its own life during the creation process. I start with an idea in mind, but what the knife becomes is more a product of the fire, the anvil, and the hammer rather than my intent."

If she understood, Khan Hazen did not show it. "We have one thing in common, the fire you play with. Fire is the cure for the Inner Sphere, I have foreseen that. Worlds will have to burn so that our new society can grow from the ashes."

The way she spoke chilled Stephanie, but she was careful not to show it. *Her Mongol Doctrine will kill billions. It violates the teachings of Nicholas Kerensky. Warriors exist to protect the weaker castes, not to burn them. Yet others follow her flag blindly because she promises to be the ilKhan, and the Jade Falcons to be the ilClan.*

"The fire is only part of the equation in shaping the metal," Chistu responded. "The anvil, the positioning of the hot metal, the striking of the hammer. They must all work in unison to create."

"I am only concerned with the hammer. That is what it is to be a Jade Falcon. We pulverize our enemies."

"As you say, my Khan," Stephanie replied. *Trying to argue my point with her would be lost. She forms her opinions and twists the facts to fit her beliefs. That is one of the weaknesses of the Mongol Doctrine.* Stephanie knew the truth. The hammer was only one part of the equation. The anvil and the positioning of the metal, merged with the right strike, were what gave the metal shape and meaning. *I would try to explain it to her, but it would only frustrate both of us.*

"You are indeed every bit a Jade Falcon that I would have command one of my Galaxies, *quiaff*? There are times I wonder where your true loyalties lie."

"Make no mistake my Khan, I am every bit a Jade Falcon." *Perhaps more than you...*

"We shall see," Malvina replied. She uncrossed her arms and handed a noteputer to Chistu.

The Galaxy Commander put her hammer down on the anvil and killed the blower to the forge, taking the device. The background sound of the fan all but disappeared, suddenly making everything else louder. "Coventry, *quiaff*?"

"Affirmative," the Khan said. "I take it you are familiar with the last battle our Clan had there, *quiaff?*"

Stephanie nodded as she eyed the long list of orders. Every Jade Falcon knew of Coventry and the events that had transpired there. Her Clan's defeat in 3058 had spawned the Whitting Conference, and the forging of a Star League that struck back at the Clans. It was a world that had set many things in motion, including the demise of the Smoke Jaguars and an infernal peace with the Inner Sphere.

The orders she read were long, detailed, and incredibly specific. *Raze Whitting, leave no structure standing? Eradicate the Coventry Military Academy? Tactical nuclear weapons use authorized?* These were military orders unlike any she had ever seen. Usually orders to field commanders were a few lines at best. This was three screens worth of specific acts of destruction and carnage.

To Stephanie Chistu, they were acts unbecoming a Clan warrior, let alone a Jade Falcon.

"Khan Hazen," she said, considering her words carefully. "These orders…"

"Are quite specific. I want House Steiner to bleed on Coventry. I want them to die there at our hands. I want to erase our past failure there. Nothing is to remain to remind anyone of our prior defeat there. You will be the instrument of that destruction."

Malvina's words stung Stephanie. Changing history was a vile act, usually done by weaker minds. *We should never be afraid of our past to the point where we desire to change or destroy it. Our past is not a scar, but a reminder of where we have come from.* "Victory can be achieved without these acts of deliberate destruction."

"You believe that, *quiaff?* I do not. Conquering Coventry is a mere footnote in *The Remembrance* if you do not take the actions I have outlined in those orders."

For a moment, Stephanie held her words and returned her gaze to the noteputer. "The authorization of nuclear weapons…it is unnecessary."

"I believe it is, even as a last resort. If you are unable to achieve conventional victory on Coventry, per your orders, these weapons will ensure it. Burn those foolish enough to stand against our Clan."

"The Jade Falcons would become the Smoke Jaguars if such weapons were employed—especially against the lower castes."

"That is one perspective. Another is that the lower castes do not deserve honor, leniency, or mercy. The bellycrawling Spheroids are a cancer that must be removed before our new society can take shape. We saw in the last campaign for Coventry that civilians took to BattleMechs right off the factory floor and fought us. Why should we risk the precious lives of trueborn Jade Falcon warriors to such people? The nuclear weapons are part of your contingent, Galaxy Commander Chistu. It is not up for debate."

She would have me be a butcher to millions. That is what she wants to turn me into...an icon for her misguided doctrine. "Perhaps another Galaxy should be used my Khan, with a commander more...attuned to your thinking on this matter."

"You would refuse a direct order of your Khan, *quineg?*" There was a hint of caged fury in Hazen's voice.

She anticipated my words and is prepared. "Negative, Khan Hazen. I am not refusing. Given the details you have in these orders, it is clear your interests might be *better* served with another commander leading this kind of assault."

Khan Hazen said nothing for a moment, but her stare spoke volumes. "I am the leader of Clan Jade Falcon, and one day all of the Clans. These are the kinds of missions that we will be undertaking—now, and until we are the ilClan. These kinds of missions are who the Jade Falcons are under my leadership. If you are unable or unwilling to follow orders, you will be replaced with a commander who will." It was not a threat, not from Malvina Hazen. It was a promise.

For a millisecond, the escape route was tempting. This was not the way to wage war that Stephanie believed in. At the same time, the thought of her command and the people loyal to her being subjected to a new commander more to Malvina's vile tastes made Stephanie wince. *I cannot put my people through that.* "Neg, my Khan. Replacement is not desired, nor do I wish replacement. I will comply."

That made Malvina grin thinly, something that did not calm Stephanie's emotions. "Excellent. I am sending along Star Colonel Yaroslav and two Clusters from Gamma Galaxy to assist you."

Yaroslav was a known warrior, an ardent supporter of the Mongol Doctrine. *He will be Malvina's eyes and ears, there to spy on the slightest deviation of my orders. He is her eyes and ears.* "It is not necessary, but I would be foolish to refuse any support you may be willing to offer."

"Exactly."

"What are the defenders of Coventry that we know of?"

Khan Hazen seemed nonplussed as her grin evaporated. "Hardly anything at all. The Seventeenth Arcturan Guards are posted there. They have some experience, but have recently been reinforced with relatively green replacement troops. I would rate them as average to below-average. There is the Coventry Military Academy, whose cadets lack any practical battle experience. If history holds true, the Coventry Metal Works will also field some defenders."

Chistu knew the full account of the last time the Jade Falcons hit Coventry, and remembered that even green units could fight furiously when pressed. "We should be more than a match for them. I will not discount that the Lyrans will throw in reinforcements, given the strategic nature of the planet."

"We have less intelligence regarding House Steiner's reserves. Our recent assaults have stripped them of their capability to easily respond to attacks. The lack of defenders on Coventry suggests that they have sent their reserves to Donegal, according to the Watch's estimates. If they do send troops in to try holding Coventry, I doubt it will be a force of any merit. The Lyrans are teetering on the edge, Galaxy Commander. You may be all that is needed to tip their precious little House over."

Stephanie doubted the Lyrans were teetering, but did not desire the inevitable argument. "Anything else, my Khan?"

"Per your written orders, you are to maintain an effective fighting force at the completion of the operations on Coventry. This is your paramount objective. The Exiled Wolves still prowl, and I need your Galaxy able to respond to any opportunities they might exploit.

"You are to deal House Steiner a blow it cannot recover from. I anticipate our enemies will see our presence there and come searching for blood. I want your force to come through this relatively intact, or a victory on that blasted world will mean nothing to me. Understood, *quiaff*?"

Chistu nodded. "Affirmative. When do we depart?"

"Three days from now."

She moved the metal she had been working on to the cooling rack and hung up her work tongs. "Then I have much to do."

"*Aff,* you do," Khan Hazen said coolly. She did a pristine about-face and left Stephanie alone at the forge. Behind the Khan, her damaged toy Cynthy followed.

Star Colonel Jagger Thastus studied the noteputer for several minutes, his mouth slightly agape. His black hair bore a hint of premature gray in his sideburns, which made him look easily a decade older than he really was.

Stephanie Chistu watched him carefully. He was one of her top field commanders, leading the First Falcon Striker Cluster of her Galaxy. She and Thastus had bled on the same ground many times. Moreover, he shared her opinion of Hazen's Mongol Doctrine.

"The Khan is setting you up," he said. "She is forcing you to act in her proxy and to wage a kind of war that is unbecoming a Jade Falcon."

Chistu nodded. "Agreed. Though I would encourage you to hold your tongue from this time forward. The walls have ears."

"And she has saddled us with Star Colonel Yaroslav of Gamma. He is here to do one thing: report on our adherence to her blasted orders. A spy, through and through."

"I have no doubt you are correct," she said. "That is something we cannot change any more than her command to take tactical nuclear weapons with us."

"You are not seriously considering using them, *quineg*?"

She shook her head. "*Neg.* I have no choice but to take them. Taking and using, however, are two different things."

Jagger studied the intel data on Coventry for the better part of three minutes before speaking again. "On paper, this should be an easy conquest. The Seventeenth Arcturan Guards are a good unit, but hardly able to successfully engage a force as large as ours. That is, of course, if the Watch has gotten their intelligence correct."

Her half-cocked grin told him she felt differently. "While Khan Hazen sees me as some sort of threat, I doubt she would send such a large force to Coventry unless she expected the Lyrans to send in reinforcements. No matter what that estimate says, Coventry is as much a symbol to the Commonwealth as it is to us. They will not let it go without a vicious fight."

"Perhaps she is right in sending those nuclear weapons with us then."

"*Neg,*" Stephanie replied quickly. "Taking the world by burning its cities, people, or defenders leaves no honor. It would serve as a rallying cry for the Commonwealth. One can almost hear Trillian Steiner screaming, 'Remember Coventry!' if I use such weapons, and rightfully so. I will not give them the moral high ground in this fight."

"Then you will be at odds with our Khan," Jagger said coyly.

"So be it." *She cannot take the Jade Falcon out of my soul. I will find victory for our Clan and our people, without tarnishing my honor.*

CHAPTER 2

LCAF COMMAND POST OBADIAH
TOCKERT, VORZEL
COVENTRY PROVINCE
LYRAN COMMONWEALTH
22 JANUARY 3148

General Roderick Steiner stepped into the command bunker of the Obadiah and was greeted by sentries that immediately snapped to attention and saluted. He saluted back as he entered the Strategic Operations module. *I have had people saluting me for some time, but not this many.* Such was the price of being the General of the Armies of the Lyran Commonwealth. He had never asked for this office—his cousin Trillian, the Archon, had thrust it upon him.

As the officers in the room parted before him, opening a path to the main holographic display table, Roderick gave the officers supporting nods and a thin smile of encouragement. He had to. The Lyran Commonwealth had been suffering strings of defeats and fighting increasingly desperate battles against Clan Wolf and now their old nemesis, Clan Jade Falcon. A big part of his role, as he learned over time, was to keep the officers' morale up.

I don't know how my grandfather dealt with all of this attention. Adam Steiner had first fought the Jade Falcons back during their initial invasion in 3050, and he did so again as Archon of the Commonwealth. *Now I command all of the armies that remain of our state. I wonder if I'm going to be the last General of the Armies—a small black footnote in some future history book.*

One officer did not step aside. His chiseled chin and muscular frame topped with blond hair made him stand out. Hauptmann-General Jasek Kelswa-Steiner.

Seeing him, Roderick stepped forward and extended his hand. "Imagine meeting you here, General Steiner." *It feels funny to say*

"General Steiner"–almost as humorous as being called that myself. He had lived under an assumed name for most of his early life. Only circumstance had finally made Roderick reveal his true last name and linage. Since then, his life had become totally different. *Sometimes I long to be Roderick Frost again.*

Jasek flashed a smile and shook his hand firmly. "A distinct pleasure, sir."

"You can drop the 'sir' with me. We're family, even if distanced by a few marriages," Roderick replied. "What you've done in the Arc-Royal Defense Cordon has been outstanding. I would offer you a commendation, but you already have most of the medals we can give."

Jasek glanced down at his ribbons and grinned slightly, then turned his blue eyes back to Roderick. "Like you, I don't do this for the glory. I do it because it is the right thing to do."

It was not a casual comment on the part of the *hauptmann*-general. His storied journey of command was one of legend. Starting as a part of the Republic's military, his Stormhammers had been a beacon for Steiner loyalists in the Republic. His original goal had been for an independent Skye, but the twists and turns of the tornado of Steiner politics had brought him back into the Commonwealth's fold. Trillian, his cousin and current Archon, trusted Jasek, and that was more than enough for Roderick.

"I'm glad you were able to get here," Roderick said, gesturing to the holographic display. The pair of them moved to it.

"No offense, Roderick, but why are we here? Vorzel is not a strategic world."

"It is *now*," the General of the Armies replied. He looked at the officer manning the holotable controls. "Captain—" his gaze dropped to the officer's name plate, "—Belcher, pull up a star map, a hundred and fifty light years centered on Vorzel."

The man's fingers flew across the controls, and the image appeared in the space above the table. The front was frightful. Tharkad, the capital of the Commonwealth, was bordered by Jade Falcon-controlled worlds. The Falcons had been bloodied there, badly, but they would strike again; it was merely a matter of time.

Roderick gestured to the map. "LIC reports that the Falcons are staging their forces on Upano." He pointed to Captain Belcher, who nodded and highlighted Upano with a pulsing green dot in the air before them. "Jasek, using Upano as your staging world, if you were Malvina Hazen, where would you strike to deliver us a devastating blow, one that would hurt is the worst?"

"That's easy. Two of our provincial capitals are within easy range for an assault—Coventry and Donegal."

Captain Belcher made the worlds pulse Steiner blue at their mention.

"Exactly," Roderick replied. "One or two jumps, and you can hit those worlds. The real question is which one?"

Hauptmann-General Kelswa-Steiner studied the map. "I would venture Donegal. You take that world, you essentially cut off a significant portion of the Commonwealth."

Roderick crossed his arms, his gaze on the map, then back to Jasek. "True, but Coventry has a history with the Jade Falcons. It was there they were given a stunning defeat in 3058. That defeat led to the Whitting Conference, the formation of the Second Star League, and the events that followed. In many respects, their defeat on Coventry has to be one the biggest blemishes in the history of their Clan—hell, all of the Clans. I would imagine they'd do almost anything to erase that stain from their damned *Remembrance*."

"So you think they'll hit Coventry?"

Roderick shrugged faintly. "We don't know for sure. I seriously doubt they will strike at both planets. Malvina Hazen understands initiative and momentum in warfare. She will want a sure victory, complete and utter— regardless of which target she goes after."

"This Malvina Hazen is not like any other Clanner we have fought," Jasek said.

"You are the master of understatement, General," Roderick agreed. "Her way of waging war—taking no prisoners, deliberately targeting civilians, wreaking utter destruction...it plays to our absolute worst fears of what the Clans can be."

"She relies on those fears as part of her arsenal. I cannot imagine what the Inner Sphere would be like under Jade Falcon rule with her as the ilKhan."

Roderick could imagine it. It was the stuff of nightmares. Hazen would grind her heel down on anyone she considered inferior, which was most of the population of the empire she might forge. Human rights would be a thing of the past. "The only good that comes from her arriving is it can galvanize the troops to fight to the end. They'll know that surrendering to her Mongol Jade Falcons is a death sentence."

"Of all of the enemies our people have faced, we have never fought one hell bent on our deaths," Jasek replied. "Even the Word of Blake was not as brutal as she, and that says a lot. So, how do we deal with this jade scourge?"

"Simple. We stage here, between the two high-probability targets. When she makes her move, we sweep in with your Fifteenth Arcturan Guards RCT and my Second Royal Guards. She will be forced to commit more troops to try wiping us out, killing any other offenses— or she will lose and we will cut off her momentum. I have ordered scouting JumpShips in both systems poised to jump here and get word to us immediately as soon as their ships show up." Gone were the years of fast HPG communications between worlds. Now there was a time lag every time a foe made a move. *ComStar and the Republic both owe all of us more than the darkness we find ourselves in.*

"I prefer option two," General Kelswa-Steiner said. "In that first scenario, we could end up dead."

Roderick smiled slightly. "'Ours is not to question why...'"

"What does the LIC say about her leading the attack?"

Roderick's grin faded slightly. "There is a high probability that Malvina will be leading the attack. Frankly, I am hopeful. If it is her, we have an opportunity to cut the head off the snake and throw the Jade Falcons into some turmoil with the loss of their Khan."

Jasek chuckled. "You may be the only person in the Inner Sphere that *wants* Malvina Hazen to show up."

Roderick pondered the fantasy of facing off against Hazen in one-on-one combat. The leaders of two armies fighting a battle to determine the fate of a war—there was a certain romanticism about it. He also knew it would never happen with the Jade Falcon leader. She saw him like everyone else, unworthy of her attention. *Her reckless disregard for humanity has shown us all the darkest side of the Clans.* "I don't want her to show up *per se.* It just might open an opportunity that we couldn't pass up." Roderick turned his gaze to the map. "What is the status of the Fifteenth Guards?"

Jasek Kelswa-Steiner pointed to Captain Belcher. "Pull up our TO&E if you would, Captain." After a few seconds of fingers flying at the controls, the organization and equipment chart for the Fifteenth Arcturan Guards appeared. "As you can see, Roderick, we are almost completely refit. The replacement troops are a bit green, but our veterans are putting them through the paces right now."

Roderick studied the data, nodding approvingly at what he saw.

"You mentioned the Second Royal Guards RCT?" General Kelswa-Steiner queried. "Did you bring them all?"

"I did," Roderick replied, handing a data cube to Belcher, who pulled up the TO&E of the Second Royal Guards. "The only problem was their CO. She had taken ill."

"Judith? That's terrible. Nothing bad I hope."

He shook his head. "It's not good." *Cancer never is.*

"Who's commanding them then?"

"*I* am," Roderick said.

There was a pause between the two men as Jasek studied Roderick's face, possibly wondering if he was joking. "Roderick...you are the General of the Armies. A General of the Armies hasn't led troops into a battle in ages."

"I am aware of that," was all Roderick could say. "That doesn't change anything. They are under my personal command."

Jasek's face reddened slightly. "Sir, if I may speak freely—"

"Always."

"Sir, if we lose you, it hurts the Commonwealth a hell of a lot more than losing another general."

Roderick had anticipated the rebuttal. He lowered his voice so that only he and Jasek could hear his words. "Two things drove this decision, General. One, to be blunt, we don't have a deep pool of officers to dip into to fill the slot—not with the experience needed to lead a RCT. Second, I am more of a field officer than a 'General of the Armies.' That is where my experience is. It's where I feel at home. If I am going to send troops in against Malvina Haven's forces, I want our people to know I am there not just in spirit but with them on the field."

General Kelswa-Steiner considered what he said before speaking. "I understand. It's just a hell of a gamble."

"I like to think it will help morale. Truth be told, I want a shot at Malvina if she shows up in person."

"You and I will have to square off for that right," Kelswa-Steiner replied. "We can't lose sight of the obvious. The Jade Falcons are not the true threat. *She* is the real enemy we have to worry about."

"I hope you're right. LIC says a lot of troops follow her banner. Based on my experience, every Jade Falcon is a deadly enemy to contend with. No matter what, if she is not there, she will send in one of her best."

"Where do you think she'll hit?" Jasek said.

"Donegal makes such a tempting target that it *should* be there. Malvina knows that too. I think it will be Coventry."

"*Ja.* They came and died there before," Jasek said. "I would make a play for Donegal myself, but I think emotions trump logic when it comes to the Falcons."

Roderick nodded. "Malvina Hazen is recasting the Jade Falcons into her own twisted mold. Part of that has to be erasing the failures of the past. Coventry represents that past. I think that will drive her more than strategy. The Jade Falcons under her have no room for Coventry in their history."

"No matter where she strikes, one thing is for sure," Jasek said with a wry grin. "She won't be expecting *two* Steiner generals hitting back."

CHAPTER 3

PORT ST. WILLIAM SPACEPORT
COVENTRY
COVENTRY PROVINCE
LYRAN COMMONWEALTH
15 FEBRUARY 3148

Galaxy Commander Stephanie Chistu opened the communications channel to her troops. "Delta and Gamma Galaxies, I bid you good luck. Follow your orders and the timeline, and we will prove ourselves more than a match for these Lyrans."

There was a hiss and snap in her neurohelmet earpiece. *"Galaxy Commander, we will be swinging over the spaceport in thirty seconds."*

"Just as planned," she responded to the Star Captain in command of the *Admiral DiFranco*, the First Falcon Striker Cluster's command ship. While the First was Star Colonel Thastus's unit, she would be acting in overall command of the Cluster. She clenched the targeting joystick and the throttle and engaged her fusion reactor for more energy. The low hum under her feet told her that her *Jade Hawk* was ready for battle.

The arrival in the Coventry system had been at a pirate point, giving the defenders little time to prepare. Leutnant-General Francine Ross, of the Seventeenth Arcturan Guards RCT defending the planet, had sent Stephanie a message, essentially asking if she was going to issue a *batchall* for the world. She had responded flatly. "Per the will of Khan Malvina Hazen, *neg.* You are not to be granted the honor of a *batchall.* Prepare to feel our wrath."

The *Admiral DiFranco* swung on its axis as it approached the spaceport. Port St. William Spaceport had been the site of the first Falcon attack in 3058. She had ordered the captain to pilot the ship on the same flight trajectory over the port for her landing. Again, Khan Hazen's orders on this point were so specific that it limited

Stephanie's ability to exercise her own military discretion. *My own Khan is attempting to ruin me, either by following or disobeying her* blitzking *orders. I have to fight her words as well as the Lyrans.*

The doors of the massive *Overlord-C* opened, and light poured into her cockpit, diffused by the ferro-armored glass. Below the moving ground whizzed past.

The Star Captain's voice came over the loudspeaker. *"Drop in five...four...three...two...one...."*

Stephanie hit the release and kicked her leg controls to activate her jump jets. The *Jade Hawk* roared as she disgorged from the ship. The tarmac was some fifty meters below, looming quickly as she controlled her descent. On the ground, she saw people running for cover while all around her, the First Falcon Striker Cluster dropped as well. Elementals rained down from the *Admiral DiFranco*, their jump jets dropping them slowly, with the precision that only a Jade Falcon warrior could appreciate.

She picked her landing spot, a patch of ferrocrete, and hit it hard, bending the knees of the seventy-five-ton war machine as she landed. The *thud* was so loud and resonant that it shook her rib cage. Her tactical display lit up with emerald dots for her troops—and crimson for the enemy.

"Falcon Strikers," she barked while pivoting her *Jade Hawk* to the right, "secure the perimeter of the spaceport one block out, just as we planned. Deploy smoke." An artillery explosion made her 'Mech quake, and a trio of autocannon shells just narrowly missed the right pseudo-wing of her *Jade Hawk*.

The source of the attack had come from a pair of Hetzers, painted gray with streaks of black and blue for urban camouflage. They were barely concealed behind a stack of cargo containers and started to back up the moment she spied them, realizing they were outmatched.

"You have chosen poorly," she said through gritted teeth. She targeted the one on the right, switching her short-range missiles to a single target interlock circuit. The moment she heard the tone of target lock as the reticle drifted over the target, she fired.

The *Jade Hawk* nudged back slightly as the two dozen short-range missiles streaked from their high racks. The missiles bore in on the Hetzer, exploding in an orange cloud of shrapnel, smoke, and death. The wheeled tank made a grinding noise as three of the missiles devastated its front tire. Two others went wide, blowing up a nearby cargo container and filling the air with burning paper that was more spectacular than deadly.

The damaged Hetzer's top hatches opened, and a billowing cloud of smoke poured skyward. If there were survivors, they never made it clear of the hot shrapnel inside the tank. Its lancemate fired its autocannon at Chistu. The shells were a blur as Stephanie sidestepped enough for several shells to whiz past her cockpit. The others hit her right torso. Their explosions were vicious, but her training and instincts paid off as she leaned slightly into the blasts—otherwise she might have toppled over from the impact.

Her damage display lit up with yellow warnings, but a quick glance showed that her armor had absorbed the impacts. *You will pay for that.* Checking for any other potential attackers, she charged the Hetzer at a full run, crossing 150 meters in a matter of seconds. The driver of the wheeled tank attempted to turn and make a break for it, but the smoldering wreck of the other vehicle blocked its escape.

Stephanie stopped in front of the vehicle and kicked. Her *Jade Hawk*'s foot hit the extended barrel of the Hetzer's Crusher SH Cannon, crumpling armor and bending the barrel almost sixty degrees from the impact. The kick was so hard that the tank skidded sideways, ripping tires from their rims and leaving bits of shredded tread in their wake.

The crew of the now-crippled vehicle bailed out. She let them go. Without their tank, they were just unarmed infantry. She spun and surveyed the spaceport. There had been a lance of light Steiner 'Mechs at the other end of the large tarmac, but they had fired only a single volley before fleeing to the city for cover. One of their number had not been so fortunate. The mangled *UrbanMech* belched crimson flames and black smoke where it had fallen. Several other rising plumes from burning vehicles and 'Mechs dotted the spaceport. Her First Falcon Strikers fired smoke rounds that mixed with the smoke from the ruined vehicles, obscuring the spaceport and the targets there. *If they have spotters, they will not get a good bead on us as targets.*

Chistu and her officers had studied the first battle on Coventry carefully—and she was sure her opposition had done the same. When the Jade Falcons had landed before, they had been hit by barrages of Long Tom artillery fire. *We will not be drawn into the same mistakes twice.* "This is Striker Prime. Deploy the fighters to the outskirts of the city, concentrate on the north. If you see enemy artillery there, destroy it."

An extremely loud explosion far off to her right made her 'Mech quake. *Artillery! Almost on cue.* From what she saw on her tactical display, the exploding rounds had missed her 'Mechs. *They are firing blind on the spaceport...I learned well from our last invasion of this accursed world.*

She toggled her command channel. "Strikers, I want triangulation of that incoming fire. Relay the coordinates to our air support. Fourth Falcon Dragoons, deploy to the south, three blocks into the city, and form a perimeter, then stand by for additional orders." More explosions went off amid the green-and-black smoke that covered the spaceport, doing little than tearing up the landing zones.

A few rumbling minutes later, word came from Star Captain McKinney that they had pinpointed the area. Unlike the previous attacks on the planet, this time the Lyrans had hidden their Sniper artillery in the city itself, in a small suburban park. It took several passes for the aerospace fighters to find them, as they had been well disguised. She heard the explosions off to the northeast of her position, and saw smoke rise in the distance, proof that her fighters had done their duty.

Stephanie signaled her DropShips to commence landing operations and asked for a sitrep. Besides her two Hetzers, there had been a platoon of hovercraft—SM1 Tank Destroyers and Bellonas—and a lance of 'Mechs. Only one of the Bellonas and a lone black-and-gray *Hatchetman* had managed to fall back before being destroyed. The rest lay as burning carcasses of war.

There had been one Falcon casualty. MechWarrior Sockwell's *Eyrie* had been caught in the Steiner crossfire from the marauding hovercraft and gone down. While he was still able to fight, his 'Mech, pockmarked from autocannon fire, would require numerous repairs. While his honor was intact, his fellow warriors did not spare him some taunting at being "First Blood."

Stephanie sent word to her Strikers and the other deployed Falcons, ordering that the enemy equipment be checked and that survivors be taken as prisoners.

"Khan Hazen would not have ordered us to take prisoners," Star Colonel Yaroslav responded.

"Our orders from the Khan say nothing about the treatment of prisoners. Khan Hazen is not here. Until I am killed, I am in command, and my orders will be followed. Understood, *quiaff*?" Her tone left little in the way of misunderstanding.

"*Aff*," Yaroslav responded flatly.

Stephanie grimaced—she knew of his leanings well before the operation. His black uniform and reputation mirrored Malvina Hazen's. The shadow of the Mongol Doctrine was already showing its brutality on Coventry, which was something Stephanie hated. *There is no honor in killing prisoners of war. We are better than that.*

She studied the tactical display. The defense at the spaceport had been a token unit. House Steiner's Leutnant-General Ross was still out there, with considerably more firepower at her disposal. *We must move swiftly but cautiously.* Memories of the last battle of Coventry tugged at her thoughts.

Her orders from Khan Hazen were clear on cer tain day-one objectives. It was now time to move off the spaceport and to go after those. She toggled her comms channel to the DropShips. "Attention DropShip *Render*, you may commence your run now. Star Captain Noonan Binetti, take the Beak Binary and execute the orders you have. Strike hard and fast, then return here to the spaceport."

"Affirmative," Star Captain Binetti replied. He was good, a trusted member of the Third Falcon Talon Cluster, still in low orbit. His mission was strategic in nature. His enthusiasm was electrifying, even over the commlink.

Stephanie switched back to the troops in the Port St. William Spaceport. "First Strikers, we are moving to the northwest through the city. I want a tight formation and good cross-covering fields of fire. Fourth Dragoons, you have spaceport security for now and are active reserves until the Third Talon Cluster lands."

Cities were the bane of every true warrior. Narrow streets and tall buildings made for excellent ambush sites. She had chosen her path through the city carefully as a result...avoiding the obvious wide highways where ambushes might normally be staged.

They had gone only ten blocks before the first signs of resistance appeared. It was a pinprick at first: three squads of Albrecht-class hoverbike infantry striking at the rear of her command. They darted out, fired a salvo of short-range missiles, peppering several of her BattleMechs, then sped away. A Star of Elementals took off after them, but only as far as her defined defensive perimeter. It took restraint and stern orders from her to keep the more rabid Mongols in her ranks from pursuing. *That is exactly what they want–for us to follow them to where the odds are even.* Stephanie was unwilling to play the Lyrans' game.

It wasn't until the edge of the urban area that Leutnant-General Ross showed her hand. Hidden in an old scrapyard that concealed their reactor signatures, a full battalion of the Seventeenth Arcturan Guards suddenly appeared, hitting the flank of her column. The rumble of autocannons and the flashes from particle projection cannons filled the air.

"This is Striker Prime, weapons free. Engage, but do not pursue more than two blocks," she barked as she drifted her targeting reticule onto a gray-and-blue striped *Marauder IIC*. She locked onto the ram's head logo of the Seventeenth Guards just below the cockpit and fired as the Lyran officer attempted to bring his arm-mounted PPCs to bear.

Her salvo of short-range missiles bore true to target, hitting the legs of the heavier BattleMech near the knee actuators. Armor plating caved in, and a few fragments flew off, crushing a nearby car.

Stephanie juked her 'Mech hard to the right in a sprint as the Lyran unleashed its trio of PPCs, their crackle drowning out the reloading cycle on her missiles. The air between the two combatants lit up white-blue as the charged particles flashed viciously at her. Lesser warriors would have flinched at the attack, but Stephanie maintained a stern concentration. Two of the energy weapons found their mark on her *Jade Hawk*, one savaging armor in her arm and the other in her left torso. Stephanie compensated for the loss of armor, maintaining her balance with ease.

She swung behind MechWarrior Schofield's *Mad Cat III*, the Emerald Ghost, painted in wisps and streaks of fading green to make it look ghost-like. Schofield was heavily engaged with a Lyran *Trebuchet,* and hardly noticed her coming around behind him. It was, as she had planned, just enough time to reload her missile racks. As her prey emerged from behind the *Mad Cat III,* she unleashed another deadly salvo, again concentrating on the lower regions of the Lyran *Marauder IIC.*

The vast majority of her missiles slammed into the right leg of the hulking 'Mech, explosions devouring armor and myomer in orange and red bursts. The *Marauder IIC* fired all three of its PPCs again. One particle beam hit Emerald Ghost, and the other found her right leg. The third shot slammed a building two blocks away, no doubt doing considerable damage.

Stephanie leaned to the side of her cockpit and saw smoke rising from the damage that had cut into her green camouflage streak pattern. Her *Jade Hawk*'s wound still glowed angrily from the hit.

Schofield's *Mad Cat III* twisted at the waist and fired a wave of long-range missiles into his new target. The missiles hit everywhere on the *Marauder IIC,* causing the pilot to reel from the impacts. The 'Mech teetered for a moment, then listed forward, coming down on one knee. Its right PPC gouged the ferrocrete road on impact with a sickening metallic grinding noise.

Chistu did not hesitate. She broke into a sprint right at the *Marauder* as its pilot struggled to stand. Her small lasers stabbed crimson beams into the 'Mech, mostly hitting the torso and extended knee, which had been her intended target.

At point-blank range, she pulled the right arm of her 'Mech back and swung it hard, aiming at the exposed and damaged knee of her attacker. Her *Jade Hawk*'s claws dug in hard and deep, ripping at the actuator controls and nearly severing the joint from the internal structure.

The *Marauder* pilot was either unaware of the severity of the damage or chose to ignore it. The Lyran 'Mech struggled against all odds to stand. The strain was too much for what was left of the knee actuator. It popped and hissed as it gave way, and the *Marauder IIC* collapsed.

She loathed having to make a physical attack...it was not the desired fighting style of a Jade Falcon, but neither was dying in battle. She rose just as Schofield downed the elusive *Trebuchet* some fifty meters distant, the Lyran 'Mech furrowing into the roadway and breaking a water main that showered it. That pilot also started to rise, refusing to give up the fight, despite the odds.

Stephanie's eyes danced across her tactical display. Her command Cluster was winning, that was obvious, but there was no way to know how many other troops were still hiding in Port St. William. It didn't matter, however—her orders were to flush and destroy every Lyran she could find, and that was exactly what she intended to do.

CROSS DIVIDE MOUNTAINS
COVENTRY

Star Captain Noonan Binetti debarked Beak Trinary from their DropShip in the steep foothills of the Cross Divide Mountains. The orders he'd been assigned were outlined by Khan Hazen herself, but their execution had been the precision work of Galaxy Commander Chistu. Having studied the history of the Jade Falcons defeat here several times in his career, he understood why they had been deployed so far away from the fighting now raging across the planet.

"Beak Trinary, this is Beak Prime. Slasher Star, take the two far entrances to the south of our position. Emerald Knight Star, take the three targets to the north. Beak Star, we get the middle. Plant the charges and set them off. Do not wait or ask for confirmation." His reinforced Binary had combat engineers and equipment normally not attached to the formation.

A wave of *"affs"* followed on the comm channel as he rushed toward the mountain. The first cavern entrance was more like a crack in the rock face of a jutting formation of stones. From the air and most angles on the ground, it was almost invisible.

One of his infantry squads carefully scouted the cave entrance and signaled that there were supplies inside, munitions and other goods. *They have prepared their little hidey-holes to wage war as they did the last time we invaded. So much the better.*

Binetti ordered MechWarrior Awtry to deploy the explosive charge in the hands of his *Griffon IIC*. The device was a fuel-air explosive. As soon as it was laid, the Star fell back and Awtry trigged the blast. The explosion, combined with the secondary blasts from the munitions inside, collapsed the cavern. In the distance he heard another *whomp* of a similar blast as other caves were destroyed.

During the last battle for Coventry, the caves had been a refuge for the Spheroids to wage a guerrilla war against his Clan. This time, if all went as planned, that option would be denied them.

"All right then, onto the next target," he commanded. "Move as if Khan Hazen herself were watching you!"

OVERLORD-C CLASS DROPSHIP *ADMIRAL DIFRANCO*
PORT ST. WILLIAM, COVENTRY
10 HOURS LATER...

Galaxy Commander Stephanie Chistu stood on the bridge and watched as the repair crews moved the mobile gantry over her *Jade Hawk* and replaced the damaged armor.

The fighting for Port St. William had finished two hours earlier. The Seventeenth Arcturan Guards RCT had fought with tenacity, far more than she had expected. Even now, the bulk of their forces were unaccounted for. Even those that struck at her had hit, then faded away.

According to the Watch, the unit's reputation had been badly tarnished in the fighting on Tharkad. Their new commander had apparently put some spine back into them, only confirming what she thought of military intelligence. It was a good strategy, hit and run. *In this case, it prolongs the inevitable.*

A line of Jade Falcon BattleMechs appeared on the edge of the spaceport. She recognized the dull green of Star Captain Noonan Binetti's *Gyrfalcon* leading them. He had followed her orders precisely, maintaining comm silence so as to not betray his isolated position to the Lyrans.

She grabbed a headset and held it to her ear. "This is Striker Prime. Beak Prime, sitrep."

"Mission accomplished, Galaxy Commander. We encountered no enemy forces. They will not be using those caves against us this time."

Stephanie allowed herself to smile. "Good work. You have honored your Clan. Please send me the battleROM footage of your mission. Then come in and get some rest. We have a busy week planned."

She paused for a moment, contemplating the victory. She had learned that even the smallest of planets were big places, often filled with surprises during times of war. Her Delta Galaxy had scored on two fronts so far, but there were plenty of battles ahead.

The Star Captain's battleROM footage came through a few moments later. The video was pristine, showing the soaring heights of the Cross Divide Mountains, unmistakable in their majesty. It also showed the fuel-air explosives going off, sucking the mountains down on top of the caves, one after another.

She looked at the communications controls and her grin broadened. *Now is as good a time as any.* Switching to an unencrypted channel, she broadcast in the clear, so that her enemy could hear. "Leutnant-General Ross of the Seventeenth Arcturan Guards. This is your enemy, Galaxy Commander Stephanie Chistu of Clan Jade Falcon."

There was almost a full minute of silence before she heard the crisp tone of the Lyran commanding officer. "This is General Ross. To what do I owe the pleasure?"

Arrogant...confident...all the better. "We have taken Port St. William and destroyed your hiding holes in the Cross Divide Mountains. I thought you should know."

"So I have heard," Ross replied coolly.

"The old ways are of no use to you." Stephanie then transmitted the battleROM footage to General Ross. Before Ross could respond, Stephanie killed the transmission at her end. *Let her contemplate that...*

CHAPTER 4

MONOLITH-CLASS JUMPSHIP *BROADHEAD*
NADIR JUMP POINT VORZEL
COVENTRY PROVINCE
LYRAN COMMONWEALTH
18 FEBRUARY 3148

From the bridge, General of the Armies Roderick Steiner watched as the last Fifteenth Arcturan Guards DropShip connected to its docking collar. He turned to the vessel's captain. "Send word, we jump within the hour."

Hauptmann-General Jasek Kelswa-Steiner strode over next to him and looked out the viewport down the spine of the JumpShip. "I hate asking, but any more word from Coventry?"

"No. The only thing we got was from the picket JumpShip we had in-system. I've had our intelligence staff enhance the images of the Jade Falcon ships." He pulled out the large photos and handed them to Jasek.

"That's enough DropShips to carry a Galaxy of Jade Falcons," he said looking at the photos.

"More than that, I fear—at least an additional Cluster of troops."

"Do you think General Ross can hold out until we get there?"

Roderick pondered the question carefully. "Francine is smart to the point of cunning. She knows that in a one-to-one fight, her forces are outnumbered, and most likely outmatched. The smart play is to drag this fight out, whittle away at the Jade Falcons, avoid a major confrontation that might cost the entire planet. If she plays this right, she can shoot and move long enough for us to arrive."

General Kelswa-Steiner smiled and handed the images back. "I rather like the image of us being the cavalry, riding in to save the besieged settlers. It hearkens back to Terran mythology of the old west in America."

Roderick understood the reference as well. "Assuming she can hold out with the Seventeenth Arcturans, our arrival really just evens the odds. If we can wreak enough havoc on the Falcons, we can kill their offensive. They will be forced to toss more troops at us or leave Coventry altogether." *Hopefully the latter.*

"If Malvina Hazen is there, the citizens will be suffering."

If Hazen is there, the citizens will be dying. "True enough. If she is there, we have a chance to take her out, and maybe put a permanent end to this slaughter-doctrine of hers. If she's not, we still need to beat the commander of those forces."

"From the DropShips, who are we up against?" Roderick pulled up a printout from an LIC report.

"The DropShips conform to Delta Galaxy—Hazen's old command. According to our intel, it is commanded by Galaxy Commander Stephanie Chistu."

"I take it since it is Hazen's old roost, this Chistu is a hardliner."

Roderick's brow raised as his eyes went through the report. "We don't have a lot on the Jade Falcon commanders, but LIC believes she is a more of an old-school traditionalist. She hasn't been seen by our operatives wearing the black uniform associated with Hazen's Mongol hordes."

"That's odd. You'd think Hazen would've sent one of her hardliners for such an attack. Especially since that is her old unit."

Roderick put the report down. "There's more going on in the Jade Falcon camp than we know. Hazen must have her reasons for sending this Chistu to the planet. One thing's for sure, the fact that she doesn't seem to be some city-burning witch might play to our advantage before this is over."

"How's that?"

He shrugged. "I don't know, Jasek. It's just one of the million things we need to keep our eyes peeled for."

The battle for Coventry was taking much longer than Galaxy Commander Chistu had hoped for. It did not surprise her—she had anticipated a staunch defense. The problem wasn't that the battles were prolonged; it was that the House Steiner forces had been using hit-and-run tactics rather than engaging in a stand-up fight. She had anticipated this based on the last campaign. Key supply cities had been early on her target lists, and her Delta Galaxy had done a good job of hitting and taking those towns.

General Ross had not crumbled, but seemed to shift where she attacked from as a result. It made for a more fluid situation, the kind Stephanie relished. It was a game of falcon and mouse, one where she had more discretion and justification for deviating from Khan Hazen's plans.

In her portable command dome, she studied a map of the region. Elements of the Seventeenth Arcturan Guards had been spotted redeploying to the Ridesein River Valley. The valley was steep and wide, with rolling hills, and the Ridesein River was difficult to cross at this time of the year. This made the bridges more strategic as she planned on moving against them.

At the edge of the holographic map was another target—Whitting. That was where Hauptmann Caradoc Trevena had offered Khan Marthe Pryde *hegira*, ending the first attempt to wrestle the world almost a century earlier. Whitting had been where the Second Star League formed. Khan Hazen had plans for the town. It was to be razed to the ground, nothing left standing. Stephanie hated those orders, but there was no way around them. There were ways to soften them, however. Malvina would level the town with all of its inhabitants. *I am not her. I will follow her orders to the letter, but I will do it* my way.

Star Colonels Yaroslav and Jagger Thastus entered the command dome and stood at attention. She waved both of them over to the table. Jagger was one of her most trusted commanders, leading the First Falcon Striker Cluster when she was not in the field. Star Colonel Yaroslav was in command of Gamma Galaxy's Ninth Falcon Talon. Donning the black jumpsuit of a Mongol supporter was not enough; he shaved his head bald, making him stand out even more. From what she heard, when he saw a gray hair, his solution was to remove all of his hair. *Odd that he would not shave his goatee as well, since it has streaks of gray in it.*

"Good morning," she began in her best command tone. Both officers nodded to her. "The time has come for us to strike in multiple directions to hopefully overtax the defenders of this world. Reconnaissance has detected the Arcturan Guards shifting to the Ridesein River Valley. I am taking the majority of Delta in pursuit of them."

"What of my warriors?" Yaroslav asked. "We did not come here to garrison spaceports."

Neg. You came because you are loyal to Khan Hazen, and you were sent to spy on me. Of this I have no doubt. "If it is a battle you seek, you have come to the right place. I am deploying a reinforced Trinary from the First Falcon Striker and your Ninth Falcon Talon. Your mission is to move against Whitting, one of the prize targets."

Jagger remained emotionless, but Yaroslav seemed excited at the mention of the town.

"Khan Hazen has specific orders for the town," Stephanie continued. "It is to be razed. We are to record its destruction and transmit it to the defenders of this world to show it to them as a motivator for them to surrender."

"I look forward to destroying this blight on our Clan's reputation," Yaroslav said.

"While we will follow the orders of our Khan, this will not be a senseless slaughter of civilians. Once you have dealt with the town's defenders, give the civilians free passage to leave the town before it is destroyed." Stephanie locked her gaze on Star Colonel Yaroslav. "Is that understood, *quiaff*?"

"*Aff*," he said firmly.

"What do we know of the defenders, Galaxy Commander?" Jagger asked.

"The Coventry Planetary Militia and students from the Coventry Military Academy. I am anticipating a reinforced Trinary's worth of troops, but only some are BattleMech equipped. We saw some academy BattleMechs in an earlier strike, and they are merely modified *Chameleon*s, rigged for hot-firing. They have a number of tanks and hovercraft as well, and at least a pair of VTOLs. You should be more than a match for them."

"We shall destroy them," Yaroslav said. "Their academy forces are whelps at best, a freebirth sibko that is gloriously outmatched. Their deaths are the only hope they have for honor."

"I want them *defeated*," Chistu said. "It is not necessary or required to destroy them. If they offer surrender, you are to accept."

Her words clearly soured the expression on Star Colonel Yaroslav's face. His cheeks reddened with her words. "This is not what Khan Hazen would want."

She is not here. "We are following her orders to the letter, Star Colonel. Where she did not provide clarity, I am exercising my discretion as the task force commander. We will accept prisoners. Whitting will be destroyed. Understood, *quiaff*?"

"Affirmative," he said with less enthusiasm than displayed earlier. "When do we depart?"

"You will go in two hours. Overall command of this mission is going to Star Colonel Thastus. You and your warriors will report to him."

Yaroslav glanced at Jagger. "I look forward for the opportunity to have the honor to be part of the destruction of Whitting. Thank you, Galaxy Commander."

She nodded to him, and the Gamma Galaxy officer left the command post. Jagger Thastus remained.

Stephanie leaned in so that only he could hear her. "Watch that one, Jagger. His ideology is two steps in front of his common sense. Such men can prove to be a handful."

"Not a problem, Commander. I will be on him like a shadow."

OUTSKIRTS OF WHITTING
COVENTRY
COVENTRY PROVINCE
LYRAN COMMONWEALTH
NINE HOURS LATER...

Twilight settled in, and the sky was a brilliant mix of orange and purple against the nearby mountains. Star Colonel Yaroslav saw from the leaves on the trees that the wind was picking up...perhaps a hint of a storm later in the night. As picturesque as the image was, his gaze settled on the town of Whitting in the distance.

Some of the Coventry Military Academy forces had retreated after the first clash with the forces of Star Colonel Thastus. Not so with the Coventry Planetary Militia. Armed with new 'Mechs from Coventry Metal Works, they were proving quite tenacious. They had sprung ambush after ambush, doggedly giving up terrain until they reached the outskirts of the town. Then they fell back, using the structures for cover, waiting. Joined by academy survivors, the Lyrans must have thought they could hold out better in the town.

To him, like most of the Clan, the town was an ugly scar in their history, and one he gladly looked forward to eradicating. It had been rebuilt since the last Falcon invasion. The structures looked new, and more numerous. Whitting...the scar...had grown. *I am sure there are statues commemorating our defeat here, mocking our Clan.*

Yaroslav shifted impatiently in his cockpit, chafing under Thastus's command. Thastus was aggressive, but it was clear he not only served under Chistu, but was devoted to her. He had taken prisoners. Blitzking *prisoners! These filthy bellycrawlers had been trying to kill us a few minutes earlier, now they ask for our mercy. Khan Hazen understands that honor should not be granted to such people. Warriors like Chistu and Thastus have no place in the future of the Jade Falcons.*

"Your orders, Star Colonel?" Yaroslav asked, suppressing his contempt as much as possible.

"They are holed up in there fairly tight and night will be settling in soon," Thastus replied. "We do not wish to give them too much opportunity to inflict casualties as we move against the town. I suggest that you swing around to the far side of town with your troops. We will move in from the east, along that small river that runs through the town rather than on the roads. You will hold there, making sure you have their full and undivided attention. They will feel the pinch of our vise."

We will be out of sight from these Delta troops...perfect. "Aff," was all Yaroslav said. He noted the wind direction. "We will be to the west-northwest of the town, right at the outskirts. They will not fail to know we are there."

Yaroslav ordered his Command Star to fall in behind his *Summoner* as they began their wide flanking maneuver. Thanks to the hills and the buildings of the town, he left Thastus's line of sight in a matter of minutes, but could follow the Delta forces on the tactical display. *If Khan Hazen were here, this city would already be in ruins—its defenders dead. Clearly that was her intent in her orders.*

The Delta Galaxy troops made it into the outskirts of the town on the shallow river, but then all hell broke loose. *"Talon Prime, we are under attack, redeploying to the south,"* came the voice of Star Colonel Thastus on the tactical channel. There was a rumble on the channel, then a hiss.

Another voice, Star Captain Myers of Delta, cut in over the static. "Striker Prime is down!"

Yaroslav's tactical display showed that Thastus's 'Mech was still operational, but it had taken substantial damage. Better yet, Thastus's 'Mech was unmoving—indicating he was unconscious.

Perfect! This makes me the ranking officer in the field. "First Striker, this is Talon Prime, I am assuming temporary command. Concentrate your fire on the structures around the enemy and begin to fall back by Star. Ninth Talon, we will advance and fulfill the orders of our Khan. Open fire on the buildings. Emerald Talon Point, open fire with Inferno rounds—hit the structures, set them ablaze. Destroy everything."

You wanted me to get their attention, and that is what I will do. Targeting a four-story structure before his *Summoner*, he fired his long-range missiles and his autocannon. The façade of the building was devastated. His Elementals had brought a handful of Inferno rounds for their shoulder-mounted missile racks—and they followed his orders perfectly, spraying several structures with the fire-producing explosives. His other 'Mechs opened fire as well, targeting other buildings. Within minutes, several structures were gutted and the flames roared in the wind, spreading from building to building, turning the town into a raging conflagration.

Yaroslav grinned broadly at the image against the setting sun in the distance—Whitting, being consumed. He fired his PPC into the carnage, aiming for buildings beyond the fires, devouring them with his beam of charged particles.

RIDESEIN RIVER VALLEY
COVENTRY
FIFTEEN HOURS LATER...

Stephanie Chistu looked at the footage while the two Star Colonels stood nearby. Her *Jade Hawk* towered over them at the makeshift field command post, its shadow looming over the trio.

Thastus had his arm in a sling and a bandage over the flash burn that had penetrated his cockpit and neurohelmet, searing his forehead. Yaroslav stood in his black jumpsuit, arms crossed, proud of what he had done. He had even handed her a charred banner of the Coventry Military Academy he had recovered from the ruins. She clenched it in her hands; the smell of smoke rose from the cloth—a nagging reminder of what had happened in Whitting.

She stared at the images from several battleROMs. Jade Falcon 'Mechs firing into Whitting, the wall of orange and yellow flames whipped by the wind, making the fires leap from structure to structure. Several 'Mechs of the Coventry Planetary Militia tried to emerge, their weapons lowered and their reactors shunted to lower power levels, likely to surrender, but instead were fired on by Falcon warriors—*her* warriors. Elemental Stars had swarmed the last holdouts of the Coventry Military Academy, ripping their 'Mechs apart, then blasting the helpless MechWarriors in their cockpits. Civilians that somehow survived the fire came out of the smoke and carnage only to be fired on by her troops. One family was beset by a Gamma Galaxy Elemental and beaten to death.

She turned to the two officers, the full fury of her temper rising, which felt like the flames that consumed Whitting had seared her own face.

"Star Colonel Yaroslav, how could you have misunderstood my orders? Civilians were to be given free passage before the town was destroyed. Those were my words, *quiaff*?"

"Aff," he replied. "The situation became fluid once Star Colonel Thastus was dispatched. It became clear that we had to take pressure off Delta Galaxy. I ordered the Ninth Talon to create a...*diversion* of sorts. I believed that destroying the structures would achieve the goals Khan Hazen laid out, and would relieve the attack on our brothers and sisters."

"You violated my explicit orders," Chistu said through gritted teeth.

"I improvised in a situation that was spiraling out of control. And I adhered to the orders of our Khan. Whitting was to be razed. It has been done. I have erased that cancer from our history. Because of my actions, Whitting is no more." Arrogance and pride rang in each word.

He believes himself safe because he followed Malvina's orders. In the end, this will be his undoing. "You took no prisoners, let no civilians survive," she spat at him, closing the distance between them. He was taller than her by thirty centimeters, but in that moment, they were locked eye-to-eye.

"In my opinion and experience, there was no way to be sure that the militia troops were ready to capitulate. Rather than risk precious Jade Falcon blood, I merely killed them," he said in a cavalier tone.

This is the Mongol way. Short-sighted, horrible, brutal, and vicious. It does not reflect the best of our people, but the evil of man. Rage stiffened her whole body as she spoke, "Star Colonel, let me ask you this. Now that you have done this, slaughtered these people, what do you think will happen when a Jade Falcon becomes a Lyran prisoner?"

"No self-respecting warrior would allow themselves to be in such a situation," he said flatly.

"Yet, it does happen," she countered. "They will remember what you have done. They may kill their prisoners as a result. By defying my orders, you have doomed any of our forces that fall into their hands."

Yaroslav was not swayed. "It will serve as further incentive for our troops to avoid capture. Besides, it is the way of the Clans. The weak, those that are captured, will die. We are a warrior-led people. Those that do not live up to our ideals, they are purged from our gene pool. It is the way of the Jade Falcon."

"The warrior caste has always existed to protect the lower castes. That is the way of Nicholas Kerensky—not your way."

The Star Colonel opened his mouth to offer a rebuttal, but she cut him off before he could say another word. "You have tainted *me* and my warriors with your actions. You will be allowed to retain your command only because I need every warrior we have. When this is over, we will settle this in a Circle of Equals. Do you understand what I am saying, Star Colonel, *quiaff*?"

"*Aff*," he said with a scowl. Dismissed by a short jerk of Stephanie's head, Yaroslav left, heading to where his troops were refitting after the fight.

"This is my fault," Thastus said wearily. "I failed you, Galaxy Commander. I was knocked out for twenty minutes or so. By the time I came to, he had already set fire to the town."

She put her hand out on his shoulder. "*Neg.* You have failed no one. You were temporarily taken out of the fight. There is no fault for doing your duty. It is my fault for sending Yaroslav in the first place. I knew his true loyalties, and knew he was a problem. I would have been better served using him for rearguard duty."

"What do we do now?"

"I have orders to fulfill, now that Whitting has been destroyed. Our Khan left me little way to avoid what follows. Go see to your troops."

As Thastus left her presence, she stuffed the burned academy banner into her jumpsuit.

TWO HOURS LATER...

Stephanie Chistu had ordered her vid-tech to edit the battleROM footage of Whitting, removing the images of slaughter that Gamma

Galaxy had perpetrated. It was still a horrible thing to watch: troops firing at building after building, each one burning or exploding, going from structure to charred rubble in a matter of minutes. Still, she had removed the footage of civilians being killed and troops being shot rather than taken prisoner. When she was as satisfied as she could be at the footage, she broadcast the video images in the clear. She eyed the orders she had printed from Khan Hazen. *A little editing is needed here as well.*

"Defenders of Coventry, I send you this footage of Whitting. I have been ordered by Khan Malvina Hazen to tell you these simple words. 'When the new Star League is born, it will be with Clan Jade Falcon as the ilClan.'"

She ended the transmission and shut the unit off. Malvina had ordered only the last line to be broadcast, but Stephanie had given herself some discretion to add the first two sentences. *The enemy needs to know that what happened there was at Malvina's bidding, not mine.*

CHAPTER 5

COVENTRY METAL WORKS
COVENTRY
COVENTRY PROVINCE
LYRAN COMMONWEALTH
7 MARCH 3148

General Roderick Steiner watched as his command battalion of the Lyran Second Royal Guards rushed the outskirts of the Coventry Metal Works industrial complex in a tidal wave of metal, myomer, and pent-up aggression. They had landed two days ago from a pirate jump point, only to learn that the factory had fallen to the Jade Falcons a day earlier. They had to act fast, or risk the defenders of Coventry falling before Roderick's troops could make planetfall.

There were few signs of previous fighting—from what he'd gathered from General Ross, the 'Mech works had been defended by all that remained of the Coventry Military Academy's cadet cadre. Their school had been destroyed, leveled by the Falcons and, from what Ross had told him, the Jade Falcons had slaughtered civilians and soldiers alike in Whitting. *This is Malvina Hazen's handiwork. Her "doctrine" is little more than terror and the destruction of anyone she sees as inferior to her...and she holds herself in very high regard.*

The cadets had struck out from the complex rather than use the structures for cover. They had held the Jade Falcons at bay for hours before being overwhelmed. Several had managed to flee from the field of battle. The entire senior class refused to yield or surrender. It was either sheer bravery or pure fear of what would happen to them as prisoners.

Their deaths had left the plant almost defenseless. Most of the workers that could pilot tanks or 'Mechs had taken what was on the production line and escaped to form up with Ross's remnant of the Seventeenth Arcturan Guards. Not trained for battle, the cadre was still warmly welcomed into the ranks of what remained of the Seventeenth. The factory fell unceremoniously to the Jade Falcons.

Francine Ross was proving herself a top-notch Lyran general. Her troops had used the factory to keep their 'Mechs and tanks operational as best they could. Cut off from those supplies, she was in a world of hurt, suffering more than 67 percent casualties. A lesser commander would have conceded, but she fought on. Much of it was by staying mobile and keeping her force split into three distinct commands. She attacked, bled the enemy, then got out before the Jade Falcons could bring the full fury of their Delta and Gamma Galaxy troops against her. It was a gutsy strategy that wreaked havoc on the enemy—and her own troops and equipment.

The Lyrans had come with one intent—to take back the factory complex. The Jade Falcon Trinary that held the production grounds had let Roderick's Royal Guards get close before unleashing a maelstrom of firepower on them. His "scout" lance, three *Atlases* and a *BattleMaster*, had been bathed in fire that would have consumed lighter 'Mechs. They had managed to skirt around the Falcons and had gotten to cover at the west end of the vast complex of buildings, but had paid a price in ferreting out the defenders.

The rest of the Royals hit from the south, while General Kelswa-Steiner and two companies hit from the flank to the east. Roderick joined his advancing battalion, going in with them despite urgings of caution from his junior officers.

As he advanced, his modified *Rifleman IIC*, a captured Clan 'Mech, was suddenly hit with a Gauss-rifle slug, nearly toppling him mid-stride. The impact tossed him forward in his command couch as the 'Mech rocked backward, and he struggled to keep it upright. The damage from the impact was considerable. From his cockpit he saw a twisted piece of armor of his right torso peeled upward and back from the impact.

The attacker, a *Vulture* in prime configuration, mounting four deadly pulse lasers and massive long-range missile racks, slid behind a building before Roderick could get a target lock on it. He spotted an emerald-green *Jupiter* firing off to the east, directing fire at Jasek's force. *We have to dislodge them from their cover, or this will get messy quickly.*

His targeting-and-tracking system beeped a warning as a strike tank emerged from behind a warehouse. His battlecomputer struggled to identify it, finally coming up with an Enyo. A Hell's Horses tank—no doubt a Jade Falcon spoil of war. He swung his arm-mounted lasers to bear as the Enyo unleashed its large pulse laser, filling the air with brilliant green bursts of death.

The laser caught his 'Mech in the left thigh and stitched a series of burns up into his left torso. Roderick stopped his gait and leveled a perfectly aimed shot from his *Rifleman IIC*, sending a dual barrage of large pulse laser fire right into the tank's turret. The bursts of green energy scored across the turret, leaving smoking holes in their wake. The Jade Falcon tank responded with a wave of Streak SRMs as the driver attempted to reposition the tank after his assault.

Roderick kept his lock on the Enyo, juking his *Rifleman IIC* hard left to get a better angle as the Enyo tried to evade him. The *Vulture* emerged from hiding, unleashing emerald lasers into his left shoulder and burning off a large piece of armor in the process.

Damn these green bastards! A wave of long-range missiles from the shoulder rack of the Jade Falcon OmniMech concentrated on the right side of his *Rifleman*, pockmarking the armor with each hit. The rumble of their explosions was drowned out with the damage warning tone in his neurohelmet.

Roderick swung his damaged arm around and fired two of his pulse lasers. They scorched a nasty pair of scars across the front of the *Vulture*, enough to force it back around the corner of a building.

Then the Enyo reappeared, letting loose with its large pulse laser and a wave of eighteen short-range missiles. The laser caught him low on the left leg, burning holes in a tight pattern—a testimony to the skill of the Jade Falcon gunner. The Streak missiles found their marks everywhere—including one that exploded just over his head on the cockpit canopy, causing a thin spiderweb of cracks in the ferroglass.

I can't play tag between these two. The *Vulture* was the more dangerous threat, and had to be dealt with quickly. Roderick swung around toward the rear of the structure where the *Vulture* had been hiding. His targeting system locked onto the enemy 'Mech's fusion reactor, as he knew his opponent was doing. It was not going to be a surprise attack, but that was never his intention. Jerking his command yoke hard, he slowed while approaching the building, arcing his run and bringing his pulse lasers to a fully charged mode.

Rounding the corner, Roderick saw the *Vulture* at nearly point-blank range, the air around him filled with its pulse laser flashes. One missed him entirely, hitting the building and sending bits of masonry ricocheting off his cockpit canopy. The other found him dead center, boring into his left torso, one pulse following the other, punching deep.

Roderick heard tone and pressed the thumb trigger on his large lasers in the same heartbeat. The quartet of large pulse lasers hit the *Vulture* in its left hip. All four shots concentrated their emerald fury in that one location, blackening the light-green-streaked armor and doing so much damage that the 'Mech staggered to the side, then fell into the building.

For a fleeting moment, Roderick felt like cheering. That abated when the *Vulture* caved in part of the wall and unleashed forty missiles into him as it went down.

The 'Mech's leg little more than a smoking and twisted piece of metal lying in a collapsed building, the Clan warrior relied on a cocktail of luck and training when firing. Beeping from Roderick's damage indicator and the multiple explosions across his canopy made him reel backward. The dense cloud of smoke from the missiles obscured his view of the *Vulture*. He strained with the foot pedals to keep his *Rifleman* upright, narrowly winning that battle. As he regained his balance, he fought the torrent of heat in his cockpit—the result of losing several heat sinks. As he focused, he could make out the outline of the *Vulture* as it somehow managed to rise on its one good leg, straining to get its weapons in line for another attack.

The pulse lasers...oh no you don't. Putting distance between them might allow a barrage from those deadly pulse lasers that he could ill afford. The tactician in his brain took over from the strategist, processing the decision in a millisecond. The option was open to fall back and swing around the building for cover, recover, and cool down. *That Falcon has to be near the end. It's up on one leg and hotter than hell.* Instead he broke into a full charge, sprinting right at the damaged OmniMech.

To the credit of the Falcon warrior, they jerked aside to try dodging the approaching *Rifleman*, hop-turning it more into a glancing blow. Armor ripped from both 'Mechs as they ground against each other, with Roderick passing his intended target. He ignored the insistent warnings of damage to his own 'Mech; all that mattered was the status of his foe.

He almost lost his balance again, fighting against momentum, gravity, and the imbalance of his damaged *Rifleman*. Spinning around, Roderick saw the *Vulture* and the damage he'd inflicted on it. The 'Mech had fallen from the impact—no surprise there, given its one good leg. Deep rents ran across the jutted-out portion of the center torso, sparks flying from one hole in particular. The hip joint he'd savaged sparked as well. One of the missile racks was so badly mangled there was no way that it could fire. He started lining up his lasers when another salvo of long-range missiles filled the air between them.

Roderick twisted at the waist, as if that might shield him. Half of the barrage plowed into a nearby building and blew in the masonry wall. The missiles that did hit him rattled his *Rifleman* hard, splattering bits of armor against the nearby buildings and ricocheting them back against his 'Mech.

Smoke and dust filled the air and as his targeting system sought out his enemy. Roderick tuned out the tactical channel chatter buzzing in his ears and swept his reticle onto the *Vulture* as the Jade Falcon warrior struggled to rise on one leg. As his thumb moved to the firing stud on the joystick, a pair of his own 'Mechs, a battered *Commando* and a light-blue *Scourge*, charged right into his line of sight only forty meters away, effectively blocking his shot. They had been pursuing another target farther down in the complex, and had rushed forward, not realizing their imminent peril.

Roderick sidestepped his 'Mech, but saw through the smoke that the *Vulture* pilot was gone. Frustrated, he hit his commlink. "This is Royal Actual. Burguess, Alsager, you nearly got shot running into my field of fire! Watch those firing angles and lanes, people."

He was also frustrated by the denied shot...it meant that the *Vulture* might still be a threat. *He's smart, this Falcon. He knows if I emerge he'll get another shot with those pulse lasers, and if he does, it might just take me down.*

His targeting system beeped a warning behind him. *The Enyo!* He pivoted in place, angling his lasers for a barrage. The pesky tank had used the fight to reposition and was angling for a kill shot. He saw it poking around a building corner, creeping out some eighty meters away. His own targeting reticle danced on the display as he tried to line up the shot.

Without warning, a *Templar* rounded the corner behind the Falcon tank and hit it with a wave of crimson beams and green pulses of laser light. The tank's large pulse laser fired a wild shot at Roderick, narrowly missing his right leg and hitting the building next to him with a resounding *whomp* that threw dust and debris into his field of vision.

He fired a large pulse laser as the *Templar* drove a devastating kick into the Enyo's rear. His own weapon hit the chassis below the turret, burning a deep, smoking hole into the armor. But the *Templar* did even more damage. Its kick penetrated the engine compartment. The ripples of heat that rose from the damaged engine blurred the gray, blue, and white streaks of the *Templar*'s camouflage paint.

The Jade Falcon vehicle was pinned. Moving forward brought it face-to-face with Roderick, and it couldn't back up because of the *Templar*. Realizing this, Roderick began to advance, his 'Mech fighting him with the heat buildup, lumbering toward the tank and jerking his *Rifleman* next to the structure that the *Vulture* had damaged, using it for immediate cover.

In true Clan tradition, the Enyo tried to blast its way out, firing its turret's pulse laser and another rack of Streak missiles at Roderick as he passed. The laser missed, blasting a building and immediately setting something on fire within.

All six of the missiles hit his right side, blasting new holes in what armor still remained there. As soon as he got behind the cover of the wall, Roderick skidded to a halt and doubled back. *I can't let that* Templar *have all of the fun.*

He let the noise of his subordinates barking orders fade into the background. Roderick saw a blur of Lyran 'Mechs rush past him, farther into the complex. He ignored them for the moment—shifting from General of the Armies to a MechWarrior. All that mattered now was the kill.

As he poked his right arm and cockpit around the corner, he saw the death of the Enyo. The *Templar* lifted its massive leg and drove it down hard into the rear of the tank again. The engine flared as it exploded, a ripple of heat and flames roaring up as the tank died. Flames and fury blew the hatches off as the Enyo's internal space became an instant blast furnace—incinerating the driver and gunner.

The *Templar* pulled its foot out of the flaming debris that had been the Jade Falcon tank and stood to face Roderick, its foot still glowing and blackened from the killing blow. Roderick's targeting system locked onto the transponder and gave him the MechWarrior's name—*Jasek Kelswa-Steiner.*

"I appreciate the assist, Jasek," Roderick broadcast as he checked to make sure no other Jade Falcons were in immediate range.

"Is that what you call it, an 'assist'?" Jasek replied, his grin evident in his voice. "From where I was standing, I thought I saved your life."

Roderick smiled at the light jab. "Sitrep," he replied.

"Changing the subject," Jasek said in a cocky tone. "Very well. We've secured this end of the plant complex. I am showing the Jade Falcons falling back, slow but sure. The problem is that they're trashing the buildings and equipment as they go."

Roderick turned and saw pillars of smoke rising in the distance to the north. It was both good and bad news. Good that the Falcons were falling back, bad they were ruining the Coventry Metal Works plant in the process. *This is that blasted Mongol Doctrine at work. In the old days, the Clans would have left this place as they found it.*

He adjusted his tactical display to give him a view at a more strategic scale. The Jade Falcons had lost some 'Mechs and armor, that was for sure—but so had the Lyrans. *We can't afford to trade them 'Mech for 'Mech in this game.* "We need to secure what we can of the plant."

"My Fifteenth Arcturans are still in relatively good order—though we ran into a swarm of damned Elementals that left one of my companies out of action—and you have plenty of troops in your Royals. We should pursue them. Let me run them down, take them out."

Roderick understood the desire—it was the same one he was keeping in check at that moment. "Our goal is to take back the plant—and we need to finish that up. I'd love to go after this Stephanie Chistu, but right now we need to be careful. Those Falcons are heading north because that's where she has the rest of her force. We'll win Coventry—not in one big battle, but by winning a lot of little ones. Today, we won."

"Yeah," Jasek replied. "I just hate the thought of the Jade Falcons slipping through our fingers like this."

"They didn't. We bled them good. If nothing else, this will force Chistu to rethink her strategy. Besides, the second part of our plan was to get to General Ross and her Seventeenth before Chistu finishes them off. We need to stick to the plan."

"Understood," General Kelswa-Steiner replied, a hint of dejection in his voice.

"Let's wrap up here and go save General Ross. That's what the cavalry does, ride in and save the day, remember?" Roderick added as he prepared to issue orders to the rest of the Lyrans in the Metal Works.

SEVENTEENTH ARCTURAN GUARDS FIELD HQ
LOWER RIDESEIN RIVER VALLEY
ELEVEN HOURS LATER...

Roderick Steiner walked away from his *Rifleman IIC* after a quick glance at the damage the tough 'Mech had taken.

The Jade Falcons had not given up the factory complex without a brutal fight. A brilliant green-and-white-striped *Ryoken* had crashed through a factory building and had come up behind him near the end of combat, riddling his rear and left-side armor. The stubborn foe had cost him one of his large pulse lasers. He looked at the sagging weapon, its barrel badly melted, seared wires hanging from its actuator joint. Repairable—but it would take time.

Just how much time do we actually have?

General Kelswa-Steiner's force had struggled to dig out a Binary of Falcons in a smelting facility. The large equipment and tight quarters had made the battles there unfold suddenly, and at point-blank range. Jasek's 'Mech had gone down three times, but each time he got back up and pounded back at the Falcons. What remained of the building was more rubble than factory when he was done, but the job had been completed.

Roderick's joints ached as he walked to the portable command dome. The sentries snapped to attention, and he gave them a quick salute as he entered. Inside, Jasek stood next to another general, still wearing her coolant vest. She turned and went to attention.

"General Ross, I presume?" Roderick said, nodding for her to relax.

"General Steiner," she replied in a raspy voice. "I hadn't expected the General of the Armies coming here to save my ass. Not that I'm complaining, it's just an unexpected surprise."

"I don't ask my people to do anything I'm unprepared to do myself," he said wearily. "So, how are your Guards holding together?"

"By the skin of our teeth," Ross replied. "I have two functional companies at this point, and a semi-operational company made up of tanks that are more spare parts than original. We've done well just to keep our equipment up and running, but I can't replace lost MechWarriors or trained tank crews."

Roderick nodded. "My Second Royals are down by a few companies, but everyone has taken some damage. We were hoping to salvage armor and weapons from the factory, but the Falcons went out of their way to destroy the facilities as we moved in. I think we can get most of our losses at least back on their feet soon."

Jasek added, "The Fifteenth is down by over a third as well. It was rough going in that factory." He extended his hand to Ross. "Apologies—General Jasek Kelswa-Steiner."

She offered the thinnest of smiles as she shook his hand. "I am well aware. Your reputation made planetfall three days before you did."

"General Ross, any signs of Malvina Hazen here?" Roderick said, locking his eyes with hers and ignoring as best he could the wrinkles on her face and the bags under her eyes. "If not, who are we up against?"

"The Butcher of Wotan isn't here," she said, using one of Malvina's nicknames. "Not yet anyway. Gentlemen, we are up against Stephanie Chistu of Delta Galaxy, along with a Cluster from Gamma. She's the field commander here."

Roderick stepped up to the portable holographic display and keyed in Chistu's name for the intelligence data on his enemy. It appeared in the space over the table along with a recent LIC photo of her from Upano. She was short and stocky, and wore her hair short. He looked over the intelligence assessment, reading the highlights aloud. "Intel says she's a tough nut to crack. She took over Delta Galaxy from Malvina herself. LIC believes Hazen took her more fanatical troops out of that Galaxy and seeded them into the other units to spread her 'Mongol Doctrine.' I'm not sure if we can use that against her or not."

He scanned the data. "Says here that in her Bloodname Trial, Stephanie Chistu took on a 'Mech that outmassed her by twenty tons. She had loaded her 'Mech with Inferno missiles. She plastered that poor bastard, some Star Colonel, lit him up. He could barely move, let alone shoot. Then she hit him in a way he never expected—punching and kicking his 'Mech into scrap."

"I thought the Clans didn't like physical attacks—that they saw them as less than honorable?" Francine asked.

"Most do. No one expected her to do it. She pilots a *Jade Hawk* fitted with close-fighting claws. It says a lot about her style of combat and tactics. Her strategies tend to be unorthodox to your average Jade Falcon." Roderick replied.

"Look at her uniform," Jasek said, pointing to the LIC image. "It isn't black like the rest of the Mongol dogs."

"According to the intel report, she's more of an old-school Clan traditionalist in terms of political thinking," Roderick confirmed.

General Ross weighed in, pulling up some holovid footage of the flattened and still-burning town of Whitting. "I'm not so sure of that. This is—*was*—Whitting. Her troops did this—killed thousands of innocent people and erased that town from the map."

Roderick scanned the images, the burned human bodies still smoking. He closed the video down and returned to the intelligence report on the holodisplay. "Which troops, specifically, did that to Whitting?"

"Mostly the Gamma Galaxy troops that came with her," Ross replied.

"LIC reports that Gamma is more hardline than Delta when it comes to Hazen's religion," he read from the report.

"That doesn't hold water with me," Ross replied angrily. "They were troops under her command—she's responsible for their actions."

"Agreed," Roderick said. "All I am implying is that she may not have issued the orders."

"Does it matter?" Jasek asked.

"It might," Roderick pondered out loud. "It makes you wonder what is going on over in the Jade Falcon camp. But at least we know who we are up against."

"I want a crack at her," Jasek said, his tone grim. "Personally."

"Me too," Roderick said.

"No offense, generals, but there's a line, and I'm way in front of you both," Ross said.

"Let's not get too wrapped up in vendettas. What they did to Whitting, they did because Coventry is a black mark on their history. A nasty scar. I'm sure the other Clans blame them for the Second Star League as a result. Even if Malvina Hazen isn't here, her doctrine certainly is. They erased Whitting from the map as a result of a defeat a century ago. She doesn't want any reminders of past failures." *It is strange that these Jade Falcons fear their own history enough to attempt to utterly destroy it.*

"Well, we finally have the numbers here to turn the tide on this Stephanie Chistu," General Ross said with a sigh of relief.

Roderick nodded. "Defeating the Falcons on Coventry again will damage them far beyond this planet. It will hurt their morale everywhere they stand. It will be something that every Jade Falcon will have to endure."

"Or," Jasek added, "it will compel them to throw more troops at us here." It was a dose of reality, one Roderick had hoped wouldn't be mentioned. *One thing about Jasek, he says what he thinks—both good and bad. With the HPG blackout, it may take them longer to call for reinforcements, and if they do, it will severely damage their honor.*

Roderick stiffened his stance, rising to his full height. "Good. If they throw more troops at us, they will not be landing those same troops on other Lyran worlds. Let this place be their Stalingrad."

"Keep in mind that a lot of defenders died in Stalingrad," Jasek replied with a wry grin.

"You and I are just two in a long line of Steiners. It is our lot to fight and possibly die for our people. But I have no intention of dying here, not yet, and neither should you. We need to organize ourselves and deliver a crippling blow to Stephanie Chistu."

Ross smiled. "Let me show you the Dales. It's not far from Lietnerton, where the green bastards seem to be concentrating. We get them in there, we might be able to give you that crippling blow, sir."

The holographic map came to life, and Roderick began drinking in every detail Francine Ross could provide him.

CHAPTER 6

The city of Lietnerton had changed hands three times in two days, and the prospect of it happening again was not something Stephanie Chistu wanted to contemplate. She had evacuated the civilians at the start of the fighting, but the damage to the city, especially its industrial sector, was staggering. The struggle for Lietnerton proved challenging, with little to yield as a result.

That was why she had deployed Delta Galaxy to outskirts of the Dales, where her enemy had been striking from. *I had my hands around the throats of the Seventeenth Arcturan Guards just a few days ago...now Coventry's fate hangs on every missile barrage.*

She stopped her *Jade Hawk* in a low dip in the wooded foothills of the Dales and took a long drink. Days of fighting meant battling dehydration as much as the enemy. Her perpetually damp shirt reeked with sweat, and the dry spots were caked with her own filth. She didn't smell her own body odor any more, but those of her fellow warriors was, at times, stomach churning. Even a lifetime of being a Jade Falcon warrior did not mask the stench of others.

She and Malvina Hazen both had anticipated reinforcements landing on Coventry. This planet was almost as important to the Commonwealth as it was to Clan Jade Falcon in terms of history and what it represented. What neither of them had anticipated was two regimental combat teams: one led by Jasek Kelswa-Steiner, hero of the Stormhammers; the other led by none other than General of the Armies Roderick Steiner. *One might think the Lyran Commonwealth does not want us to take this world.* Their arrival could even be considered as something of a compliment. *House Steiner sends two of its best to face me. That will bother Khan Hazen when she finds out. The Lyrans have never sent such high-ranking officers after her.*

Stephanie had avoided rushing into the Dales for a number of reasons. First, she suspected a trap. The Dales were wooded, rolling hills, some of which twisted and snaked for kilometers. Lowland creeks and bogs in some areas impeded mobility, which would prevent her from using her preferred tactics. The trees were some form of cedar, and from what she had seen, quite flammable. The area provided a defender with the perfect masking of their movements. The fact that the Lyrans struck at Lietnerton, took it, and then retreated to the Dales pointed to a potential ambush...one she could ill afford to stumble into.

I let myself become anchored to Lietnerton, and that was a mistake. It is time to cut that cord. No matter how much my "beloved" Khan wants that town leveled, it is more important to win this battle first. There is no honor in merely blowing up a city, killing innocents and combatants in the process. Warriors, even those using the city for cover, are worthy of killing in battle—not in wanton mass destruction.

Second, if it wasn't a trap, it meant leaving very little force in the city, making it ripe for the taking. Stephanie had already kept her forces and supplies mobile because of the seesaw battles. *I cannot afford to put my rear areas at risk.*

So she had devised a solution: abandon Lietnerton altogether. Strategically, the city offered her little other than the fact that Malvina Hazen wanted it razed. Chistu moved her supply base to Port St. William Spaceport, where her DropShips and aerospace fighters could provide adequate protection for her rear area. Star Colonel Yaroslav had protested, claiming she was disobeying orders, as she still had not completely destroyed Lietnerton per the direction of Khan Hazen. The Gamma officer's desire to wreak wanton destruction was growing more annoying with each passing day.

Since his actions at Whitting, Stephanie had kept him on a tight leash. She "reminded" him that she was more than aware of the Khan's orders. *There will be plenty of time for me to deal with him incessantly challenging my orders before this campaign is done.* It was the only thing about Coventry she found herself looking forward to.

The other issue she juggled was staying on the offensive and maintaining the state of her combat force, something Yaroslav seemed to ignore. The battles for Coventry had cost her quite a bit of equipment so far. Spare parts, creative salvaging, and downright ingenuity had allowed her to keep her force near full operational strength. However, it was impossible to replace dead warriors or those injured so badly they could not pilot a 'Mech. As such, she had more 'Mechs than MechWarriors—and was still down 28 percent as a result. *True Jade Falcons know that often logistics and technicians determine victories in campaigns, not cunning strategies.*

My enemies are also injured, but they still outnumber us. The Seventeenth Arcturan Guards existed more on paper than in reality. While she had mauled Jasek Kelswa-Steiner's Fifteenth Arcturan Guards, they were still operational. The Second Royals had lost two or three companies of 'Mechs and armor, but Roderick Steiner kept the rest in the field, constantly nipping at her right flank, then fading back into the Dales to lure her there.

The odds fall in their favor, not mine. That meant she had to avoid mistakes because it could tip not only a battle, but the fate of Coventry itself. *I have no desire to be the person that lost this accursed planet a second time in the name of the Jade Falcons.* She eyed the Dales in the distance and wondered what surprises the Steiners had planned for her there. Her aerospace recon flights had found the Second Royals and Ross's Arcturan Guards, but there was no hint of Jasek Kelswa-Steiner's forces. That made her even more suspicious.

Star Colonel Jagger Thastus marched his temporary replacement 'Mech, a *Hellbringer*, next to hers. Thastus was a dogged fighter. His arm fracture had not fully mended yet, so he took shots of painkillers—right through the cast—to stay in the battle. Oddly enough, his 'Mech bore a similar injury—its right arm was a dull primer-gray replacement for the one blown off in an earlier battle.

"Galaxy Commander," he said calmly. "You look to the hills. Are we going to move on the Dales, *quiaff*?"

"Affirmative," she replied.

"It is a trap, you know that."

"I do. The Lyrans will assume we are going to leave a force to hold the city. We are not. We are going *all in*. They will not have contemplated that. Their assumption that we need to hold Lietnerton will unbalance them. You know my philosophy about traps and ambushes."

"*Aff*, I do," his voice came back. "You prefer to go into them—and through them."

She grinned in response. *That is because I am a true Jade Falcon.*

Stephanie Chistu studied the lines of retreat from the last three times she had driven the Lyrans into the Dales. They were from diverging areas, but the paths of their withdrawals seemed to converge at a point some twenty-four kilometers in. *We never took that bait before, but now we shall surprise them and come at them from a direction they will not anticipate.* Moving along the Parish Highway some fifty kilometers east, then cutting north, she could arrive where she thought the Lyrans were, but catch them on their flank.

There was a temptation to send in aerospace elements to provide aerial reconnaissance, but doing so would tip off her enemies the moment they were spotted. *I need complete surprise to hit them hard where they will not expect it.*

She barked orders to her subordinates, who understood her thinking and complied. As usual, only Star Colonel Yaroslav pushed back. He demanded that if she was sure where the Lyrans were, they should go straight there. When warned of the clear risk of ambush, he shrugged it off.

"True Jade Falcons do not fear engaging the enemy. We should head right at them, destroy them, crush their support staff, and put an end to these hit-and-run attacks."

Strong words—yet no call for a Circle of Equals against my orders... such is the fury of the Mongol Doctrine outside Malvina's direct influence. Yaroslav accepted his orders and complied, albeit begrudgingly. It took the better part of a day to prepare—but once Stephanie began moving her force, they traveled with a swiftness that would have pleased even the most seasoned Falcon warrior.

The Parish Highway ran along the south edge of the Dales, curving with the contours of the foothills. A low drizzle began to fall and the skies turned gray. Chistu knew the rain would turn the sod in the Dales into a potentially slippery mess. A running BattleMech tore up ground with ease, even more so when it is wet. Her plan was to use the highway to extend and swing around, enabling a flank attack on her would-be ambushers.

When she reached the first waypoint, where her force would leave the highway on their flanking march, she stopped. There had been no sign of the Lyrans. Lietnerton was empty—but they had no way of knowing that unless they had sneaked scouts into the city. Even if they had, they would have no idea where her warriors were going, or what her intentions were.

Stephanie toggled her broadcast to the Falcons' secure tactical channel. "All right, from here, we move in standard wide-*w* formation. When we encounter the Lyrans, the flank positions will move wide, give us a good interlocking field of fire. These Spheroids love their artillery—and they are bound to have some hidden nearby. I'll bring in our CAP to seek and destroy these dishonorable weapons, but if you pinpoint the origin of incoming fire, engage and destroy at your discretion.

"I mean this to be the last fight with these *blitzking surats*. They have fought with honor thus far, but far too many of our warriors have paid a price for the respect we have shown them. Fight well, but I do *not* wish this to be a bloodbath. Any surrender will be met with acceptance. I know some of you feel differently, but I am in command here, and my orders stand." The last bit was leveled at Yaroslav and the others who harbored Khan Hazen's Mongol thinking. "Understood, *quiaff*?"

"The channel lit up with multiple *"Affs!"* in response.

"Then let us bring Coventry into our nest." She set off from the highway and into the Dales as her Jade Falcons fell into good order, making an almost perfect wide-w formation. They moved out to the next waypoint, thirty-two kilometers to the north. Galaxy Commander Chistu ordered her troops to wheel to the left. *If my calculations are correct, we should land on their flank shortly.*

As they advanced, the far left of her Galaxy suddenly opened fire. Her targeting-and-tracking system lit up with targets, fed by their tactical feeds. JES II Strategic Missile Carriers. *We've stumbled into their artillery reserve, no doubt.*

The air to her left flashed with explosions that flared brilliantly against the gray skies and slow rain. The reports made the ground quake slightly. One of her OmniMechs, a *Fire Moth* piloted by MechWarrior Lafreniere of the Buhallin bloodline, was taken down almost instantly as she crested the hill that had concealed the tanks, a wave of missiles seeming to home in on her center torso. Her fusion reactor erupted as the light 'Mech became tiny bits of shrapnel and a huge fireball rising in the air. Radioactive flames consumed her cockpit instantly, giving no chance to eject. The smoking remains of her ejection seat crashed to the ground some thirty meters from her position, no parachute, just burning debris.

Seyla, Lafreniere. Stephanie angled her *Jade Hawk* toward the blast as a number of her 'Mechs reached the hilltops and poured fire down the other side. As she reached the top of the hill, Star Captain Bressel Helmer's *Warhawk*, who had moved alongside her, was bathed in two-dozen long-range missile hits, most ripping into his patched upper torso armor and blowing bits back down the hill. Looking down, she saw one of the JES launchers already ablaze, the flames illuminating the others that were backing away from the swarming Jade Falcons.

She found one JES that no one had claimed as a target and brought her reticle onto the boxy missile racks that dominated the vehicle. Her short-range missiles twisted in the air and tore open one of the racks. The reloading LRMs spilled out, falling into a deadly pile near the vehicle.

The driver tried to adjust his retreat to dodge her, but her short-range lasers scored several searing hits, the emerald beams slashing the frontal armor with deep glowing furrows. Stephanie advanced as the carriers unleashed wave after wave of short- and long-range missiles. They filled the air like swarms of angry and deadly hornets. She heard the blasts and felt her 'Mech rock under the impact of at least six missiles across her right side. It did not shake her determination or her gait. *That JES is mine.*

The moment her targeting system indicated she had reloaded, she fired another deadly volley of short-range missiles. Eight tore into the carrier's left tread, blowing off a bogie and sending it bouncing down the hill towards the burning JES. The track was little more than shattered bits of metal now, and its loss made the JES suddenly jerk around, exposing its flank. One flight of LRMs roared toward her but missed widely, slamming into Bressel Helmer's *Warhawk* and the hillside.

Her *Jade Hawk* closed the distance even more, and she fired at the vulnerable flank with her extended-range small lasers. The searing crimson beams furrowed the thinner armor of the now stationary target. Rather than leaving scars, they seared deep holes into the missile tank. There was a low rumble, then the JES exploded. A moment later, another one some eighty meters away went up in an orange fireball.

A squad of Lyran infantry appeared from concealment, unleashing a volley of shoulder-launched short-range missiles at Tholburn Pryde's *Viper*. The missiles hit in an uneven cascade and against the gray rain clouds, and the *Viper* lit up with flames. *Inferno rounds!* Tholburn fell back to deal with the flames from the flammable-gel-filled missiles as one of the Gamma Galaxy 'Mechs unleashed a salvo of SRMs into the retreating infantry. The explosions tossed Lyran body parts into the air. It was far from fair. *That unit was brave to take on an approaching 'Mech force in such a manner. Killing such troops is a waste.*

The firefight was over a few heartbeats later; the shattered artillery tanks never really stood a chance. "All right, Delta and Gamma, charge!" Stephanie broke her *Jade Hawk* into a trot past the burning vehicles and up the next hill.

As she rose over the crest of the steep ridge, a mass of 'Mechs and armor all turned to face her, alerted by their comrades and the staccato of battle. Yelling with guttural rage, Stephanie rushed at the Lyran forces. Gone were Clan rules of engagement; the Lyrans fired pell-mell at the approaching enemies.

Her *Jade Hawk* was hit by a PPC shot to the left leg, making her stumble. The flash of white-and-blue charged particles sent arcs of discharging energy dancing across the wet armor. She reeled, fighting to shake the impact.

There was no time for revenge; she sought out the biggest and nearest foe, an *Axman*, and unleashed a full barrage of short-range missile fire at it. The missiles caught the right side and leg of the sixty-five-ton killing machine, punching two dozen craters in the armor. The *Axman* pivoted to her and let loose with its massive Luxor-Devastator autocannon.

The stream of large-caliber shells hit her center torso, killing the momentum of her charge and knocking her backward. She hit the wet sod and tore a wide furrow into the hillside. Her sense of balance evaporated as she was tossed about wildly in her seat, the restraining straps digging into her upper body.

Chistu tried to get her bearings; she had to fight her battlecomputer, the gyro attempting to recalibrate her position, and what her body and mind were telling her about how her 'Mech came to rest. It took precious seconds to overcome the disorientation.

Instincts honed with a lifetime of training kicked in. She flexed her knees and pushed with her arms, getting up on her right knee. The *Axman* fired its jump jets, closing the distance between them, raising its massive hatchet.

Stephanie needed time to stand, and could buy that with firepower. She unleashed everything she had at the looming war machine that was about to land before her. There was no concentration of fire in her alpha strike—the Lyran BattleMech was riddled everywhere at once. One moment that made her smile was seeing one laser hit the *Axman*'s sloping head, searing the cockpit's armored glass. The heat in her cockpit was searing, but she pushed her bruised body through it to keep fighting.

She got to her feet as the *Axman* landed. The hatchet in its right hand came down like an executioner about to behead a criminal. Stephanie pivoted hard, testing every bit of her skills as a warrior. The blade only nicked one of her extended wings, bending it badly.

She lunged with her *Jade Hawk*'s claw, aiming right at the *Axman*'s cockpit. The armored claw hit squarely, punching deep, right through the weakened glass. The *Axman* stopped all movement, then toppled over backward. As it fell, her claw freed itself from the cockpit. Looking at it, she saw a maroon smear of blood on one of the talons. That was distasteful. Clan warriors did not like close combat. They trained for it, but did not seek it out.

Stephanie swung her 'Mech around just in time to see Star Colonel Jagger Thastus's *Hellbringer* get hit with a Gauss-rifle round. The ferro-nickel slug was a blur of silver in the air until it hit his left elbow, mangling the actuator into worthless scrap. Still in the fight, Jagger fired his functional ER PPC into a Lyran *Blackjack*. The gray-and-blue-streaked 'Mech swung around like a dancer on one foot, then fell over, thudding hard into the wet grass.

Pivoting her 'Mech at the waist, Stephanie saw the first line of Lyran 'Mechs had either been defeated or were falling back. *Exactly as I had hoped.* If she pressed her advantage now, continued to drive into them, they would rout or surrender.

Suddenly off to her right, a company of enemy 'Mechs rose over the hill, their reactor signatures making her targeting system bark out proximity warnings. *"BattleMechs approaching inner defense zone,"* the battlecomputer's voice said in her neurohelmet. She killed the warning.

"Galaxy Commander Chistu, I am General Jasek Kelswa-Steiner of the Stormhammers. I am coming for you. Prepare to die!" a voice said on an open channel. The source, a hulking *Templar*, formed the center of the Lyran formation.

"Striker Prime to Striker Command Star, form up on me!" Stephanie said.

She expected the Lyrans to hold the high ground and rain fire on her. Some did. Many followed the unexpected charge led by General Kelswa-Steiner. They did not just rush the Jade Falcons; they were headed right for her.

The *Templar* fired as she swung to face it. The Gauss-rifle round was a barely visible silver-blur as it slammed into her 'Mech's left thigh. His missiles missed, but his pulse lasers did not, peppering her *Jade Hawk* everywhere.

She focused on the rushing behemoth, aiming for the center of its mass. Her short-range missiles exploded almost simultaneously, blasting at the thick armor. Her lasers targeted high on the 'Mech as well. While they found their mark, they did pitiful damage.

Kelswa-Steiner ran forward, right at her. She juked right, breaking into her own jagged run to shift to his side. Turning the *Templar* in a full run was like trying to pivot a battleship—it was impossible.

General Kelswa-Steiner pivoted his 'Mech at the waist and fired his medium lasers, one of which tore into her right arm. His Gauss rifle fired, not at her, but at Thastus's *Hellbringer*, which was moving in to join her. The hit caught the OmniMech dead center, cratering the 'Mech hard and deep.

Stephanie fired another volley of short-range missiles as Steiner's 'Mech came to an abrupt stop. A third of her missiles spiraled on past her target, hitting the hillside in the distance. The rest struck his upper left torso. The yellow and orange explosions offered some satisfaction, but not enough.

He unleashed pulse lasers as she toggled her jump jets and jammed her feet on the control pedals. His large pulse laser missed, the emerald beams searing the air only a meter from her cockpit.

The medium pulse laser wracked her *Jade Hawk*. Her damage display flashed yellow in a vain attempt to get her attention, but she ignored it. All that mattered now was Jasek Kelswa-Steiner and this fight within the battle. It was the way of the Clans.

Thastus fired his medium lasers and PPC into the gray-and-blue blur. Stephanie only saw the particle cannon hit. The blast of artificial lightning ripped into the chest of the *Templar*, sending superheated armor shards flying into the rain-filled sky. The raindrops steamed as they hit her 'Mech, but she ignored both the exterior and interior heat.

She landed farther up the hill her enemy had charged down, almost completely changing positions with him. As she flexed her knees to stand upright, she unleashed another salvo of missiles at the Steiner general.

Another Jade Falcon fired at him as well, blasting him with auto-cannon rounds.

"*Neg*!" she called into the microphone, broadcasting in the clear. "This one is mine!"

Kelswa-Steiner must have heard her, she was sure of that. The *Templar* turned and fired another silver slug of carnage into her 'Mech, slamming her left leg hard. The damage warning went from yellow to red.

Attempting to move, she found the leg sluggish. *Myomer has been severed...the actuators are still intact.* The leg still fought her attempts to move faster. *Damn!*

Her small lasers concentrated on her opponent's mangled upper torso, easily finding their marks. While less powerful, the lasers kept nipping at the armor in their way. She saw a dull orange glow in the *Templar*'s center torso and knew she'd hit his fusion reactor shielding.

Chistu limped backward in an uneven gait as her enemy un-leashed pulse laser fire and short-range missiles. She pivoted at the last moment, exposing her thinly armored but somewhat intact rear armor. The shots consumed the armor there and hit her *Jade Hawk*'s left arm. The cockpit temperature soared instantly. She didn't even have to look at her damage display to know she had lost a heat sink or two.

Jasek started closing the distance, accelerating from a walk to full sprint right at her. Chistu let go a snap shot of short-range missiles. Gone were the blue-and-gray streaks on his upper torso, replaced by holes, charred and black, some still smoking as he charged. He rocked under this fusillade, unlike the previous ones, clearly strug-gling to maintain his balance.

An explosion to her left marked the end of two 'Mechs, MechWarrior Odekirk Pryde and one of General Steiner's command, a mangled *BattleMaster*. Both pilots punched out as their grappling 'Mechs disintegrated in twin fusion-engine explosions. Chistu tuned out the casualties. None of that would matter if Jasek Kelswa-Steiner killed her.

In that moment, she realized that could very well happen. Kelswa-Steiner was a formidable and tenacious warrior. *He will not break off. He wants only one thing–my death.* Stephanie Chistu never feared her own death; that had been conditioned out of her after a lifetime of combat. At the same time, she had a respect for death, one that amped up her combat instincts to a whole new level. *I am the true Jade Falcon...*

Jasek Kelswa-Steiner's voice sang out over the open frequency for all to hear. "For Skye! For the Commonwealth. For House Steiner!"

Stephanie's eyes stung with sweat as it seemed he was rushing right at her personally—not at her 'Mech.

The *Templar* was on her just as she fired a pair of her small lasers. Kelswa-Steiner collided hard with her, and she leaned her *Jade Hawk* into the rushing 'Mech—partially to keep her balance, partially out of pure aggression.

The two BattleMechs ground against each other in a groan of scraping metal, their mass and armor merging for a moment. The heat spiked around her, some of it no doubt from the enemy. She should have fallen—a lesser warrior would have. But Stephanie Chistu did not. A wave of nausea rose over her, and she felt the taste of bile in her mouth. Neural feedback. Her senses blurred for a moment as she struggled against tunnel vision.

Slowly, bit by bit, she regained control. Damage warning lights showed almost all crimson, but she ignored them. At that moment Stephanie did not need damage displays to tell her what was happening: she was living it. In that moment, the armor around her became a second layer of skin. She was one with her 'Mech.

Her cockpit was right across from General Steiner's. She saw him in his command couch; like hers, his cockpit glass was cracked. He was struggling with his joysticks.

At this range he's going to kick, use his weight against me.

For a millisecond the two warriors, only meters apart, locked gazes. Stephanie swore she saw him grin and wink at her through the faceplate of his neurohelmet.

Not this time. Her *Jade Hawk* was built for close combat, and she used his own mass against him. She dug her clawed fists into the *Templar*, grappling, twisting, and turning...allowing him to scrape past her. Momentum and mass worked against Jasek's *Templar* as he stumbled, falling off balance.

She fired her jump jets as he passed, his 'Mech awash in her jet flare as she rose. This time it felt like she was under the thrust as well, as the heat boiled so intense around her. Her *Jade Hawk* ground against the *Templar* as she rose straight into the air.

Leaning forward as far as her restraints would allow, she saw the general's missed punch swing into the space where she had been. Smoke rose from her enemy as he staggered a half-step forward, almost drunkenly. Angling her damaged 'Mech, she hovered over him by a good ten meters.

Then she cut the jets.

The Lyran general was under her jump-jet thrust, no doubt blinding him to what she was doing. The full seventy-five tons of her *Jade Hawk* dropped on Kelswa-Steiner's 'Mech. One of her thick feet hit a shoulder, while the other crashed into his cockpit. She did not see him die—she did not have to. The sudden twist from the imbalance of her descent offset the grinding under her feet.

She fell off to her left side, hard. More armor tore and shattered, and her left arm would not respond at all. A coppery taste flooded her tongue, and she realized she must have bit her lip or hit it on the inside of her neurohelmet.

The blood did not matter to her. She was alive. The same could not be said of her foe. His auto-shutdown sequence had cut in with the pilot's death. As she rolled to one side, she saw the fallen *Templar*, its cockpit crushed beneath her 'Mech's massive foot. She did not rejoice this time, as she had in other victories. *This Steiner general was more than a worthy foe. To rejoice would deny him the honor he earned here today. Had he lived, he would have been a worthy bondsman.*

Trying to stand was a struggle, as if she were drunk and armpit deep in mud. More nausea made her head ring and her vision narrow. Every hot breath she drew was a reminder of the heat in her cockpit. Rocking her *Jade Hawk* to the side, she managed to get a rough sense of bearing. Using her right arm, she pushed and twisted and fought to get to her knees, then to her feet.

Her *Jade Hawk* was in bad shape, but still operational. The remaining Falcon forces secured the ground where she had been fighting. According the sensor feeds, the Lyrans were pulling back, concentrating to the west. *They saw their best warrior fall, and it has shaken them.*

Checking her own forces, Stephanie was staggered by the losses. She and Thastus were all that remained as a result of Jasek's charge on her command Star. Her other units had suffered significant casualties as well. *The odds are not in our favor...and our element of surprise has been lost.*

It has been said that Jade Falcon commanders do not care about the odds. That was only partially true. There was another adage they did adhere to: do not fight the math. Stephanie quickly calculated the respective firepower and losses on both sides and came to one conclusion: let the Lyrans fall back.

She hated it. This was to have been their last battle, their last confrontation. It was slipping through her fingers, and it galled her to have to issue the order. "Secure our casualties and fallen 'Mechs, leave nothing for these vultures. We will tactically redeploy to Port St. William."

"We are retreating, *quineg*?" Star Colonel Yaroslav asked. "This is not the way of the Jade Falcon."

She tried to tune out his accusatory tone, to no avail. "*Neg*, we are not retreating—we are assuming a new defensive position. My orders stand, Star Colonel."

"You have fifteen tactical nuclear weapons at your disposal," Yaroslav pressed for all of the Jade Falcons to hear. "Give the order. Fire one or two where the Lyrans are regrouping. Fire them, and this world will be ours."

"*Neg*," she said, straining to handle her *Jade Hawk*'s uneasy gait. The torrid heat of her cockpit told her that she had lost a number of heat sinks in the fight. *It is bad enough I have to fight this damage, this enemy—now I have to fight my own warriors.* "Those weapons are at my disposal and mine alone." In that one moment, she understood the allure of the Mongol Doctrine. *It would be so easy to give the order, to end the bloodshed. Easy is not the path of the Jade Falcon. We have never been a people seduced by slaughter. I can see why Malvina's followers are so drunk with her way of waging war.*

"*Stravag!*" Yaroslav retorted. "If you have no stomach for that, then fire a nuke at Lietnerton. Let the Lyrans see the mushroom cloud rising from the city. They will fold and surrender to us."

Unlikely. "After your actions in Whitting, Star Colonel, no Lyran will surrender to us willingly. I will not destroy a city, wipe out its culture and heritage, just to sow seeds of terror. My orders stand."

"*Perhaps you have been injured, Galaxy Commander. If you lack the will of the Falcon, let me take command. I will show you what it is to be a true Jade Falcon.*"

The arrogance in his voice only added to her nausea. "There is nothing wrong with me, nothing that cannot be cured by removing you from command. Star Colonel, you are relieved of duty."

"I do not acknowledge your authority to do so, Galaxy Commander Chistu."

Despite her weariness, Stephanie grinned at his insubordination. "Good. When we get back and prepare for our defense at Port St. William, we will settle this matter once and for all in a Circle of Equals. Until then, you will follow my commands—all of you. Retrograde by Stars *now*. I want good tight formations. Give cover and suppression fire for the recovery teams to salvage our people and gear."

A low rumble of thunder signaled an increase in the rain's intensity and further accentuated her orders. She paused for a moment, then continued. "We still have to take this bloody planet. It will simply take more time than we had planned. And we will do it with honor, not savagery."

With those last words she licked the clotted blood in the corner of her mouth and swallowed it, feeling the sting on her lip.

CHAPTER 7

LYRAN FIELD HQ
THE DALES
COVENTRY
COVENTRY PROVINCE
LYRAN COMMONWEALTH
12 MARCH 3148

Roderick stared at what was left of Jasek Kelswa-Steiner's blood-stained uniform.

He had ordered the man's remains cremated; a death so horrific made it impossible to embalm him to take him back to his family. *Death from above–a horrible way to die.* The uniform bore testimony to the violence of the general's death. Even with a quick washing, it was stained with the dull maroon of blood and gore. Holes and tears were evident everywhere.

Rain pelted the roof of the portable command dome. The storm had grown after the battle that had cost his distant cousin's life. It was as if Coventry itself was attempting to wash away the blood from the field. The cool rains and gusts of wind only seemed to add to everyone's misery. The air was humid and cool, but stuffy.

Roderick studied every fold, every drop of dried blood, his eyes settling on the general's insignia Jasek had worn. The four-pointed star was attached to the collar with special adhesive strips. The star bore his blood as well.

He crossed his arms and stared, trying to clear his mind, but the questions plagued him. Why Jasek had rushed straight at the Jade Falcon command Star, despite the odds? *After all the battles with the Stormhammers, he thought himself invulnerable. He did what I wanted to do, go right after Chistu. He did something that was beyond brave. We all pledge to give our lives to defend the Commonwealth. The difference is, he fulfilled that pledge, willingly...boldly.*

Part of his mental struggle was the guilt he personally bore. He had underestimated Stephanie Chistu. She had deliberately gone into his trap with her entire force, hitting his thinly protected flank. Roderick hadn't thought she would readily abandon Lietnerton and commit her entire force—a critical miscalculation of his enemy's strategy.

The battle had been furious. Jasek's charge at Chistu had compelled her to punch out of the encirclement, right through the left flank of the Second Royal Guards. Now his forces were at just over 50 percent operational readiness. The only bit of satisfaction he could cling to was that the Jade Falcons had suffered heavy losses as well. The Clan had hauled off the most useful gear in their retreat, leaving bits and pieces of salvageable equipment in their wake, but that was little solace for dead Lyrans. *The odds are in our favor, but these are Jade Falcons we're fighting. Odds mean nothing to them; I learned that in the Dales. I made a terrible mistake. I was arrogant and this was the cost—one of our best tactical leaders.*

Even so, Jasek had almost taken out Chistu. *If he had, this might all be over. Instead, we have to continue this fight right up to the bloody end.* Roderick had not come to die on Coventry, but looking at the bloodstained uniform of his fiercest general, he momentarily wondered if it was his destiny to die here too.

He shook his head. *No. I will not die here, not now—and* not *at the hands of the Jade Falcons.*

General Ross entered the tent, wearing her field jumpsuit. Her hair was slick with sweat; her eyes looked tired. She walked up next to Roderick and said nothing for a moment, looking down at the uniform. "His men are taking it hard."

"We all are," Roderick replied.

"His second-in-command, Colonel Ostrowski, is hospitalized. Punctured lung and burns. He was taken down when the Fifteenth was pursuing that Chistu bitch out of the Dales."

In the wake of Jasek's death, the Fifteenth Arcturan Guards had recoiled at first, then regrouped and went off seeking vengeance, against orders. Galaxy Commander Chistu had bloodied them badly for their efforts. *I understand why they did what they did, but it only cost us more men and equipment.*

Roderick forced his thoughts away from Jasek for a moment, focusing on the art of war. "We will roll the Seventeenth into the Fifteenth. I want you to assume command of the Fifteenth."

She hesitated. "Sir...?"

"Francine," Roderick said with his most assuring tone. "I know these troops loved Jasek. A lot of them were with him in the Stormhammers. They saw him as some sort of god, and I don't blame them. But I need *you* there. You know Coventry best—you've got more experience with Jade Falcons than I do at this point. They will see that, too. Trust me, you're the best person for the job." He meant every word.

"Yes, sir," she replied, her voice firming up with his encouragement.

A sergeant from the Fifteenth Arcturan Guards, his name tag reading *Havener*, entered the tent, holding a small container. "Begging your pardons, sirs, I wasn't sure if you wanted these for some sort of ceremony." At Roderick's nod, he put the container of ashes on the table before the two generals and departed the room. The solemn look on his face spoke louder than any words.

Roderick let the silence hang as he carefully thought. *A ceremony? The men under his command deserve that much, and he certainly earned it. Their morale is low. They didn't just lose a commanding officer, they lost a hero of the Commonwealth. How do I turn that around?* Bad morale was toxic for troops in the field. His mind raced trying to find the answer—it was the key between saving and losing Coventry.

General Ross stared at the makeshift urn. "If this can happen to him, what chance do any of us have? He was one of the Commonwealth's best field commanders."

"Do you think that's what the troops feel?" he asked.

She nodded. "I do, sir."

Then we may be doomed. "I refuse to believe that. Do you know why?"

"Why?"

"History is replete with moments when defeat is inevitable, when victory can slip through your fingers like sand. I've spent my life defying those moments. Most of my youth was spent hiding from being a Steiner, pretending to be someone else. My cousin Trillian changed that in me. She didn't just make me go public, she let me be what I was born to be—a member of our House. We don't exist in the Inner Sphere to be witnesses to history. We exist to *make* history."

"We are not all Steiners, General."

You are wrong. Steiner is not a drop of blood or a name, it is something more. "Perhaps we are, we just don't know it yet."

Ross nodded. "Well, you are right about one thing—we need a spark, something for the troops to hold onto, something that will convince them they can succeed. Men and women who are convinced they are going to be beaten have a way of making that happen."

Roderick knew she was right. "You must have studied desperate battles in history, Francine. They are won by soldiers that do extraordinary things at just the right moment."

"What do you have in mind?"

"Have you read about the War of Texas Independence?"

"Of course, sir, required reading at the Nagelring. I remember reading a paper on the Battle of the Alamo."

"Good—the Alamo is the key to this. It was a lost cause, doomed from the very start. It was that loss that allowed Sam Houston to galvanize his forces and eventually turn the tide of the war. When the Alamo fell, their entire campaign could have crumbled—turned into an obscure footnote in history. Houston took advantage of that loss and made it their battle cry. The Texans charged into battle scream-ing, 'Remember the Alamo!' Houston understood that a defeat can inspire as much as a victory." As he spoke, he stared not at her, but at the urn. *There is a way to turn this around...to turn Jasek's loss into a victory...*

"I'm listening, sir..."

Roderick stood erect, squaring his shoulders. He reached out into the urn and touched the ashes that had once been Jasek Kelswa-Steiner. He pinched some of those mortal remains between his fin-gertips. *General, you have one more mission to fulfill—and that is to help me defeat the Jade Falcons.* "First, call me Roderick. We have spilled the blood of our enemies on the same battlefields—we can shitcan the 'sir' and 'general' talk between us. I trust you, Francine. The Seventeenth was a battered and beaten unit, and you turned them around. Your work here has been remarkable." *I have more remarkable things for you to do still.*

"Thank you, Roderick," she said. He saw a slight blush in her expression.

"We need to turn things around just like Sam Houston did after the fall of the Alamo. We need to light a fire in their bellies."

She stood straighter at his words. "Agreed. What do you have in mind?"

"Leadership, plain and simple—you and me. We will give our people a rallying cry. Actually, Jasek did that already. We will give them a symbol to turn them into raging fanatics. Stephanie Chistu may think she has us beat, but I think she's already lost this planet—she just doesn't know it yet. All we have to do is convince her."

"I'm with you, si—Roderick."

"You know those black-cotton ammo bags we wrap inferno rounds in? I want you to round up a bunch of them, get your hands on as many as you can. Get a couple of privates working on it. Get some gray spray paint and our best artist. I want them cut into sashes, one for every soldier in our command. Get those ready, then I want you to assemble our force—everyone. I'll tell you what I want stenciled on them. We can use that big hill in the Dales, the one to the south. I want everyone there."

"What are you planning? Armbands won't change anything."

"I think you're wrong. We don't know for sure what Sam Houston told his men, verbatim, but we can look to literature and history for inspiration. Are you familiar with Shakespeare's *Henry V*?"

She shook her head. "I'm afraid I wasn't a big fan of the classics in school. I favored mathematics."

"Fair enough. Look up the St. Crispin's Day speech."

"Okay. How does an ancient play figure into all of this? What are you thinking?"

Roderick allowed himself a thin smile. "'If we are marked to die, we are enough to do our country loss; and if to live, the fewer men, the greater share of honor.'" He quoted from his memory of the English king's speech.

"You have me at a disadvantage, sir."

"I have come to believe that William Shakespeare understood the Clans. That speech may just be the key to us beating the Jade Falcons on Coventry."

SIX HOURS LATER...

The weather cleared slowly, with the sun breaking through more often. The rays of light gleamed as moisture evaporated from the Dales. Roderick had organized the event carefully, deliberately designed it for maximum impact. He walked to a small collapsible table that had been brought out to the hilltop overlooking the large natural bowl of the ground. In some areas, the sod had been churned into mud by BattleMech footprints, which were now large puddles of water. In other places, tracks from tanks snaked through the grass and dirt, leaving a distinct river-like pattern on the hillsides. BattleMechs and armor had been placed along the hillside like silent sentinels.

Roderick surveyed the survivors of the three regimental combat teams. Their faces were weary, drawn, almost devoid of expression. Many were covered with lubricant, dirt, sweat, and mud, and all wore masks of exhaustion and fatigue. Their eyes were all locked onto him, staring dully at his every move. He could feel the presence of each remaining man and woman, as if their breaths were his own.

At Roderick's side stood General Ross. While both of them had managed a quick field shower, Francine had changed the most in appearance. She looked ten years younger than she had just a few hours earlier. *It is important for them to see us here, recovered, shaved, refreshed, and ready to fight. It will help give them strength to see us this way. It shows them that things can and will change.*

As he faced them, an unspoken command was transmitted, and all of them snapped to attention. "At ease," he ordered, and a wave swept the Lyran soldiers as they resumed their casual, weary stances.

Also standing on the hilltop were the two highest-ranking survivors of the Fifteenth Arcturan Guards: Major Troy Cowell and Captain Krzysztof Krecislaw. Their jumpsuits had been washed, and the men themselves were presentable, although Krecislaw was heavily bandaged. His 'Mech had been destroyed, and he had been burned during punchout. Roderick had honored him by telling him he would pilot Jasek's *Templar* as soon as it was repaired. The grizzled Krecislaw had nearly burst into tears. Major Cowell wore a grim expression that mixed angst and anger.

The General of the Armies adjusted the mike on his jumpsuit and surveyed the survivors one more time. Thanks to large speakers that had been placed, he knew the crowd would hear his speech, his conviction. These were good soldiers, good Lyrans, one and all. Now was the time to turn their grief and depression into furious rage.

He had made notes on the back of a supply requisition form. Ross had asked him what he was going to say, but he kept the words private. He had rehearsed the speech twice while the memorial was being arranged, mostly to ensure he could drive home the key points with respect. Roderick had filled Francine in on the rest of his plans, but not the speech itself. The words would come from him—from the depths of his heart. The notes were merely props, an unnecessary safety cushion. *These words need to come from me, not from a piece of paper.*

"Good day. You know me, but I don't know most of you. I'm the General of the Armies—and you are the men and women who follow me into battle. Despite our differences in rank, I am not nearly as important as each of you. While I may be the head of this combat force, you are its heart—its soul."

"My grandfather was Archon of the Commonwealth. If he were here, I'm sure he'd have something inspiring to say like, 'The Jade Falcons made one big mistake. They attacked my home planet.'" A few of the weary troops—those that had seen documentaries of Adam Steiner's years on Somerset during the first Clan invasion—chuckled at that comment.

"Well, I am not my grandfather. Rank and blood doesn't matter on days like this. I am here like you, a citizen of the Lyran Commonwealth. And today, we come together to mourn Jasek Kelswa-Steiner—one of the greatest MechWarriors and field commanders of his era.

"Many of you came with him from the Stormhammers, and you probably knew him a lot better than I did. If he were here, I'm sure he would tell you all to never give in to despair. He'd probably tell you not to grieve him, but to avenge his death. He would probably say his death didn't matter. He was humble that way. Most legends are.

"Well, I will tell you today that his death *does* matter. It matters to me, and I am sure that it matters to you." Roderick cast his eyes down to the urn on the table. "This is all that is left of him—that, and our memories of him." Roderick saluted the container, and the entire mass of his troops did the same. He held it for a moment, letting everyone have this one moment of grief and respect.

"I am sure that you are all wondering what happens next. I could order in the DropShips and we could leave. We could retreat from Coventry, let the Jade Falcons have it. It's just a planet, after all. God knows the Commonwealth has others. But we would be abandoning the civilians to the most brutal of enemies—a foe that flattens cities and kills the innocent. We would survive, but the people of this world might not.

"We could go, regroup, and wait for our foe to hit another world, and another. They will keep coming, and we will keep fighting them. We might live for a few months, a few years, but in the end, the Falcons will eventually come for each and every one of us." He paused long enough to let that sink into the host before him.

"But I'm here to tell you that I won't be doing that. The enemy is here, and by God and the Archon, I intend to fight them here. To *stop* them here. You all heard what happened to Whitting—thousands of innocents killed. I have seen the footage myself, and it is a war crime beyond the pale. That is the Mongol-horde thinking of the Jade Falcons now. There are no innocents—no honor—not in the eyes of the Mongols. If we leave now, they will eventually hit our home worlds, one by one. Then the dead will be your wives, your husbands, your brothers, your mothers, your lovers, your families, and your friends. We need to stop them here—*now*. If we can do that, we kill their offensive right here. They cannot leave Coventry in our hands—it galls them. They seek to erase their past defeats, to change history. I say, fuck them!'" There were many nods of agreement from the gathered troops.

"So, the choice is clear, and it is one we must all face. This is not a democracy. I can order you into battle. I will fight them alone if I have to. But I put it to each one of you now. Do any of you want to turn tail and run?"

"No!" came a low roar from the crowd. As if on cue, the clouds parted, and brilliant rays of sunshine bathed the Lyrans.

"Do any of you want General Jasek Kelswa-Steiner's death to be wasted?"

"*No!*" This time it was louder—firmer.

"Do you want the Jade Falcons to claim any scrap of glory in his death? Do you want them to sing about his fall in their damned *Remembrance?*"

"*NO!*"

"Neither do I. Jasek Kelswa-Steiner wouldn't have retreated in the face of these Jade Falcons. You know that, and so do I. In fact, he went after the Jade Falcon commander right here in the Dales. His attack forced the enemy to withdraw. He and his command lance broke their assault. He gave his life so that we could all survive and be here today, this day, on this spot. If he were here, he would insist that we fight on." Murmurs of agreement rose from the troops below him.

"You may think he is no longer with us. You may think all that remains of him is in this urn." He gestured to the simple burial urn on the table. "You may believe that his death means he's gone. I'm here to tell you that you are wrong. General Kelswa-Steiner is *not* gone. He is here, today, with each and every one of you."

Roderick saw new energy return to the men and women under him. Their faces, once gaunt, seemed to glow red with anger and fury.

"I will not let my cousin be some footnote in a history book under a chapter about the fall of Coventry. Hell no! I intend to carry him with me into battle." He reached out and carefully lifted the urn, raising it so they all could see.

"These are his mortal remains, the ashes of a great man." He set the urn back down and opened it. He dipped his thumb into the gray dust. Then he put his thumb on his forehead, grinding the remains of Jasek Kelswa-Steiner there, leaving behind a bold, dark gray mark. He could see their faces following his every move. *Good.* "Jasek is with me now. He will ride into combat one more time. He will be there to lead us all to victory."

He motioned to Major Cowell, who bent down and pulled out a strip of cloth from a shipping container. Made from the ammunition bags, the black cotton had been cut into a crude sash some ten centimeters wide and sixty centimeters long. Spray-painted with a crude stencil in gray in the middle of each sash was the star-and-shield insignia of the Archon's Shield, the Stormhammers' elite unit.

Roderick extended his right arm, and General Ross took the cloth and tied it around his biceps so that the insignia was clearly visible. Roderick then turned back to the troops.

"This sash represents mourning for General Kelswa-Steiner, but it is more than that. It will serve as a reminder to you and anyone who ever sees it. In the years to come, many people will claim to have been here on this day, on Coventry, when we drove the Jade Falcons off this world again. They will brag about being here when we defeated the invaders. They will tell lies of their heroic deeds. It always happens, those who reap a false harvest of honor. They will never have the proof that they were here, which is this armband I wear.

"But when you are in your later years, bouncing your grandchildren on your knee, you will tell them the truth of what happened on Coventry, when *you* saved the Commonwealth. You will tell them that *you were there.* You will have proof—the black sash you wore into battle that day. It will be one of your most prized possessions. It is something that no other Lyran will ever wear again. You will remember the ashes of Jasek Kelswa-Steiner on your forehead, and the spirit he inspired you with. People will remember what you did, and that simple band of cloth you have will forever link you to the men and women around you. We are not just Arcturan Guards or Royals today, we are part of something bigger, something those that aren't here will never understand. In your old age, this sash will be a reminder of your greatest victory, and how each of you took Jasek into battle for his last and greatest victory."

Roderick turned to General Ross and dipped his thumb into the ashes, making a mark on her forehead similar to his own. He then tied another sash from the container on her right arm. Francine turned did the same with Major Cowell and Captain Krecislaw. Tears ran down Krecislaw's round face as she did so.

Roderick heard several men and women crying in the hollow. But the expression on every one of their faces was grim determination.

"Today, we are all Jasek's pallbearers!" he shouted. "Today, we carry him to the victory he earned! Form up lines, and prepare to be part of history!"

The troops moved, no longer with a weary trudge, but scrambling to get into lines leading up the hill. Roderick grabbed a handful of armbands, as did the other officers. As each Lyran trooper stepped forward, they were given a smear of gray ash on their foreheads by one of the officers at the table. Those with injured arms had the bands tied across their brows like headbands. Some touched the cloth as if it were somehow blessed. Every one of them understood the significance.

As they passed through, Roderick shook hands with every one of them. The armbands, the ash—it made them all equals.

The entire process took over an hour. Tears flowed, but what the General of the Armies saw was inspiration, faith, and most importantly—hope.

They milled about the great depression in the hills until the last of them had been honored. Roderick turned on his microphone again. "Atten-*hut!*"

In unison, his reinvigorated troops snapped to attention in perfect rows before him. "Look to your right," he ordered, and they complied. "Now to the left." He paused. "Now eyes front."

"Those men and women you saw, they are your brothers and your sisters. We all bear the mark of Jasek Kelswa-Steiner on us. That makes each one of you my blood and kin. That same blood flows through the Archon, and into our past. Today, I am proud—" his voice wavered for a moment, but he steadied it and continued, "—to call all of you my brothers and sisters. Today, we are *all* Steiners." Smiles through gritted teeth came back to him. *Fury!*

There was one more artifact on the table that needed to be addressed, the pair of rank stars. Roderick picked up the bloodstained star insignias that had been removed from Jasek's uniform. He held them up in the air. "These are Jasek's *hauptmann*-general stars. He died wearing them. General Ross and I would like to wear these in the coming battle. But Jasek was *your* general first and foremost. If we do this, we do it together. So I ask you all, may I put these on?"

"*JA!*" The thunderous roar of cheers echoed into the Coventry sky. Roderick put one star on next to Francine's, then she placed his.

Roderick then turned back to the troops. "The Falcons think they have us beat. That is a mistake, one I intend to take advantage of. I will go and face them alone if I have to."

"Over my dead body!" Francine Ross said, loud enough for the microphone to pick it up. "Even if it is just the two of us, I'm with you, sir."

Another huge cheer rose from the Dales.

"General," Major Scott said. "For Jasek and for the Archon, I will go and fight at your side."

"Get me a 'Mech sir, any 'Mech," Captain Krecislaw said, his voice carrying to the crowd. "I will make them pay for Whitting—pay for murdering my commanding officer."

There was another unified roar from the troops—one that Roderick did not interrupt.

After a full minute, he spoke again. "Very well, brothers and sisters. Let's get ready to take the fight to them."

The crowd dispersed with renewed energy and vigor. The malaise was shaken from them. The weariness and sorrow that had weighed them down was gone. The officers that helped with the distribution of the sashes crisply saluted and asked to go and get their troops ready for the coming fight. Each and every one seemed to move with a new snap and energy. Even the wounded shook off their limps and pain.

Francine Ross moved in front of him and shook his hand. "Roderick...I've never seen anything like it. You did it. You reinvigorated them."

"No, *we* did. They will follow you now as if you were Jasek himself."

"It was amazing. I mean those words...people don't talk like that."

"Yes they do, in their hearts and souls. I just tapped that."

"I think you just turned the tide of this fight."

Roderick allowed himself a thin smile. "Like I told you earlier, Steiners *make* history. You heard the speech. You are a Steiner now—so you had better get used to it."

"What's next?"

"If I were Stephanie Chistu, I'd be heading for Port St. William to lick my wounds and prepare to go on the offense again. It's the Jade Falcon way. We need to hit her before she makes us dance to her tune."

"You have an idea, I take it?"

Roderick's smile grew broader. "In fact, I do..."

CHAPTER 8

JADE FALCON HEADQUARTERS
PORT ST. WILLIAM SPACEPORT
COVENTRY
COVENTRY PROVINCE, LYRAN COMMONWEALTH
13 MARCH 3148

In the hotel room she had commandeered, Galaxy Commander Stephanie Chistu went over the current state of her troops on the noteputer. Despite the damage done by the Lyrans, she still had an effective combat force, though some disparaging gaps in the Jade Falcon ranks concerned her. *We have enough in us for one more good fight. After that I may not have an ongoing, operable force.* Giving Malvina any reason to say she wasn't following orders was something she refused to face, and her Khan insisted that her command be still able to fight.

She had dispatched the Savage Claw Trinary of the Fourth Falcon Dragoons to the town of Guite, some twenty kilometers to the southwest. Their role was to act as a tripwire if the Lyrans got aggressive. The town was just south of the Ochoa River, accessible via a single highway bridge back to Port St. William. The plains surrounding Guite were rolling, but offered little cover except to the forested region fifteen kilometers away. It was the perfect place for a sentry post. *If you come for me, Roderick Steiner, you will find that I have plenty of time to react.*

Chistu looked at the noteputer, wincing at some of the losses. *We have been able to keep our combat force operational in terms of equipment, but replacing warriors is not as easy.* The Mongols of Gamma Galaxy had suffered staggering losses in the Battle of the Dales. *Their brutal fighting style damages them as much as it does the enemy.* When Jasek Kelswa-Steiner's Fifteen Arcturan Guards had pursued her force, Gamma exceeded her orders and turned to give them battle—bloodying both sides.

She had managed to get a quick shower as the technicians struggled over her *Jade Hawk*. Her tech, Helgeson, finally told her the grim truth: the OmniMech could be repaired, but not without extensive time and parts, both of which they lacked on Coventry. *If we still held the Metal Works, he would have been able to fix it.* A replacement would be pulled from those available. *I have taken out this Jasek Kelswa-Steiner. It will either break their morale—or fill them with a resolve I may yet regret.* She did not cringe from the fight she felt coming; in fact, she looked forward to it. *Khan Hazen will never admit it, but these Lyrans are worthy foes for our Clan.*

Stephanie's muscles still ached from the battle, and her head throbbed from the neural feedback she had suffered. Her sense of balance was coming around, thanks to the medication the medtechs had given her. She had suffered worse in her lifetime, but not in recent years. The battle had taken a physical toll on her, but the shower, a warm meal, and a cup of hot coffee had performed a remarkable revitalization.

A knock on the door announced Star Colonel Jagger Thastus' arrival. "My apologies for disturbing you, Galaxy Commander, but I think the time has come to deal with the 'problem.'"

"Is he causing issues, *quiaff*?"

"*Aff*," Thastus replied. "You have removed Star Colonel Yaroslav from command, but his mouth runneth over. He comments about you and your lack of, well, fortitude, in the battle. He has been openly expressing his opinions to our warriors. He has suggested that you lack the will to utilize the weapons at our disposal."

The nuclear missiles. Stephanie cocked one eyebrow at his words. "His words do not cut me, but I will not allow such a contamination with my troops. The man is a virus, and he cannot be allowed to spread."

"You are up for combat, *quiaff*?" Thastus asked.

She rotated her shoulder to stretch the muscles. "I have fought Trials in worse condition." *Of course, I was younger then.*

"He cannot win. If he does, he will declare a Trial of Possession for your rank, and try and take over your Galaxy."

He is probably correct, but I cannot show concern to him. "You worry too much, Jagger," she said, taking out her sheath of throwing knives and strapping them to her right shin. "I have not lost a Trial in years. I do not plan on starting with this *blitzking* murderer. Have him brought to the tarmac. I will be there shortly. I want a mix of Delta and Gamma warriors for the Circle of Equals. When he is defeated, I want them to witness it as well."

"As you command," Thastus said, saluting then departing.

Chistu went to her duffel and pulled out a large bowie knife, "Tickler." It had taken her weeks to forge and polish. She had balanced it perfectly, cut the handle to conform to her hands. Tickler had never let her down. She put it into the leather sheath and threaded her belt through the sheath, wearing it at her side. If all went as planned, Yaroslav would soon feel the cut of its edge.

Star Colonel Yaroslav stroked his goatee as Stephanie stepped out confidently in front of him. He was a full thirty centimeters taller than her. His bald spot was in need of a shave; she could see blackish stubble showing. A bandage on his hand, running through into the wrist of his uniform, told her that he too had been injured in the recent battle. His black jumpsuit stood out in contrast to her own green one. *My uniform is steeped in tradition. Yours is a political statement.*

"You had no right to remove me from command of my troops," he said defiantly. "For that, you will pay dearly."

"I always welcome the useful opinions of officers in my command. That is not an invitation for critique. You have crossed a line that requires honor be served."

"I prefer to fight you here," he said, gesturing with a sweep of his hand. "No subterfuge. We will battle in the open."

"Agreed," she replied. "I say we battle with melee weapons," she patted Tickler at her side. "We need not damage our 'Mechs. Nor do we need to waste pistol ammunition. This should be done up front and personal."

Yaroslav smiled. "Well bargained and done!" He nodded at one of the black-jumpsuited Gamma warriors, who stepped forward with a large spear. "You are too predictable, Galaxy Commander." The Star Colonel took the spear in hand. "Everyone knows of your fondness for knives. I will fight with the weapon my *sibko* trained us with for years, a coursing spear."

The blade at the end of the spear was straight on once side, curved on the other, with a slight hook near the haft. It was more of a guisarme than a true spear, a true Jade Falcon melee weapon. The shaft was thick duro-aluminum. She had seen such weapons, and had fought with one herself in her youth. Yaroslav's looked custom-made, no doubt a weapon he had made for such fights. *It gives him reach against me. He thinks that gives him the advantage.*

She gritted her teeth and offered him a thin, confident smile. "You will find that I am full of surprises, Star Colonel. I trust you find these warriors suitable for a Circle of Equals, *quiaff*?"

"*Aff*," he said, offering his own feral grin in response. The warriors backed off and formed a wide circle about ten meters in diameter. She felt their eyes on her as she lowered her stance and pulled out Tickler. It felt comfortable in her grip.

"Let us begin," Chistu said.

Yaroslav did not strike quick or fast. Instead he spun the large spear around like a propeller as he began to stalk her. Stephanie was familiar with the form; it helped him gauge the balance of the polearm. She shifted to counter him, watching his every spin. He was left-handed, she noted. His arrogant grin made her want to lash out at him and draw first blood, but that would be a mistake.

"I will kill you today," he said, stopping the spinning of the spear and holding it with both hands in front of him, pointing the tip of the sharp, hooked blade right at her head. "And when I do, I will fulfill the will of Khan Hazen. I will burn the surviving Lyrans and cities to cinders."

"Hollow words," she replied, tossing Tickler between her hands. "From a hollow warrior."

Anger swept his face and bald head, turning them red. He jabbed at her with the spear, coming within half a meter. Then, like a dancer, he spun, sweeping the weapon around, advancing at the same time. The blade-like spear point came right at her face in a long arc. Chistu's years of experience kicked in, and she leaned backward, feeling the blade narrowly miss her face.

Yaroslav swept the blade back, and this time she deflected it with Tickler, forcing the blade over her head. She was surprised when he jerked the blade and the small hook caught Ticker and wrenched it hard in her hand.

He lunged forward, and the blade cut her jumpsuit and sliced her forearm. She felt the cut but ignored it, springing at the Star Colonel and swinging Tickler at him, catching him low on his thigh. Some blood flew, but the black jumpsuit concealed the true amount of damage she had caused.

Yaroslav spun again, reeling and bringing the spear back, resting it on his extended right arm, which he pointed at her. She jumped back and balanced her stance. She was tempted to look at the cut on her arm, but focused on her opponent instead. Her hand ached from his weapon jerking the knife, but she ignored it as well.

"You bleed, Galaxy Commander. You can end this at any time."

"Honor demands that I see this through," she said, grinning at her foe simply to irritate him.

It worked. Yaroslav lunged twice, advancing like a fencing master. The spear came in close, and she knocked it hard with Tickler, this time making sure to avoid letting it get hooked. He surprised her again by jerking the blade to the side, hitting her collar and cutting her there.

I have to close the distance. She jumped at him and somersaulted, springing to her feet right in front of Yaroslav. She lunged at him and he recoiled as Tickler hit him in the stomach. The cut was not deep, but it didn't have to be. He grunted as she slashed again, this time cutting his chest. The uniform parted, and she saw the cut across his ribs and upper abdomen. Blood oozed from the wound.

The Gamma Galaxy officer slammed the spear's shaft down onto her head hard...and Stephanie pivoted out and put some distance between them again before he could smack her a second time. Yaroslav thrust at her again and nearly cut her in the process.

With her free hand, she grabbed his spear and pulled it toward her, the blade going past her. Her foe had not anticipated that; she saw that on his face. She brought Tickler at him, slashing his right cheek and cutting off the end of his goatee.

The Star Colonel jerked the spear from her grip and reversed it, hitting her again in the head with the shaft as he retreated. Her skull rang. Stephanie was glad to have the distance between them. His wounds were bleeding and painful. Each passing moment would weaken both of them, hopefully him more than her.

"You have lost your beard, Star Colonel," she said with a broadening smile. "Perhaps you can shave it smooth like your head."

He wiped the cut on his face and glanced at the blood all over his hand. "Little woman, I grow tired of this sparring as if we were *sibkin* wrestling over dinner." He spun the spear around again, this time pointing the butt of the weapon at her.

For a millisecond, Chistu was puzzled—then she heard a *click* and felt something hit her in the right breast. Almost instantly, a sudden chill swept her right side.

She backed up several steps before glancing down. Four needles stuck in her breast. *A hidden needler!* Her breath became strangely labored. She pulled the needles from her chest but felt no relief.

"You freebirth scum," she cursed, keeping some distance between them. "You have violated the terms of our Circle of Equals. We agreed to melee weapons. You have brought a projectile weapon." It hit her as she struggled to breathe—these were not just needles, they were something more.

Her fellow Delta warriors stepped into the Circle. Violating a Circle of Equals was something unheard of. The black-suited Gamma warriors turned towards her warriors, then back to the pair of them. There was no formal protocol for someone that broke the bond of a Circle of Equals.

"An oversight on my part," he blatantly lied, spinning his spear around to a traditional low fighting stance. "We adherents of the Mongol Doctrine believe in complete victory by any means. I am confident that Khan Hazen will overlook my slight breach of honor, especially when I tell her what I have done to Coventry in her name.

"By now you should feel the poison starting to paralyze your body. It is a special cocktail, Galaxy Commander, made from goliath scorpion venom. Admit defeat now, and you may yet survive.

Continue, and I will take your command from you after I plant this spear in your dead body."

The poison was working fast. *Too fast.* Her breath became ragged. Slowly, she dropped to her right knee, still holding Tickler in front of her, though she could see it wavering. Her vision tunneled, and she fought it with every bit of her strength, somehow staying conscious. She felt cold, but beads of sweat stung her eyes. *I cannot let this monster win.*

"Give up, Galaxy Commander," he gloated. "This is a fight you cannot win."

If he threw his spear at her, she was in no condition to dodge or parry it. Her head swam. A wave of dizziness gripped her hard.

"You honorless freebirth!" cursed Thastus from the edge of the Circle. "You will pay for your actions!" He moved forward, but two Gamma warriors blocked him.

"I think not," Yaroslav said, turning toward Thastus—and away from Stephanie.

Now!

As his gaze left her, she summoned the last bit of her strength. Dropping Tickler, she reached for the sheath on her lower leg. Her body almost toppled over from the dizziness, but she fought it back with the same fury she had used to fight Yaroslav. She reached down and felt the three throwing knives strapped to her shin.

Yaroslav turned to face Thastus and the commotion from the edge of the Circle of Equals. Stephanie knew his arrogance had overridden his common sense.

She raised the three blades over her head as the ferrocrete tarmac seemed to suck her downward. With a precise snap of her wrist, she hurled the three blades as she had thousands of times before in practice.

The blades separated in flight but flew true. One hit in the Star Colonel's side just below his rib cage. Another embedded itself in his beefy biceps. The last one struck his throat from the side, entering one side and stabbing out the other.

Dropping his spear, Yaroslav made a choked, *"Ack!"* and reached for his throat. Hitting the blade with his palm, he only worsened his wound. The spear *clang*ed on the ground as he turned to her, stark terror in his eyes. His hands quaked, and he fell to his knees, eye to eye with her. A gurgle rose to his lips, and blood splattered out of his half-opened mouth.

One of his hands fell to the knife in his abdomen and pulled it out, tossing it in her direction. Yaroslav listed forward, breaking his fall with his left arm. Blood flowed from his throat wound to the ground. He wavered, and her full attention and concentration focused on him as he collapsed.

For a moment, all eyes shifted to her. She felt them, drew from their energy. With her last bit of strength, she stood up. She was wavering, teetering side to side. It was hard to breathe, and her tunnel vision surged as she rose unsteadily to her feet.

"This fight is concluded," she hissed. "Get that *surat* some medical attention."

Chistu started to collapse, but hands grabbed her from behind, preventing her from falling face-first on the ground. Darkness and dizziness consumed her, and the lights of the spaceport went instantly dark.

Stephanie heard voices, but could not make out the words or who was speaking. It was a garble, half-dream, half-reality to her. She forced her eyes open, and the white light above made her head throb.

I am alive. That self-acknowledgment was enough to cause her to shift. Her joints protested and ached like she had not felt before. She opened her mouth and tried to speak, but her throat was bone dry. Coughing, she felt the presence of others around her, outside her field of vision. The coughing made her whole chest especially her right chest, throb.

"How long?" she managed to say.

A medtech moved into her field of vision. "Please try to relax, Galaxy Commander. You've been through quite a bit."

Stephanie tried to clear her throat, but it hurt. "How...long?" she repeated slowly.

"Ten hours," another voice from outside her field of vision spoke.

Jagger! She turned her head slowly and saw him. "We performed a temporary dermal patch," the medtech said. "You shouldn't move too much, Galaxy Commander."

"Sitrep," she said, ignoring him and focusing on Star Colonel Thastus.

"I had the Ninth Talons launch the Emerald Eyes Wing and do a pass over the Dales. The Lyrans have moved out."

"To where?" she said, shifting and half sitting up.

"Unknown. I believe they moved into the Jukka Forest. It is not far from the Dales and thick enough to obscure their activities."

Stephanie brought up a mental map of Coventry. Thastus's theory made sense. If it was true, she had been wise to put a Trinary in Guite. *This Roderick Steiner is unlikely to break easily, even with the death of his bloodkin. His bloodline is known for its tenacity. He will keep coming at me.*

Stephanie's mind danced. "Yaroslav?"

Thastus's right eyebrow cocked. "Alive—barely. The doctors were able to save him, against my better judgment. We all saw him violate the Circle of Equals. Even his own troops disapproved of his actions. Poison is unbefitting true warriors, especially Jade Falcons. The use of a needler...that was wrong. He was trying to assassinate you. You know that, *quiaff*?"

I do now. "Aff," she replied. The medtech handed her a cup of ice-cold water, which she drank. Her aching throat calmed on the third sip. *Yaroslav meant to kill me, not just fight me. How much of Malvina was behind his actions?* If Malvina wanted someone dead, she and her Mongol followers did it in the open, with no need for underhanded tactics. Stephanie did not want to believe that her Khan would stoop to assassinating her own commanders, but she had dark doubts—doubts she dare not speak aloud.

She put the cup down. "I will see him."

"He cannot speak," Jagger said. "Your last attack saw to that. It permanently damaged his vocal cords. The best he can likely do is whisper."

"Good. It means I will not need to have him gagged." She slowly swung her legs off the bed and felt the tug of the synthskin bandage on her right breast. The medtech moved to stop her, but Stephanie shot him an icy glare, and he stepped back.

The hospital floor was cold beneath her feet. There was a hint of imbalance, but she felt better than expected after such a savage fight. Jagger moved in at her side, not offering to help her at all.

They went two doors down the hall, to where two *solahma* infantry in the green uniforms of Delta Galaxy stood guard. *Jagger was wise to put him under guard. We do not know the level of mischief he is capable of.*

She entered his room and saw Yaroslav on the bed. His throat was wrapped in a thick pad of gauze tint ed pink where her blade had found its mark. A darker shade of synthskin covered the cut on his chest, but she saw for the first time the sheer size of the wound Tickler had inflicted. *I hope it hurt then and now, you surat-suckling freebreeder.*

The moment he saw her, the Star Colonel's body stiffened, and his face turned red. His throat was wrapped so thickly that he could not open his mouth fully, but he did force out some air and spittle.

Good. He fears me. As it should be after what he has done.

"You live, Star Colonel," she said. "But your life is forfeit. You violated centuries of Clan tradition by breaking the sanctity of the Circle of Equals. By taking that needler in with you, it is clear you intended to do so from the very start. Your use of poison, the kind of killing tool that only a member of the bandit caste uses, is unworthy of a warrior."

He said nothing but seemed uncomfortable. He shifted on the bed, and for the first time she noticed that he was strapped down. *One thing about Jagger, he is thorough.*

She leaned over him so her face dominated his view. "Your Mongol Doctrine of winning at all costs has cost you your honor, and likely your life. I came here because I want you to know who beat you.

Witness the extent of your failure. Khan Hazen is not here to protect you."

She leaned in closer and lowered her voice. "I also want you to know that your violation of the Circle of Equals means your life is in my hands. As you lie here, consider what fate is befitting a warrior who has cast aside every shred of honor." She then smiled, broadly, proudly.

I am a true Jade Falcon. Stephanie stood up and walked out of the room as Yaroslav strained against the straps holding to the bed.

TEN HOURS LATER...

Putting on a fresh jumpsuit and tossing aside the worthless hospital gown made Stephanie feel better. *This is where I belong, in warrior's gear, doing warrior's work.* She had allowed herself a night of rest. *It is time my Galaxy sees me back at my duties.*

Stephanie found Tickler on the nightstand and strapped it to her side. The blade was thankfully clean of Yaroslav's blood. *I want nothing of that man to taint this weapon.*

As she stepped into the corridor, Turco, a warrior from the First Falcon Striker Cluster, ran up to her. "Galaxy Commander, you are needed at the HQ immediately."

"What is happening?" she demanded as the two of them started down the hospital hallway.

"We just received a partial message from our Trinary in Guite." Turco increased his gait to keep up with her.

Stephanie shook off the aches and pains. *It is beginning...the Lyrans are emerging.*

"Go on," she commanded.

"They are outnumbered and surrounded in the town."

By Aidan Pryde's blood! "Why was I not informed earlier?"

"Their communications were jammed. We just got an uplink via laser to our JumpShip that relayed it to us," Turco said. "Apparently they were attacked an hour ago."

"Force estimates?"

"Unknown. Initial reports are two Lyran regimental combat teams." He paused as they flew through a pair of doors and out onto the street where a command car waited. "There is more, Galaxy Commander."

Chistu did not slow down. "Go on."

"General Roderick Steiner sent a message to you personally. Transmitted on our command channel unencrypted."

He held out a noteputer as she climbed into the passenger seat. The vehicle lurched, but she ignored it. Instead, she stared at the image of Roderick Steiner on the screen; his chiseled featured and blue eyes marked his bloodline well. He was in a 'Mech cockpit, that much she could make out. She stabbed her thumb on the play icon.

"Galaxy Commander Stephanie Chistu, I am General of the Armies Roderick Steiner," he began. "I will admit, you surprised us in the Dales. We now have your Trinary surrounded and will wipe them out, just as you did to Whitting if you do not come and face us here, now.

"I trust you are game for a rematch," he said with a confident grin she could see through his neurohelmet's visor. "Or you can suffer defeat at the hands of someone who was freeborn—the choice is yours. If you want your little hatchlings in Guite, come and get them."

Stephanie just glared at the screen as she sped toward her 'Mech and the soon-to-be-joined battle. *Well bargained and done, Roderick Steiner!*

CHAPTER 9

Smoke rolled out of the heart of Guite as Roderick surveyed the devastation. The original plan had been to use it as a forward observation post, but two squads of *Himmelsfahrtkommandos* that infiltrated the small town had reported that a Jade Falcon Trinary had already beaten him to the position. Roderick had amended his plan to take advantage of the town. He had hoped to move in and force the Falcons to capitulate once they were surrounded and outgunned. Jade Falcon prisoners would have been the perfect bait to move Galaxy Commander Chistu out of Port St. William. He had given those orders to the Second Royals, specifically to secure prisoners.

For the first time ever, his troops had defied those orders.

I made a mistake. I didn't fully factor in just how much rage and fury I had instilled in my force. Roderick had suspected that Chistu would put a recon unit in Guite. In a rushed wave of wrath and ferocity he had rarely experienced, the Lyrans had encircled the Trinary in the town square before they had a chance to even deploy. After surrounding the enemy, his forces rushed in, screaming, "Remember Jasek!" and "Remember Whitting!"

The Falcons fought incredibly well, but Lyrans filled with battle-frenzy hit them from all sides at once. Formations and tactics gave way to pure rage. The fighting lasted only a few short minutes before the Jade Falcons had all succumbed. Only a few of the Clanners had been taken alive, and if it had not been for his personal intervention, even that wouldn't have happened.

While Roderick knew the Falcon defenders had been utterly defeated, he was sure Stephanie Chistu did not know that. *I don't need live Falcons as bait to lure her in, only the illusion of them.* He ordered ECM thrown up and had his troops prop up some of the downed enemy 'Mechs, in case the Falcons flew aerial reconnaissance sorties to verify. The fires were allowed to burn, generating smoke to make it look like fighting still raged. The Lyrans evacuated the surviving civilians, getting them clear of the battle about to come.

The plan had been devised by Roderick and General Ross. First, they would lure the Jade Falcons away from Port St. William. By placing her troops in Guite, Chistu had given Roderick the perfect incentive to induce her to come—a rescue mission. *She would have come anyway...the bulk of our force is here. She knows if she defeats us here, now, Coventry is hers.*

The second part of the plan involved the Ochoa River. The wide waterway was not quite at flood stage, but the water level was up due to recent rains in the mountains to the east. It was fast flowing, too fast for 'Mechs to ford. That left only the single highway bridge between the two armies. If Chistu wanted him, there was only one way to reach him, and that was across that lone bridge.

Francine Ross had summed it up best: "She will see it for the bottleneck it is, but will be compelled to come at us with expediency. She's a Jade Falcon. We are far too tempting a target to disregard."

The bridge would separate her forces, those north of the river and those crossing to the south to reach Guite to rescue their comrades and get at the Lyran troops. *Then we drop the hammer on her.* He had few resources left. There were no reserves for him to tap into.

He had not told Francine Ross or anyone else that he intended to deal with Stephanie Chistu personally. The odds in the fight were far too even for his liking. Even if his forces were victorious, he risked decimating troops on both sides. This was one of those rare times that the Clan way of fighting was best—a duel of honor, warrior to warrior.

Given the chance, I will call her out and we will end this once and for all. Francine doesn't need to know my intent. She will only protest and demand the right to face Chistu herself. The Battle for Coventry will end at my hand.

He had transmitted his taunt to the Jade Falcons in the clear. *They will come in force.* "Francine, post your troops as we planned," he sent on the command channel. "The rest of you, remember, we don't open up until they have at least a Cluster over that bridge. Wait for my command."

"Understood, sir," Francine replied.

Hasty trenches were being dug, with tanks concealed under mud, sod, and carefully placed tarps. In Guite, 'Mechs with long-range weapons were targeting the highway bridge and its approaches.

Others, hidden in the outskirts of the town, aimed at the close end of the bridge.

A voice came over his commlink. "This is Galaxy Commander Stephanie Chistu of the Gyrfalcon Galaxy of Clan Jade Falcon, the one true Clan. Who are you to take our warriors prisoner, General Steiner? You are unworthy."

"Coming from someone who kills innocent civilians, I will take that as a compliment," he replied on the open frequency.

"We are en route to your position now," she said firmly. "You will pay for your audacity."

Roderick's lower jaw clenched. "It ends here, today, Galaxy Commander Chistu."

"We shall see."

Indeed we shall...

The Ninth Talon Cluster came down the road first, followed by the First Falcon Strikers. There was no attempt at stealth, no attempt to conceal their approach. They came down the highway at a full run, 'Mechs on the road, tanks on the side. A low cloud of dust kicked up, and the thudding of 'Mech feet could be felt even across the river.

Roderick watched from his *Rifleman IIC* concealed in Guite. He switched to the tactical channel and broadcast to all of his troops. "This is General Steiner. I know you have your blood up, but we need to be foxy to beat these birds. Hold your fire until I give the word. Remember, our goal is to pinch them at the bridge, take out that first Cluster that comes across. You all know your missions. If you want to honor Jasek, do as I say, and you will have your vengeance."

The 'Mechs crossed the bridge in pairs, slowing considerably when they reached the span. *They are suspicious, expecting to be hit on the bridge where they are the most exposed.* The Ninth began crossing toward the still-smoking town.

General Steiner wanted to fire, but held himself back. *If it is this hard for me, I can't imagine how the troops are doing it.* His tactical display gave him a full readout of the approaching forces. There was no sign of the *Jade Hawk* that Stephanie Chistu piloted. She would not send them without coming herself. For a moment, some self-doubt crept in. *Has she found some way to flank me? Am I the trapper–or the victim?*

As the First Falcon Striker Cluster began crossing the bridge, the Ninth was almost at Guite. *Now is as good a time as any.*

"This is General Steiner. All units attack! For Jasek!"

"FOR JASEK!" came a hundred cries at once in his neurohelmet. They kept chanting it as the barrage opened up.

He stepped out and brought his targeting reticle past the obvious targets, aiming for a *Gyrfalcon* on his side of the bridge. A wave of emerald pulses shot forth, all hitting the left leg and hip of the fifty-five-ton Jade Falcon 'Mech. It twisted in mid-step, bumping into an *Uller* next to it. White wisps of smoke rose from the holes his lasers had seared into the green armor.

From a concealed slip trench near the bridge, a pair of Lyran SM1 Tank Destroyers burst forth, hitting the *Uller* from the opposite direction. Their autocannons blasted streams of armor-piercing hell into the 'Mech, sending fragments flying into the *Gyrfalcon* and the raging brown waters of the Ochoa River. Between autocannon shells and the bump from the heavier *Gyrfalcon*, the *Uller* pilot lost their footing and toppled over at the feet of their comrade's 'Mech.

A trio of Bellona hovertanks unleashed a wave of long-range missiles into a Jade Falcon *Loki*, riddling the 'Mech with explosions. Lasers filled the air around the Ninth Talon Cluster. From behind every ramshackle building in the town, 'Mechs stepped out and opened fire. From the low rises in the distance, Lyran 'Mechs that had been lying prone sat up, then stood and fired.

The Bellonas drove right into the middle of the Jade Falcon troop concentration, firing everywhere at once. Their howls of *"Remember Jasek!"* filled the comm channels. One collided with the legs of a *Vulture* at full speed, ruining its hover skirt but tearing a horrible gash in the *Vulture*'s shin. As the Bellona spun, its lasers and machine guns fired wildly, hitting at least three 'Mechs before being kicked hard by a *Mad Cat*, which sent it twirling out of control.

The *Gyrfalcon* fired its jump jets, rising up and over the downed *Uller*. Roderick maintained his target lock and fired three of his four lasers as the Falcon rose. One beam dug deep into the *Gyrfalcon*'s already-damaged leg; the others sizzled on its upper torso as it reached the apex of its jump.

It landed just on the south side the bridge with a *thump*, then its damaged leg shrieked in metallic agony and collapsed under the 'Mech's weight. It fell hard, face first on the road, tearing deep ruts in the ferrocrete upon impact. Bits of armor clattered as the *Gyrfalcon* struggled to right itself.

The *Uller* was less lucky. A hidden infantry squad burst forth from under the bridge and launched short-range missiles filled with flammable gel. The Inferno rounds turned the downed 'Mech into a raging conflagration. Somewhere in the middle of the yellow-and-orange flames, the Jade Falcon warrior was roasting in their cockpit. Roderick did not think on that for long. All that mattered was that the bridge was clogged.

A Lyran *Atlas* rushed at a *Mad Cat* trying to take out a Demon tank. There was no pretext to its intent. At minimum range, it unleashed a Gauss-rifle slug right into the Falcon's left-side missile rack, furrowing deep and ruining several launch tubes. The *Atlas*'s lasers and long-range missiles poured into the *Mad Cat*, sending the Jade Falcon 'Mech staggering, then toppling over from the onslaught.

The Falcon pilot rolled the ungainly 'Mech, no small task, trying to rise. Roderick locked onto it and fired two pulse lasers, peppering the head and body with smoking white gashes in its armor. The *Atlas* closed the distance at a full run, pulling its right leg back, and delivering a devastating kick to the fallen 'Mech's head. The huge foot crushed through the armored glass and deep to the rear of the cockpit. No MechWarrior could have survived such a blow.

The Bellona tank that had driven into the middle of the Jade Falcons emerged on fire, bursting forth like a bat out of hell. From the bridge, Roderick saw several Falcons attempting to force a crossing, only to be caught in crossfire from both sides of the bridge. One *Man O' War* pumped a stream of autocannon rounds across the river and into Guite. A building near Roderick exploded from long-range missiles, raining bricks onto his *Rifleman IIC*. He sidestepped to take more cover.

A green *Loki* bathed the *Atlas* in PPC fire and Streak missiles, shredding armor plating. Roderick locked onto it and fired all four of his large pulse lasers. The air became brilliant green as they tore into the *Loki*'s arm and torso. The *Atlas* fired its Gauss rifle, and the slug slammed into the enemy Mech's right arm, ripping it off and sending it spinning into the grass.

The *Loki* turned to face Roderick, swinging its PPC around, when Captain Krecislaw burst through the smoke to his left. He was piloting Jasek's repaired *Templar*, and was flanked by two other Lyran 'Mechs that seemed to be protecting him. The *Templar*, with light gray-primered replacement armor and cockpit, looked like a ghost in the haze.

All three Lyrans poured fire into the Falcon 'Mech. For a moment, Roderick lost it amid the haze and orange fireballs from missile and autocannon rounds hitting it. Seeing the *Templar* there, in the battle, brought back memories of the Battle of the Dales. This time it was different.

As the haze lifted, the *Loki* looked as if it had been viciously bear-hugged by the *Atlas*. Its armor was blackened, and smoke poured from a large glowing hole in its right side near the fusion reactor. Every bit of the armor was either crumbled, slagged, or ripped apart. Its pilot punched out, rising over the raging battle.

Roderick shifted his position to focus on the Jade Falcons deploying across the river. *The bridge is partially blocked, so now they wish to help their comrades.* He targeted a *Thor* on the far side and fired two of his large pulse lasers. One missed, but one hit the center of the Falcon 'Mech, melting and blackening armor plating. He faded back behind a building for cover, offering the *Thor* no chance at retribution.

He saw one Lyran 'Mech fall, a *Commando*, blasted in half at the waist by a *Ryoken*. There was no ejection as it went down, which meant its MechWarrior might still be alive. That hope was dashed when a *Mad Cat* rushed across the remains of the *Commando*, its bird-like foot crushing the cockpit. It did not seem deliberate, but it didn't matter to Roderick. The action infuriated him.

Four long-range missiles from across the river slapped into his side with low grumbles as they chewed into his armor. Roderick pivoted to keep targeting the *Mad Cat* and let go with all four lasers, despite the rising heat in his cockpit. Three found their mark on the Falcon's flank as Captain Krecislaw swung his *Templar* on the Falcon 'Mech. His short-range missiles, lasers, and Gauss-rifle shots enveloped the Falcon warrior in a wave of destruction. Smoke and armor fragments filled the air, and the *Mad Cat* fell backward. A gray-and-blue streaked Demon tank passed the fallen 'Mech, pouring in laser fire at point-blank range. The red beams tore deeper scars on the armor of the green 'Mech.

The *Mad Cat* pilot was a savant of some sort, ignoring the incoming fire and somehow contorting and rising to its feet. Its pilot sent a wave of long-range missiles into Krecislaw's *Templar*, momentarily obscuring the 'Mech. The Lyran 'Mech emerged from the whitish-gray smoke like a ghost, unleashing its own wave of fire as it closed with the *Mad Cat*. Roderick held his fire out of fear that he might hit his own man, instead, firing a barrage across the river at the *Thor*.

A running *Fenris* saw him take the shot, and angled to fire at him. Its extended-range PPC missed his cockpit by less than a meter, hitting the building next to his *Rifleman*. Roderick drifted his targeting reticle on the fast-moving 'Mech but held his fire for a few seconds, hoping it would allow his 'Mech some precious time to cool.

When he was ready, he aimed low and fired. Three of his large pulse lasers riddled the Falcon 'Mech's legs. The pilot juked to avoid another salvo as a *Blackjack* ripped into it from across the battlefield. Two crimson beams gored the *Fenris* on its side and legs. One knee locked up, fused by the laser blast. The *Fenris* suddenly picked up a horrible limp, its speed dropping dramatically. Its PPC fired at a passing Savannah Master, disintegrating the tiny hovercraft in a spray of melted armor and tiny bits of metal.

The *Atlas* reappeared through the haze of the firefight, its armor rent and gouged deeply, but still operational. Its skull-shaped head had been damaged, and as a result looked as if it were grinning. Roderick couldn't help smiling at the sight. As a *Vulture* rounded on it, the *Atlas* sent a Gauss slug into its spindly legs, ripping a trench-like gouge out of the armor. Myomer cables flapped from the gaping wound.

Roderick hit the *Vulture* with two of his lasers, diverting the Falcon warrior's attention from the *Atlas* at the wrong instant. Long-range missiles soaked the *Vulture* in explosions and smoke. It emerged, firing its own LRMs at the *Atlas* as it faced the most immediate threat.

The missiles shrouded the massive gray-and-blue OmniMech as the Clanner tried to put some distance between them.

A Lyran *Hatchetman* sprang into the fray behind it, swinging its axe down, ruining one of the *Vulture*'s missile racks. The handheld weapon stuck in the rack. As the Clanner tried to flee, it dragged the *Hatchetman* with it. The Lyran's autocannons riddled the Jade Falcon's rear until it twisted hard, ripping the axe from the *Hatchetman*'s hand, but leaving it stuck in the crippled missile rack. The deep holes in the OmniMech's rear armor glowed from where they had shredded fusion reactor insulation.

Both 'Mechs fired at point-blank range with everything they had. The few meters of air between them filled with fire and death until BattleMechs toppled backward, plowing into the ground.

Unable to track all of the destruction happening everywhere, Roderick turned back to the river. A *Puma* fired into Guite, where it had detected one of the Second Royals, so Roderick fired a salvo of all four pulse lasers into the squat OmniMech across the river. The *Puma*'s left leg blew off at the knee, and the 'Mech toppled over next to the *Thor* Roderick had exchanged volleys with.

His tactical display told him the Ninth Talon Cluster was in tatters. Only a few stragglers were still fiercely blasting away, falling back to the bridge littered with fallen Clan 'Mechs and the remains of blown-off limbs and armor plating. The First Striker Cluster had formed up along the riverbank but was unwilling to press forward across the bridge. Not yet, at least.

Now.

"General Steiner to General Ross," he spoke clearly on the command channel, "initiate Gauntlet. I say again, initiate Gauntlet."

"Jawohl," Francine Ross said. "See you across the river, Roderick."

The battle continued for another five minutes as the Second Royals and some of the Fifteenth found problems with their pursuit. The closer the Falcons withdrew toward the river, the more cover fire they got from the other side. The stubborn Ninth's 'Mechs and troops on his side of the river refused to try reaching the bridge. For a millisecond he admired them, until he saw another Lyran *Commando* collapse under a wave of short-range missiles.

The air above him roared—not like thunder, but continuous and rolling. Roderick looked up and saw them—Lyran DropShips loaded with troops under Francine Ross's command. They were headed toward Port St. William.

General Steiner smiled in that moment as the DropShips soared over his force and the Jade Falcons along the river. He knew every eye was looking upward, realizing that they were facing a new battle, one that none of them had anticipated. That feeling of complete surprise...that awe his enemies were experiencing...Roderick relished it.

Activating an open channel, he broadcast to the Jade Falcons. "Galaxy Commander Chistu, this is General Steiner. Your troops across the river are nearly gone, and by now you have seen my DropShips heading for the spaceport along with a full RCT. They will not attack your DropShips yet, but they will take out your support teams and technicians. You are surrounded."

Roderick paused. *She is a Jade Falcon, and if nothing else, is proud.* His grandfather had taught him that if you corner someone, you give them no alternative but to try fighting their way out. "We have both shed a great deal of blood. There is no need for us to die here for no reason. I am sure we can find a way to end this fight."

Roderick waited as the combat along the riverbank continued. A handful of adventurous Falcons stepped onto the bridge and laid down steady barrages of longrange missiles, giving some relief to the warriors of the Ninth Talon Cluster on the bank. He moved toward the pocket of Falcons on the south bank. If she did not answer soon, he would join in on the final thrust to wipe out the Ninth.

Why doesn't she respond, damn it?

The silence from his foe seemed to last forever, though in reality less than a minute had passed.

But then there was a hiss and pop as her stern voice came over the channel.

"General Roderick Steiner—"

CHAPTER 10

NORTH OF THE OCHOA RIVER
COVENTRY
COVENTRY PROVINCE
LYRAN COMMONWEALTH
15 MARCH 3148
TWO MINUTES EARLIER...

The DropShips roaring overhead made Stephanie Chistu's stomach knot for a long moment. She heard Roderick Steiner's words and nodded. *Well played...you are worthy of the Steiner blood in your veins.*

She was piloting Yaroslav's *Summoner*, and hating it every moment of it. She had claimed it as part of his punishment for breaking the rules of the Circle of Equals. The 'Mech lacked any definable shape. It was old-Clan style—utilitarian. Worse, she found it ungainly to pilot. How much of that was her hatred of the 'Mech's former pilot, she could not say. She watched the DropShips fly past her for Port St. William.

"Your orders, Galaxy Commander?" came the high-pitched voice of Star Colonel Molen Hazen of the Third Talon Cluster.

Her options were daunting. Staying and fighting to relieve the Ninth across the river meant losing more troops, with more Lyrans landing in her rear. Breaking off and heading back to her DropShips to deal with the troops there meant Roderick Steiner would pursue her. As she sat in her command couch, she tried to devise a solution, a plan, anything that might help alleviate her sudden plight.

Then her communications system flashed red. *What now?* It was coded as Flash Traffic from the JumpShip *Eyasses Brood*. "This is Striker Prime, what is it?"

The voice of Star Captain Broccán came into her neurohelmet. "Galaxy Commander, one of our JumpShips arrived in-system with a message for you from Khan Hazen. It is emergency Flash Traffic. Your eyes only."

Flash Traffic–that means one thing, a crisis. "Transmit to this 'Mech," she commanded. A second later, the image of Khan Malvina Hazen appeared on the screen. Her pale skin and long platinum braid betrayed the danger she represented.

"Galaxy Commander Chistu. You are ordered immediately to Pobeda. The accursed Wolves-in-Exile have captured our staging world, Upano, and are poised to hit several other planets. You are ordered to depart immediately to stave off any further losses." The image of her Khan disappeared.

Her face grew hot with anger and raw frustration. *Freebirth! Is it not enough that I must contend with this battle and now these orders?* In the course of five minutes, the tactical situation had changed—twice. *Stravag!* Fury made her muscles ache, and the synthskin bandage on her breast strained with each breath.

What is the answer? Her mind went to the tactical nuclear weapons. Unleashing them on the Lyrans in Guite might take them out, along with whatever was left of the Ninth Talon Cluster. *Malvina would not hesitate to unleash them, even if it kills our own forces in the process. I am not Malvina. I am a true Jade Falcon. My path is one of honor and glorious battle.*

Even if she did use nukes on the Lyrans across the river, she could not use them against the force landing in her rear without damaging or destroying her own DropShips. *Neg–the use of nuclear weapons is not the answer.*

To win, I must fight as an honorable Jade Falcon would... and fast. The solution came to her in that thought, all tied to the word "honor." *Yes, that might work...if Roderick Steiner is willing to consider it.*

She switched to a clear channel. "General Roderick Steiner, this is Galaxy Commander Stephanie Chistu of Delta Galaxy of Clan Jade Falcon, the one true Clan. I salute you on your tactical deployment and the battle thus far. You have proven yourself worthy of the honor that I am about to bestow upon you.

"I agree that the further loss of life is undesirable for both of us. So much has been shed for this world already. Let us end this in the traditions of our people. I challenge you to a Trial of Possession for Coventry—you and I alone, together in a Circle of Equals."

Chistu stopped transmitting as another of her 'Mechs across the river exploded under a vicious Lyran barrage. The flash explosion of the fusion reactor blew what was left of the 'Mech into the muddy waters of the fast-moving river; it disappeared in a plume of steam from superheated metal hitting cold water.

The waiting ate at her nerves. *If he refuses, my options are limited.* Each passing minute worked to the Lyrans' advantage. Their troops were debarking somewhere in her rear at Port St. William. *Will this*

Roderick Steiner stall, inflict more damage, and use my inaction against me?

His voice came back, oddly calm. "This is General of the Armies Roderick Steiner. I accept your gracious offer. I propose an immediate ceasefire. I will come across the river and meet with you. But I warn you, Galaxy Commander...if this is some ploy to kill me, I will not be responsible for what my troops do to you as a result."

It was an odd threat. *Such animosity these Lyrans have toward us. What will his troops do?* Memories of Whitting and what had transpired there came back to haunt her. "Agreed. I will order my troops to stand down. Despite what you think, General, you will be treated honorably."

"That remains to be seen," Steiner replied.

Stephanie ordered her troops to cease fire, and they did instantly. A few moments later, all weapons fire stopped. She moved to her end of the bridge and spotted a *Rifleman IIC* climbing through the debris at the other end. *He pilots one of our 'Mechs, battlefield* isorla, *no doubt.* General Steiner came alone, across the bridge, moving without caution.

"Roderick Steiner," she said as their two 'Mechs came within twenty meters of each other. "You may not be familiar with our customs. As the challenged, the choice of how and where we fight falls to you."

"I know your customs," he replied. "We study the ways of the Clans at our academies. I say we fight near the spaceport, some place large and flat."

"Agreed," she replied. "Do you wish to fight augmented?"

"We are both MechWarriors. I say we fight with our 'Mechs."

"Well bargained and done," Chistu said. "Follow me, and we shall adjourn to Port St. William."

The journey took an hour. As they approached, she saw the gray-and-blue Lyran DropShips first, blocking the view of her own ships. On the ground she saw most of a regimental combat team deployed.

Jagger's voice came onto her commlink. "Galaxy Commander, this is unwise. You were nearly killed a day ago in a Circle of Equals. Your wounds have not healed. You are exhausted. You have also suffered damage in the fighting at the river. These are not the ideal conditions for another trial."

He does not see it, but I am a true Jade Falcon. "Irrelevant. I received orders from Khan Hazen. We are to withdraw immediately for Pobeda. Clan Wolf has exploited our assault as a sign of weakness, and has struck."

His voice took on a pleading tone. "Then we should depart this accursed world! This trial is pointless."

"*Neg*, Thastus, it is not!" she snapped. "If we win, I can tell our illustrious Khan that we took this world and did it with honor, my way, *our* way."

"But we cannot hold it! We have been ordered back to Pobeda."

"That does not matter now. What matters is honor."

"Allow me to fight in your stead," he countered. "I am more rested that you. We cannot afford to lose you."

"*Neg*, Jagger. Malvina sent me here to die. She wanted to prove the weakness of the honorable road. This was about her and her accursed doctrine. Having you fight for me would show me as weak, and this is no time for perceived weakness among our people. If they are to have an alternative to the Mongol way, they must see it as a shining beacon. *I* have to do this, no one else."

"What if you lose?"

She grinned, if only for a moment. "If I lose, we leave. I will tell our Khan that I departed due to her orders."

"Malvina Hazen will not let you get by without the destruction of Lyrans, orders or not."

"I will not use those nuclear weapons, if that is what you imply. Such weapons are devoid of honor. She will not put another drop of blood on my hands in the name of her twisted belief system. I am not a Mongol—I am Jade Falcon."

"As you say, Galaxy Commander. I wish you well."

They arrived on the flat plateau where Port St. William rested. General Steiner asked for space, and a Circle of Equals over a kilometer in diameter was established. Stephanie invited his own troops to be part of the Circle with her own. Roderick introduced the 'Mech piloted by General Ross. She introduced Star Colonel Thastus. There was an awkwardness about the introductions. *He knows our traditions, but not the nuances of them.*

"We will enter the Circle. Star Colonel Thastus will act as Loremaster, and say when we begin. At any point, you may submit. This does not need to be a battle to the death."

"I understand. There will be no submission on my part, Galaxy Commander. I am the General of the Armies of the Lyran Commonwealth. If this must go to the death, then so be it."

He trotted his *Rifleman IIC* off across the wide-open field. When he reached the far end, he turned to face her, his 'Mech's arms raised and pointing at her. She looked through the magnified image and had to admire him. *It would be a shame to kill such a man.*

Jagger Thastus's voice came over the commlink to everyone gathered there. "*In keeping with the rede of our people, this is a Trial of Possession for the world of Coventry. May your fight be one worthy of a line in our* Remembrance. *You may begin.*"

Stephanie broke into a run to the right; Roderick trotted to the left. With her joystick she brought the ER PPC in line with his jogging 'Mech and switched the weapon to her thumb trigger...then fired. There was a deep whine, and a burst of manmade lightning stabbed through the air, hitting the *Rifleman* on the right side. The excess energy discharged as blue sparks across the Lyran war machine.

Roderick tightened the arc of his run to bring him closer and fired a barrage with all four of his large pulse lasers. Green bursts of destruction hit her boxy *Summoner* in its torso. Warning lights flared yellow as the lasers burned deep and melted armor.

Leaning forward, she brought her LB 10-X autocannon in line and fired, just as Roderick juked his *Rifleman IIC*. Most of the stream of shells missed, but the few that hit tore into his legs.

General Steiner fired only two of his weapons in response. One missed, but the other tore into her 'Mech's chest. Stephanie felt the 'Mech rock hard under the impact, the restraining strap tearing at her chest wound. She could tell it was bleeding again. *Not now...*

Unleashing a salvo of long-range missiles staggered Roderick's *Rifleman* hard, with the majority of them finding their target. The hits peeled back armor from his left shoulder as he burst through the smoke of the explosions. Her cockpit grew warm, but she ignored it. *If I am feeling it, surely he is as well.*

The *Rifleman IIC* changed directions suddenly and charged. She pivoted her torso to keep her targeting reticle on him and fired her extended-range particle projection cannon. This time she hit him in the left leg. A blackened scar appeared, and Roderick slowed his 'Mech's gait. Her tactical display did not show enough damage to have caused it. *Have I hurt him more than my sensors tell me?*

He fired another blast with the pair of pulse lasers in his left arm. One went wide, just above her cockpit. The other hit her armored canopy, searing black marks across it.

Her *Summoner* rocked backward. Her ears rang, and a wave of heat enveloped her neurohelmet. She popped the visor open to let cooler air in. Memories of the neural feedback she had endured during the Battle of the Dales came back to her, though this time it was not as bad. *I cannot take another head hit like that.* As if to validate her point, her cockpit glass suddenly cracked, a large spiderweb appearing in front of her.

She struggled to keep the targeting reticle on him, but the moment she got tone, she fired her LB 10-X autocannon and long-range missiles. It was a snap shot, she knew it. The autocannon missed, tearing up the flat grass of the plateau to his right, but the missiles found their target, hitting him everywhere. Orange and yellow bursts of the exploding warheads gave her some degree of satisfaction.

The heat in her cockpit rose further, and her cooling vest strained to keep her alive. Roderick held his fire for a several long moments, and she knew he was venting heat as well. He started to close distance with her and then unleashed all four of his pulse lasers.

The air glowed green around her. Three of the bursts hit her square in the torso, just under the cockpit. The other shot punctured her already-damaged right side, burrowing deep into the 'Mech's torso. The *Summon er* reeled, and the warning klaxon alerted her of critical damage. As her OmniMech staggered backward, she saw that her gyro and fusion reactor had been hit.

The *Summoner* pitched forward—the gyro was knocked out of alignment, and she was suddenly fighting not only gravity, but the ungainly 'Mech itself and the advancing Lyran general. Despite wrenching the throttle back, she could not get her 'Mech to respond in reverse fast enough.

The *Summoner* toppled, falling on its right side, crunching more armor in the process. She smelled burning myomer, and knew it was from her 'Mech. The *Summoner*'s right arm was pinned, and an amber warning light for her PPC illuminated; no doubt it had been damaged in the fall.

Chistu rocked the *Summoner*, but its response was unlike that of her sleeker *Jade Hawk*. It seemed to resist her every motion. She started to rise, getting one leg bent under her, but the gyro damage shifted her 'Mech's center of gravity. The *Summoner* fell again, this time doing more damage to her right side and arm. The PPC, which had been flashing yellow, turned red. A muffled blast of the particle capacitor blew her elbow actuator as well.

The roasting air in her cockpit was stifling from the loss of several heat sinks. The fusion reactor insulation had been damaged, and the reactor's heat was baking her OmniMech from within. None of that could be dealt with now. She checked her targeting system and saw that Roderick Steiner had stopped moving altogether. *I can only hope he is struggling with heat as well.*

She rocked the *Summoner* hard to her left and strained to stand. Her muscles protested as she worked the foot pedals and joysticks to get the 'Mech kneeling, then standing. As she rose she realized she was not facing the *Rifleman*, and turned to face her foe.

What greeted her was a trio of blasts from General Steiner's 'Mech. Emerald laser bursts scorched her legs and left arm. Despite the risks of heat, she brought her targeting reticle on the now dangerously close *Rifleman* and fired her autocannon. The shells tore into his legs, rocking him hard, but he managed to stay upright.

Stephanie moved her long-range missiles to a separate firing trigger as the temperature spiked from the autocannon fusillade she had unleashed. Roderick remained standing, unmoving, as if daring her to fire. She didn't move either, mostly because she didn't want to risk losing what little balance she had. Her 'Mech was badly damaged, and it fought every motion she made.

I cannot wait to fire. She triggered another wave of long-range missiles at the looming *Rifleman*, and her cockpit felt like a furnace. Almost all of the warheads found their mark, and the ungainly 'Mech reeled back as General Steiner fought the explosions trying to tumble him to the ground. For a moment, however brief, she thought he was going to fall...she was sure of it. At the last moment, he got one foot behind him, enough to keep standing upright.

As the *Rifleman* rose to its full height, she saw the damage she had inflicted. Almost every bit of its armor was pitted and furrowed. Smoke billowed from one hole in his left torso. Her tactical feeds told her that his armor was savaged, but he was still in the fight. She desperately wanted to employ her jump jets, try another death from above. The thought of killing two Steiner generals with that attack would be worthy of a line in *The Remembrance*. But the fighting at the bridgehead had damaged her jets, removing that option.

Stephanie's heart sank as Roderick fired two of his large lasers and his small extended-range laser at her. The salvo was devastating. The small laser bored into the holes under her cockpit, right at the engine. The heat level soared. She didn't see where the other hits were; they did not matter.

The *Summoner* sagged on its left side, and she leaned hard against it, pulling with every bit of her might, but to no avail. Once more the *Summoner* dropped to the ground, metallic grinding and warnings sounding all around her.

For a moment, she blacked out. When she opened her eyes, she saw darkness. She had fallen face forward, somehow twisting at the last moment. Dirt and sod were crushed against her shattered cockpit glass. She licked her lips and tasted a crusty, salty film on them. The ride side of her chest throbbed, and looking down she saw blood under her coolant vest.

A voice came over the commlink. "You have fought bravely, Galaxy Commander, but your 'Mech is badly damaged. I strongly advise to you yield, but if you force me to kill you, I will."

There was no gloating in Roderick Steiner's words, no arrogance that she would have expected from a fellow Jade Falcon. If anything, he too sounded weary and exhausted.

Malvina Hazen would try to stand, make him kill her. I am not Malvina Hazen.

"General Steiner," she said, her throat wracked and dry, "I yield this Trial of Possession to you. You have won Coventry fairly and with honor."

It had taken the techs a good twenty minutes to painfully extract her from what was left of the *Summoner*. The medtechs laid her on the ground and treated her reopened wounds with field bandages.

As they worked, she saw a man in a green jumpsuit, not too dissimilar to hers, watching them. He held a neurohelmet under his arm, and his body was wet with sweat. On his forehead was what looked like a bruise, a dark gray mark. His sweat-soaked blond hair and blue eyes told her it was Roderick Steiner.

Next to him stood another general, who Stephanie assumed was General Ross. She too had a gray smear above her brow. Both wore crude black armbands on their upper arms.

"Is she going to be okay?" he asked.

The medtech looked to Stephanie and nodded. "She will. The Galaxy Commander is tougher than her size belies."

"I believe you," General Steiner said.

As well you should, Stephanie thought. "You are Roderick Steiner, *quiaff?*"

"I am," he replied. "And this is General Francine Ross."

Stephanie looked at the woman and nodded. "I tried to trap and crush you for days, General Ross, and you always managed to stay one step ahead of me. I so looked forward to defeating you on the field of battle."

"I'm not sure how to take that," Ross replied.

"As a sign of respect, I assure you," Stephanie said, handing her neurohelmet to a nearby tech. "Jade Falcons are not good at compliments. The competitive nature of our people does not yield itself to extending accolades to our enemies."

"Very well," Ross said, her furrowed brow relaxing a bit.

Chistu turned to Roderick, who seemed to tower over her. "What of my warriors captured in Guite? Are they to be held as prisoners of war or released?"

Roderick Steiner's face reddened. "Only three survived. I am afraid my troops had their blood up, and your Trinary fought right to the end. I would be willing to arrange for a full exchange of prisoners, though."

"Well bargained," she replied. *I understand their hatred of us after Whitting and the Dales.* "Losing Coventry to you is not easy for me. Better to have done it this way than by senseless slaughter."

"After what your forces did to Whitting, I'm surprised you did not opt for the slaughter," Roderick replied coarsely.

I deserve that. "Much of what transpired here was not my design, but the orders of our Khan, Malvina Hazen. I gave orders for Whitting to be evacuated of civilians, and your troops would be offered a chance to surrender. Only *then* would the city be destroyed, per the orders of our Khan. Those orders were not followed."

Roderick Steiner's head went back slightly, and a sign of puzzlement rose to his face. "I have never heard of Clan warriors refusing to follow orders."

"We live in times of change. Some resist that change. It seems both of us struggled with keeping our forces on task. Know that what occurred at Whitting was not the actions of an honorable Jade Falcon, but of a miscreant who cast aside his personal integrity and the laws of our people to take actions I refused to sanction. In this case, I humbled this dishonorable warrior in a Circle of Equals. He has paid a dear price for his callous actions."

"That is all well and good," Roderick said. "It does not bring back the dead."

"*Neg*, it does not. I thought you should know."

Roderick crossed his arms in defiance. "Yet he willfully committed a war crime very different from overzealous troops in the heat of battle. And as a leader, you are responsible for the actions of those under your command."

"*Aff*," she replied. *If he seeks recompense, there is little I can offer him.* "I do not molt that responsibility, General. His taint is mine. Yet in the end, you have won Coventry from me. That is another disgrace I must bear."

An awkward silence reigned for a few moments. When Roderick finally spoke again, he drove straight to the point. "So where does that leave us, Galaxy Commander?"

He should know the whole truth, not just about me, but about the Jade Falcons and what Malvina represents. "Generals, I know you have little reason to trust me. My hands have been tied with orders I was given before I arrived here. I have had to walk a fine line between honor and my orders. I believe I have done that well, but I know you do not agree. If you will accompany me, I want to show you the full extent of what Malvina Hazen had planned for Coventry. Perhaps it will help convince you."

Steiner nodded, and Stephanie rose unsteadily to her feet, but waved off any hint of assistance. The two generals followed her to a nearby hover transport. Stephanie took a seat in the rear, granting Roderick the honor of the front seat, and she ordered the driver to take them to Port St. William.

They passed the Lyran DropShips, and in their shadows of the setting afternoon sun, the transport parked under one of her massive *Overlord-C* DropShips. The air reeked of fuel, lubricant, and baked ferrocrete tarmac.

As they got out, General Ross paused for a moment, looking up at the big DropShip from within its massive shadow.

"Is there a problem, General Ross?"

"No," she said, turning her gaze back down to the other woman. "I've just never been this close before."

On the ground, under the belly of the ship, were theater-range missile launchers, fully loaded, with more missiles stacked beside them. Galaxy Commander Chistu walked over to the launchers and pointed to them. "This is what I wanted you to see, General Steiner."

"Tactical missiles?"

"*Aff.* The warheads are nuclear," she said, pausing to let the admission settle in with her guests. "Khan Hazen sent fifteen of these with me with orders to use them on either your forces or the cities she identified."

Generals Ross and Steiner locked gazes with each other, then turned to her.

"You were going to use nukes on our troops?" Roderick asked.

She met both of their stares a cool one of her own. "*Neg.* I was given the authorization. I could have done so in the Battle of the Dales, or at Guite. Malvina Hazen would have loved that. I could have burned you all away and taken Coventry."

"But...you didn't?" Roderick said.

"*Neg.* It is not my way—not the true way of the Jade Falcon. Malvina has lost that way, as have her followers. She believes the only way to achieve true victory is to destroy the Inner Sphere and remake it in her own image."

"You could have destroyed us at any time," Francine Ross said in an astonished tone.

"I was authorized to. To your point, I did not. I would not just burn your troops, I would burn my soul. I did not wish to be a Jade Falcon remembered for senseless and honorless slaughter. I follow the true Way of the Clans, one where honor and tradition still have meaning. I thought you should know what I was ordered to do—and why I did not follow those orders."

"I have defeated you in a Circle of Equals—" Roderick began when she cut him off.

"*Our* Circle of Equals."

"I stand corrected. Our Circle of Equals," Roderick said. "So, what now? I have won Coventry, but you are still here. I'm not entirely sure of the protocol."

"I will ask you for *hegira*, a withdrawal from this place. It is yours—fairly won in honorable battle."

Roderick rubbed his chiseled chin in thought. "I am not so sure, Galaxy Commander. I do not want to release you simply so you can go attack another Commonwealth world. All that would change is where we would face each other next."

He is smart, this general. "I understand. It would be a breach of security for me to tell you where I am headed. I will tell you, however, that I have been ordered to fight another foe. The exiled Clan Wolf has attacked a planet we hold. I have been ordered to deal with them."

"That doesn't mean we won't face you again," General Ross said.

"Affirmative, General. If your worry is that I am going to leave here and further raid your Commonwealth, that is not the orders I have been given."

"I'm afraid it isn't quite that easy, Galaxy Commander. What happened in Whitting...the Archon, my cousin Trillian, will want justice. She will want someone held accountable, as will the Lyran people. Letting you simply depart will not be enough. Someone has to pay for the innocent civilians that died there. I am sure you see my predicament."

She pondered his words for a moment, then nodded. "If you grant me a few minutes, I believe I can honor your request." She signaled for the driver and gave him some orders. He sped off into the city of Port St. William, returning a few minutes later with a stretcher bearing a man in a hospital gown.

On the stretcher was Star Colonel Yaroslav.

Stephanie walked over to him, and the two Lyran generals followed. "This is Star Colonel Yaroslav of the Hazen Bloodline. He defied my orders and razed Whitting, killing innocent civilians and combatants alike. In fighting me in a Circle of Equals, he broke his honor by attempting to poison me. His life is forfeit, his fate mine to choose. I choose to give him to you. You want justice? Let it be meted out to the man that deserves it. He stained the Jade Falcons and your people both. If you take him, I will list him as a casualty of battle." *Your taking him will actually assist me in dealing with Malvina.*

Roderick looked down at Yaroslav while he strained helplessly at his restraints, still unable to speak. Then the General of the Armies nodded reluctantly. "That will do. I am sure that our intelligence people will want to spend time with him, and in the end, he will feel the full wrath of Lyran justice, I assure you."

"Then we have an agreement, *quiaff*?"

"In showing us these missiles and giving us this Star Colonel, you have demonstrated to me that you have honor. In the tradition of Caradoc Trevena, I offer you *hegira*."

"I accept," she said, bowing her head slightly.

Roderick surprised her by offering his hand for a shake. She did not take it. Instead, she snapped to attention and saluted. Honor would be granted with honor.

Steiner and Ross both saluted her back.

"Very well. We will be underway in the next six hours," she finally said. *I have an appointment to keep on Pobeda, and I would not wish to be late.*

"Galaxy Commander, don't take it the wrong way, but I hope to never see you across a battlefield again," Roderick said with a hint of relief in his voice.

"Time will tell, General. I do have a question for you. Both of you have a gray smudge across your forehead. What does that signify?"

"These are the ashes of the man you killed, *Hauptmann*-General Jasek Kelswa-Steiner. It was the desire of our troops that he go into battle one final time—that he lead us to victory."

"I see," she replied with a thoughtful nod. *It is a symbol to them. That is why I lost. One cannot defeat a symbol. By killing him, I gave them something to rally behind.* An important lesson for the future.

"One more question," Roderick said. "What will happen to you when you tell your Khan that you didn't burn us in nuclear fire?"

"I am sure she will not be pleased, not at all." The Galaxy Commander allowed herself a wry smile.

EPILOGUE

Khan Malvina Hazen had not announced her arrival on-planet. Her flair for the dramatic was always part of the image she wanted her fellow Jade Falcon warriors to see. When Stephanie Chistu got word that her Khan was waiting in her office, she was polishing the knife she had been working on in her spare time since the departure of the Exiled Wolves.

The blade was not a combat knife, nor a hunting weapon—it was simple. Its dark ebony handle had a handcarved emerald falcon mounted in it. The blade was as long as a bowie knife but not as wide. There was an eloquence to it, a grace. *I made it for smaller hands than my own.*

Each blade she made spoke to her as she made it, telling her who it would belong to. For all of the knives she made, only a few remained in her possession. The others were gifts to fellow warriors. This blade was no different. The Damascus-steel pattern had fought her with every hammer blow. It was stubborn, tough, and when complete—deadly. Carved into the blade was a quote from one of the Jade Falcon founders, Khan Lisa Buhallin: *"Honor is not bestowed, but is taken."* She wanted to name this knife, but that was something best left to its new owner.

Before she headed to her office to meet with the Khan, Stephanie wrapped the blade in a simple cloth banner she had carried with her since Coventry: a banner from the Coventry Military Academy, one her troops had taken from the rubble of Whitting. Burned along one edge, it bore the academy's orange and blue colors and the Lyran gauntlet insignia. Stephanie could still smell the charred edges as she handled it. She wrapped the knife carefully in the cloth and put the card with it. She put the gift in a box from her quarters, then went to meet with Khan Hazen.

Stephanie knocked on her own office door and was ordered to enter. She stood at attention, facing Hazen across her own desk. Malvina wore a short-sleeved shirt, exposing her polished, black bionic arm. Her almost white ponytail, draped over her shoulder, was longer than Stephanie remembered from their last meeting. The door closed behind her.

"Your work in dealing the Exiled Wolves a blow here on Pobeda does you merit," Hazen said, gesturing to the chair opposite her.

Stephanie took the seat and faced her Khan squarely. *She has not come to speak about Pobeda, but about Coventry.* "Thank you, my Khan," was all she offered in response.

"Which leaves me puzzled as to why you failed so abysmally on Coventry."

"You are correct that I did not successfully conquer that world," Stephanie offered, ensuring her contempt did not reach her voice. "I did, however, honor your orders."

"If you had," Malvina said, "Roderick Steiner would be ashes now, and our flag would fly over that planet."

"Your orders, Khan Hazen, were quite specific. I was to raze Whitting, destroy the Coventry Military Academy, and seize or destroy the Coventry Metal Works. Those deeds were done." *Despite how I felt about them.*

"Yes, but you lost the planet—despite having nuclear weapons at your disposal and the means to achieve victory," Malvina spat back.

"Your orders were specific at the end. If I remember correctly, 'You are to maintain an effective fighting force at the completion of the operations on Coventry. This is—and these are your words—'your paramount objective.'" Did I get that right, *quiaff?*"

"Affirmative. That still is no excuse for your actions."

"To have used tactical nuclear weapons in the Dales or at Guite would have also killed Jade Falcon warriors, greatly reducing my combat effectiveness. Your criteria for finishing operations with an effective force required that."

"The loss of a few warriors would have been acceptable and expected." Hazen leaned back in the chair and crossed her arms.

"Not in my judgment as the field commander."

"If you wish to hide behind your written orders, then what of this? You were ordered to 'deal House Steiner a blow it cannot recover from.' *Aff*, you mauled several of their precious RCTs, but you did not cripple them the way I desired."

This was something Stephanie had prepared for. "You are incorrect, Khan Hazen. I personally killed Hauptmann-General Jasek

Kelswa-Steiner, former commander of the Stormhammers—a hero to the Lyran people. He died at my hand on the field of battle."

"One warrior is not a loss they cannot recover from," Malvina countered.

Chistu was also prepared for her verbal parry. "*Neg*. He is dead. His death ruined the morale of many Lyran troops. The Commonwealth is stretched thin, you know that. A general of his caliber cannot be quickly or easily replaced. His death is that blow. An icon of the Republic era is gone—his flame extinguished."

Her words bore in on Hazen like a salvo of Arrow IV missiles. The Jade Falcon Khan changed her approach entirely, opening a new avenue in their sparring. "Regardless, your high and honorable path is what cost us Coventry. You lost your Trial of Possession against General Steiner. The failure on Coventry is on your hands."

Coventry was not a failure. She does not see that, though, because of her hatred for what I stand for. In that moment, Stephanie Chistu realized that this was not about her, but her ideals. *I am a symbol for everything that is not Malvina Hazen, and she despises that. Very well then, my Khan, let us continue this debate.* "Except for the timing, Khan Hazen."

"What?" A hint of fury rose in Malvina's voice.

"Prior to that Trial of Possession, I received orders from you to depart immediately for this planet to stave off the Exiled Wolves."

"Those were my orders."

"I received them *prior* to my Trial of Possession. As such, I was bound by those orders. Not having finished combat operations on Coventry, I was ordered to leave. My trial was an attempt on my part to find some honor and perhaps secure a moral victory for our people—but win or lose, I was ordered to depart."

"There was a presumption that you had already conquered the planet," Malvina fired back. The usually white skin of her cheeks glowed pink with anger.

"You told me to follow your orders explicitly. I did. None of your orders specifically told me to use nuclear weapons—only that they were at my disposal. When I received your direct orders to leave Coventry, I was honor bound to follow them."

Hazen slowly rose from her seat, and Stephanie did the same. They stared into each other's eyes intently. "The game you are playing with me is a dangerous one, Galaxy Commander."

Stephanie maintained her emotions and control. She felt the box with the knife in her hand and, for a millisecond, craved the blade she had forged. Neg, *that knife has another destiny, another time and wielder.* "I do not play games where my personal honor or the honor of the Clan is at stake, my Khan."

Malvina glared at her for a long, silent minute. "Dismissed," she finally snapped.

Still clenching the white box in her hand, Stephanie saluted, then pivoted perfectly, leaving the office, closing the door behind her.

Seated in the foyer was Cynthy, the abused young girl Malvina had been brutalizing for years. Her sunken eyes, almost devoid of emotion, glanced fearfully at Chistu as she approached. Cynthy's body recoiled. *Abuse has left this one scarred worse than any battlefield wound.*

Stephanie extended the box to the younger woman. "I made this for you. It is a gift."

Cynthy opened the box and unwrapped the cloth. When she saw the blade, her eyes darted back up to the Galaxy Commander.

"Honor is not bestowed, but is taken," Stephanie said, repeating the words on the blade.

Cynthy took the cloth and the blade and immediately hid it in the cushions, as if it were something very precious to her—that she did not want her adoptive mother and tormentor to see.

That is right, child. Not all Jade Falcons are like your mistress. If you are to survive here, you must become your own form of Jade Falcon. Stephanie left without another word. She walked back to the artisan's sector and removed her uniform in favor of a leather smock. She lit her forge and waited for it to roar to life. A new project was just what she needed to clear her mind over the war of words she had endured with her Khan.

Malvina may believe herself to be the hammer, remaking an Inner Sphere in her image, but if that is the scenario, I am her anvil.

And in the struggle to shape the future of the Jade Falcons, the anvil always prevails.

PORT ST. WILLIAM, COVENTRY
COVENTRY PROVINCE
LYRAN COMMONWEALTH
23 JULY 3148

"Package came in for you on the courier JumpShip, sir," Captain Belcher said, handing the box to Roderick Steiner. It was white and unmarked, other than a familiar handwriting with his name on it. *Trillian.* His cousin the Archon. What would she be sending him?

He opened the box and inside there was a note and something else, something metallic. He read the note.

Dear Cousin,

Despite my urgings that you not go to the front, I see from your report that you have disregarded my counsel. We are all saddened by the death of Jasek. Several of your troops filmed your speech on Coventry, and it is playing throughout the Commonwealth. You have inspired not just those under your command, but all of our people.

I have ordered this medal be cast for everyone that fought on Coventry. I have personally signed each commendation myself. This is the Order of Jasek Kelswa-Steiner. I trust you will see that these are properly awarded to the new members of our House.

Roderick pulled out the medal. A Steiner fist clenching a hammer, with a blue ribbon. *Perfect as always, Trillian.*

He read the rest of her note.

As for the gift you sent me, LIC has informed me that he is a treasure trove of information, once he was properly persuaded to speak. We have learned a lot about the Jade Falcons as a result.

Take care, Roderick. You won a singular battle, but the fighting is far from over. Please heed my caution and stay out of the fighting we both know is to come.

Roderick put the box and letter down and looked at the medal for a long moment. Then he shook his head. "Sorry, Trillian. The Commonwealth needs me now more than ever."

ABOUT THE AUTHORS

Philip A. Lee is a freelance writer and editor whose many writing contributions to the *BattleTech* universe include more than a dozen pieces of *BattleTech* short fiction and various sourcebook writing. He has also contributed fiction and sourcebook material for the *Shadowrun, Cosmic Patrol, Valiant Universe Roleplaying Game, Pathfinder, Steamcraft*, and more. He lives in Dayton, Ohio, with his wife and four cats. To learn more about his work, look for @joechummer on Twitter and visit philipleewriting.com.

Blaine Lee Pardoe is a *New York Times* Bestselling and award-winning author of numerous books in the true crime, science fiction, military nonfiction, paranormal, and business management genres. He has appeared on a number of national television and radio shows to speak about his books.

He has been writing *BattleTech* since the first technical readout in 1986, writing or contributing to eighteen *BattleTech* sourcebooks, two computer game books, and twelve novels.

Mr. Pardoe has been a featured speaker at the US National Archives, the United States Navy Museum, and the New York Military Affairs Symposium. He was awarded the State History Award in 2011 by the Historical Society of Michigan and is a silver medal winner from the Military Writers Society of America in 2010. In 2013 Mr. Pardoe won the Harriet Quimby Award from the Michigan Aviation Hall of Fame for his contributions to aviation history. Mr. Pardoe has been a speaker at CrimeCon 2018 speaking about the Colonial Parkway Murders.

SANTA FE, NEW MEXICO
TERRA
REPUBLIC OF THE SPHERE
10 DECEMBER 3130

Paladin Victor Steiner-Davion looked at the screen and drew a long, deep breath. His study was loneliest at night. There was a hint of smoke in the air from the fireplace, the kind of aroma that invited an afternoon nap. There were always people who wanted his time or opinion, but the number of friends was dwindling as the years passed.

That is part of the price I must pay for outliving so many of my contemporaries. While comrades had crumbled in time, it seemed that enemies were always easily replaced. *We always felt that the Clansmen were bred for war, but in reality, it turns out it is a trait we all share.* Memories of the Clan invasion, the Word of Blake Jihad, and the subsequent wars tugged at him like ghosts, beckoning him to remember them. Victor suppressed those thoughts. *It would be unworthy of me to remember fondly the battles I've fought.*

His knee ached as he adjusted his position in the thick leather chair. *Old injuries, like memories, have a way of coming back when you least expect them.*

The former Archon-Prince of the Federated Commonwealth had been working on his memoirs for three years, and there was a gap in his material that he sought to fill. Tackling the task alone in the dark of night seemed most appropriate to Victor. It was not easy to face. He had skipped over it during his first pass of the text, secretly hoping the memory of the events would have faded, or that no one would notice the omission. *Maybe no one will care about that now. It really was worthy of a footnote–little more.*

His editor felt differently, and had insisted that more be said about the planning for the strike on Huntress that destroyed the Smoke Jaguars and bought the Inner Sphere some much-needed peace. In particular, the editor wanted to know the story of Trent, the former Smoke Jaguar who had betrayed his Clan.

Old guilt washed over Victor every time he thought of that man. *I was young still, I didn't realize what I was setting in motion. How could I have known?* Memories of his behavior then, of the anguish he had caused, gnawed at him along with regret. *I should have been more understanding at the time. Not as rash...*

Now the time had come. *People will judge me by my actions and the repercussions.* Some of the information he knew he could not put in print. *Stone and I struck a devil's bargain, one that still binds me to some degree of secrecy.* Still, the story of the Exodus Road needed to be clarified for the readers—at least, that was the prodding of his editor. *I am one of the few alive who knows the details, knows the full truth.*

Victor cleared his throat and hit the transcribe button.

"The opportunity for us to strike at the Clan Smoke Jaguar homeworld came to us fortuitously, at just the right time. One of their warriors, Trent, believed the ways of his people to be corrupt. According to reports provided by a ComStar agent who had infiltrated the Clan with the purpose of turning some of their troops, the Jaguars were pompous, political pariahs. They had twisted the words of Nicholas Kerensky into a cudgel and used it to pummel their best warriors.

"Trent had fought in the Battle of Tukayyid, and was horribly injured during the Jaguars' loss there. The scalp on the right side of his head was so scarred that no hair grew there. His cheek- and jawbones were disfigured, and he had a bionic eye and an arm replacement.

"From what Precentor Focht told me, Trent was tormented by his commanding officer, an Elemental named Paul Moon. He deemed Trent too old to be of use to the Jaguars, and sent him back to the homeworld of Huntress. Trent, with the help of his ComStar handler, created a rudimentary chart of the Exodus Road. He managed to get himself rotated back to Inner Sphere duty—while carrying a map of General Kerensky's route.

"When Trent defected to ComStar, Focht struck a deal with him. He would be given a command of his own and a chance to fight in battle, in exchange for the map to Huntress. Focht understood the man better than I, understood the MechWarrior he was, the man whose honor was beyond reproach. I was so focused on defeating the Clans, challenging their invasion of the Inner Sphere, I couldn't see past the fact that Trent was a traitor to his own people.

"When we reached Strana Mechty for our inevitable confrontation with the Clans, I did something that I regret to this day. I denied Trent his chance to fight with us. I believed we couldn't have a traitor on the field of battle. Doing so would introduce an unknown and possibly unstable element to the fighting. I mistook his desire to lead troops into a battle for revenge against his former Clan. At the time, I didn't understand that all he wanted was the opportunity to prove himself a worthy MechWarrior. I assumed what drove him was vengeance.

"I was naïve, now that I look back at the entire affair. I was so fixated on finishing our quest, bringing an end to the Smoke Jaguars and stopping the Clan invasion, that I failed to comprehend the desires or heart of a single warrior—one who had made the entire operation and invasion possible. Instead, I treated him as a pariah. One man, one warrior, who gave up his people for all the right reasons, was denied what he desired—merely a chance to prove himself worthy. I labeled him 'traitor' without fully understanding him. I won't justify my thinking with hindsight. Anyone might have made the same call I did and revoked the promise Focht made to him.

"What I didn't factor in was that entirely destroying one Clan had consequences. Our actions to protect the Inner Sphere were like casting a stone in a pond. There were ripples. Destroying the Smoke Jaguars in such a brutal manner caused events years later. Destroying them created a void that had to be filled in some way.

"Nature abhors imbalances like that. The universe always finds ways to set things back into balance...I know that now. My denial of Trent set things in motion that I never could have foreseen. It's odd how one moment of letting your emotions get ahead of your logic can have ramifications for decades. I tipped over the first domino with Trent, and once the rest started to topple, the reaction was impossible to stop. This string of reactions I set in motion impacted the Jihad years later."

After a moment, Victor deleted the last sentence. Some secrets still needed to be kept.

"Little did I realize the role he had to play in affairs, and how one day I, and the entire Republic of the Sphere, might be indebted to him. But on that day in 3060, on the sacred soil of Strana Mechty, all I saw was a vile traitor.

"Rarely have I been so wrong."

CHAPTER ONE

STAR LEAGUE EXPEDITIONARY FORCE HEADQUARTERS
NICHOLAS'S FORD, STRANA MECHTY
KERENSKY CLUSTER, CLAN SPACE
19 APRIL 3060

Trent, formerly of Clan Smoke Jaguar, stood awash in anger as he glared at the short Inner Sphere prince. Trent had long seen the corruption of his people, how they had twisted the teachings of Nicholas Kerensky, turning it into a justification for naked brutality. Gone was the path where honor had prevailed. Now petty politics and backstabbing were the norm. *We have wandered so far from the tenets of honor that we are now just brutality.*

This depravity had driven him to do the unthinkable. He had provided ComStar with the route to the Clan homeworlds, the Exodus Road. It was to be an exchange. He provided the Inner Sphere with the first chance to strike at the heart of the Clans and purge his former people, and they were to provide him a chance to fight in battle once more. He had assumed the role of traitor to regain honor. The irony was not lost on him.

And now Victor Steiner-Davion was denying him that. The shorter man looked at him as a lesser man. The Inner Sphere warlord didn't understand him at all. He wanted to join battle again; not out of vengeance, but to purge the anger and guilt that boiled within him. Trent's returning to battle had nothing to do with revenge. But the glare he got from the prince was that of a man who saw him as an untrustworthy traitor—nothing more.

Worse, while Victor denied Trent his chance to join the fight against the remaining Smoke Jaguars, he was accepting the help of Clan Nova Cat. *Are they not traitors as well,* quiaff? It was too much to bear. Trent's heart pounded in his ears, and he felt his face flush.

"Do you have *no* honor, Victor Davion?" He stepped forward, reaching for the prince's throat. Davion's Elemental bondsman shifted, but Trent's warrior mind had already calculated that he would be on top of the prince before she could react. *She will try to protect him, and I will need to incapacitate her quickly.*

Suddenly a blow struck him in the face, just under his bionic ocular implant, sending him reeling before he reached his target. Khan Severen Leroux of the Nova Cats had slapped his face so hard he lost his balance in mid-lunge and tumbled to the floor. He felt something land on top of him. A knee to his solar plexus drove the air out of his lungs, and in a moment of panic he struggled to get air.

Trent felt Leroux grab his right wrist, felt something wrap around it. His bionic arm, cocooned in myomer muscle, picked up only a faint sensation of something there. Looking at his hand, he saw a bondcord wrapped around his skinny wrist, its ends in the hands of the Nova Cat Khan. If it had been his real arm, he would have felt the cord digging into his skin. As it was, the image of the cord there and what it symbolized was clear. They had taken him as one of their own. *Neg! This is not supposed to happen!* He struggled for the words as he gasped for air.

"Trent, you are my bondsman. You belong to the Nova Cats." The bald Khan rose from his chest and let the bondcord fall off...the symbolic gesture when a bondsman becomes a full-fledged warrior. "I now accept you as a warrior in our Clan. If you wish, you may join us in fighting the Ice Hellions."

Trent coughed once to get air back into his lungs and rubbed his still-stinging cheek. Victor Steiner-Davion had misinterpreted his motivation; worse, he had refused to listen. *This was never about revenge; all I desired was the chance to fight in battle. The Nova Cats are offering me that.* "Ice Hellions? I will fight them for you."

"Good. Go to Alpha Galaxy headquarters. They are waiting for you."

Hands reached out to help Trent up: Precentor Martial Anastasius Focht. Trent staggered to his feet, allowing one more icy glance back at Victor Steiner-Davion.

His new Khan, Leroux, turned to the precentor martial as well. "You have no objections?"

Focht shook his head. "He will fight well for you. Go, Trent, you have what you wanted. Finish what you have started."

Trent saw another Nova Cat warrior near the entrance to the tent. She opened the flap and gestured for Trent to walk with her.

"Finish what you have started..." Focht's words dug deeply into his mind as he pushed through the tent flap. *What I started was to set the Smoke Jaguars on the right path. What I have done is become the instrument of their destruction.*

The Nova Cat warrior walked alongside him. She was younger than he, much younger, and shorter. Yet she looked up at him with wide eyes, as if he were some sort of celebrity. Her short black hair caught the wind and fluttered in the breeze. She was small but muscular, her chest solid, making her breasts look small. For a moment, Trent remembered Judith, the ComStar operative who had helped him find his way to ComStar with the Exodus Road. He wondered for a moment where she was...if he would ever see her again.

"I am Star Captain Inanna," she said as she led him off toward a waiting Anhur VTOL transport. Once away from the tent where Victor Steiner-Davion had so grossly disrespected him, Trent suddenly felt a sense of familiarity and comfort with a military tarmac, a *Clan* military base. As they walked at a brisk pace along the ferrocrete, he allowed himself to drink in, if only for a few moments, the feeling of belonging. The air stank of coolant, lubricant, and the slight sting of sweat as he passed other warriors. Those who spoke as they passed spoke like brethren, using Clan language and proper wording. Trent suddenly realized, in that moment, how much he had missed such places. Two years huddled in seclusion with ComStar made him long for the life he once had. It made Khan Leroux's gesture feel like a welcome gift.

Trent unconsciously rubbed his wrist where the bondcord should have dug into his skin, but instead had only tugged at myomer replacement muscle. "Why did he do that? Why take me into your Clan?"

The younger warrior's grin only broadened. "We are Nova Cats. Our journey is different than the Jaguars', which brought you into the world. Your role in affairs was, dare I say, foreseen."

Trent had heard since his inception that the Nova Cats gave credence to mysticism, but he had never experienced it firsthand. "How could he have known what would happen?" *It was all so fast, I am not sure I fully understand just yet.*

"He was told of your arrival by one of us who pierced the mists of the future."

Trent looked at her and saw her wide-eyed gaze on him. "It was you, *quiaff*?"

"*Aff*," she replied. "My vision is why I am here. It is also why preparations were made in advance."

His brow furrowed at the thought of someone predicting that he was coming with the Star League Defense Force; yet there he walked, into his new Clan. *Perhaps I need to challenge my own beliefs.* "Where are you taking me?"

"Your new home, of course," Inanna responded. "You will serve in Khan Leroux's Star."

"Such a place should be reserved for those who have earned honor in the Nova Cats—not for a new warrior." To fight alongside a Khan in battle was a right for which many warriors vied. Now it was being given to him. While Trent was grateful, it did not feel right.

"The honor is yours, Warrior Trent," Inanna replied, her tone light, almost casual. "Who other than you is worthy? If our Watch is to be believed, you alone are responsible for the events that are unfolding. Our Clan's destiny, indeed, the future of the Clans, is changed because of the actions you have taken. None of our warriors have held such sway over the power structure of known space."

Trent had never framed his actions in such a way. *I never set out to change the universe. I simply wanted to restore the honor of my Clan, and for the Jaguars who strayed from the true path of Kerensky to pay the price for their insolence. That was all. Not...not what she is saying.*

Despite his resistance, there was no point in debating his life choices with Inanna. She saw him through her own goggles, attuned to the views of the Nova Cats. *Now that I am one of this Clan, I need to adopt their perspective.*

"You give me too much credit," he said in a low tone that betrayed his dark feelings. "What I am responsible for is the death of many warriors."

"*Neg*," Inanna replied. "You are responsible for the destruction of Clan Smoke Jaguar. You and you alone." Her voice held no judgment. Instead it was calm, factual, as if reading a passage from a book.

Trent stopped in mid-stride, as did his guide. "I prefer to believe that I have set matters right. The Jaguars had wandered far from the teachings of Nicholas Kerensky. They had lost every shred of honor. My leaders—*neg*—*their* leaders were brutal, and had sold their honor for power and prestige. I was left with no choice."

Inanna nodded once. "We all have a choice. I understand, as do your brothers and sisters in your new Clan. We saw what the Jaguars had become. As I saw matters unfold in my darkest dreams, others made your choice for you. You were the instrument that set many things in motion."

They passed two Nova Cat Star Commanders who saw him and nodded as if they knew him. His gaze lingered on them; their complete lack of surprise at seeing someone in the base wearing a ComStar jumpsuit confused him.

Inanna stopped in front of the Anhur. Above the personnel hatch was stenciled the logo of Alpha Galaxy. The motto, *Victory Over Delusion*, caught his eye more than the insignia's image of a Nova Cat twisted into a dragon's tail. *It will take time to get used to their customs and beliefs.* As a Smoke Jaguar warrior, he had learned to dismiss the mystical ways of the Nova Cats as proof of their weakness. He was beginning to see that their belief system intertwined with their path as warriors.

"They will shuttle you to our encampment," Inanna said.

Trent paused and looked inside, feeling almost wary of how he was being treated. *I have been called traitor for so long that I have allowed myself to believe it.*

"The Khan will expect you to be properly equipped with a 'Mech. What is your preferred configuration?"

Trent nearly chuckled aloud. It had been more than two years since he had piloted a BattleMech. ComStar had granted him access to simulators, but it wasn't the same as sitting in the cockpit. He was excited by the thought that he would pilot a 'Mech again. "My last one was an *Ebon Jaguar*. I also have experience in a *Timber Wolf*—at Tukayyid."

Inanna's forehead wrinkled. "The *Ebon Jaguar* is of Smoke Jaguar design, and is not one that we have available."

"I understand." He allowed himself a wry grin.

"Why the smile?"

"You seem to have such a grasp on things, so I assumed you already knew what kind of BattleMech I prefer."

Inanna's face stiffened. "My gift is a view through the veil of the future, Trent. I have remarkably little control over what I see. The past is for others to view, usually our Loremasters."

"I meant no offense, Inanna. I have only been a Nova Cat for a few minutes."

She nodded. "I sometimes forget that you have undergone a number of changes. 'The man who fights under four flags.'"

"Four flags?"

"I knew you were the one because I saw four flags in my vision, and a lone warrior beneath them. It is you. Smoke Jaguar, ComStar, Star League Defense Force, and now Nova Cat."

He had not thought of his journey in that context. "I sometimes forget the road I have chosen to walk. I hope your insight saw that this was the last flag I would fight under."

Inanna said nothing for a few seconds, enough to disturb him. *She is not telling me everything.* She checked her noteputer quickly, then locked her green eyes onto his own eye. "If you are to be of use to our Khan, you will need a BattleMech to pilot. I ask again, what is your preference, Star Captain?"

"I will be pleased with whatever 'Mech is available." Just talking about it made his excitement rise again. The time spent in simulators had honed his skill, but that was nothing compared to the feeling of raw power that a real BattleMech provided. *It is finally happening. I am fulfilling my dream of returning to battle.*

Inanna studied her pad. "We have a *Timber Wolf,* captured *isorla* from a trial with Clan Wolf. It is operational, but an older model. I also have a *Supernova* available for your use. Perhaps that will fulfill your needs better, *quiaff?*"

"*Neg,*" Trent replied. He had never piloted a 'Mech that large, but knew that it was a killing machine at ninety tons, and jump-capable. "As much as I would be honored to pilot a *Supernova*, I will take the smaller *Timber Wolf*. I am accustomed to it, and I am sure there are others more worthy of an assault-class 'Mech."

"You must do as you wish. If you are concerned that others would feel slighted by your taking the larger 'Mech, dismiss that thought. I doubt any would challenge you to a trial for it." Her voice rang with confidence.

"Is that not the Clan way, *quiaff?*"

Inanna offered another flash of a smile. "*Aff.* It is the Nova Cat way, however, to respect another's vision. Word of your arrival preceded you."

I must learn the ways of this Clan, and soon. Their reliance on visions and mysticism seems archaic. If this is indeed my new home, I must learn to trust their ways. "I would be wrong to refuse such an opportunity then. I accept the *Supernova*, if it is agreeable to those of my new Clan."

"Smartly bargained and done. I will arrange for us to train together, and I will brief you on our fighting formations and style differences. I will arrange for your codex to be updated, and that will grant you access to our entire complex."

Trent nodded. "Thank you."

"Thanks are unnecessary. You are a Nova Cat now, we share a bond that others cannot see or comprehend. I will be joining you shortly, after I take care of a few matters here on which the Khan has asked for my perspective. Should you need anything, contact me over our Galaxy's net." She bowed her head, as if he were somehow revered in her eyes.

If I need anything? Trent pondered. *I have been a foreigner, a traitor in the eyes of the Inner Sphere for the last two years. Now I am welcomed back into the Clans, albeit a Clan fighting against the other Crusader Clans.* It was almost too good to be true. The only thing that tempered his excitement was Khan Leroux's commitment that he would be fighting Clan Ice Hellion.

CHAPTER TWO

Trent juked hard right and felt the *Supernova* skid on the soil, digging a furrow with the side torque of his turn. The low center of gravity threw off his sense of balance, but he immediately realized his mistake and compensated, nearly to the point of overcompensating. The 'Mech listed uneasily in the high-speed turn, and for a millisecond he wondered if he was going to fall.

A lifetime of training took over his body. He maneuvered his left leg further out mid-stride, pushing the hip actuator to its maximum but giving him the support he needed on the turn. The ninety-ton 'Mech swayed but stayed upright as he turned his attention to the next leg of the course. Sweat formed on the left side of his face under his neurohelmet as he focused on sprinting ahead 200 meters, making a mental note on how to compensate for the next high-speed turn, based on his new understanding of the *Supernova*'s handling.

He made it through the next set of turns with no problem, gaining a little more confidence in handling tight turns at higher speeds. The assault 'Mech was no sprinter to begin with, but he had to learn its feel, its characteristics, and its limits if he was going to take on the Ice Hellions.

He came to a stop twenty minutes later in front of Inanna's *Mad Dog*. Her 'Mech was painted the same as his, a base of canvas tan with camouflaged streaks of browns and greens. The Jaguars in his former Cluster favored gray patterns, so seeing the *Mad Dog* standing in front of him reinforced that he was no longer in his former Clan.

The earpiece in his neurohelmet snapped as Inanna's voice came on. "Your pace was better than your last run, but still off from where it needs to be, Star Captain."

"*Aff*, I am aware," he replied with disappointment. Inanna had partnered with him to assist him in mastering his new 'Mech; in many respects, she was as demanding as a sibko trainer—minus the abuse. "The gait on this *Supernova* is taking me some time to master. It rides much lower than a *Timber Wolf* and its mass changes the energy it builds up in a sprint. I am having to unlearn as much as adapt to it."

"I suggest a break. You have done eleven laps...progressively faster and better on each one."

Trent wanted to press on, but as he flexed his legs, he felt an ache in his muscles. *I forget at times that I am older than many warriors. I do not want her or anyone else to think of me as anything other than prime.* Clearly, two years out of the cockpit had softened him, dulling some of his skills. "I agree. Let us run back to the bivouac and take in liquids there." He didn't wait for a response, immediately thrusting the massive *Supernova* forward into a run, its birdlike feet thundering on the ground under him.

Twenty minutes later, the pair arrived at the Nova Cat bivouac on the fringe of the rolling Duergar Plains. Trent felt the wash from the heat sinks as he climbed down. When he reached the ground, he patted the leg of the *Supernova* reassuringly, as if it were a pet rather than a machine of war. After hours of training in the simulator and the cockpit, he was developing a fondness for the capabilities of the 'Mech. With six extended-range large lasers, it could inflict considerable damage at long distances. After two full salvos on the move, however, the *Supernova* became an oven, overwhelming its heat sinks. He had already learned the key was to manage his heat carefully. It was easy to do in simulated combat: in a real firefight, the tendency to shoot whenever he had a shot could lead to the 'Mech shutting down if he was not careful.

They put their neurohelmets and coolant vests next to other warriors' gear on a table outside of a hard-shell temporary structure. Stripped down to their shorts, Trent saw the tight muscles on the compact Inanna. She caught him looking and flashed a narrow smile back. *It has been years since I have coupled with another.* That thought hit him like a well-aimed shot. *I have been so consumed with my circumstances in life, I have forgotten how to live.*

Looking down to avoid her gaze, he saw his right arm, a replacement for the one he had lost on Tukayyid. It was skinnier, wrapped in synthskin, looking more robotic than human. He reached up and touched his sunken right cheek, then lowered his hand. He did not need a mirror to remember the horrific damage he had suffered in the name of the Jaguars. *I am deformed. A twisted survivor of a failed crusade. While the scars mark my duty as a warrior, I am repulsive.* Thoughts of coupling with Inanna evaporated with the mental acknowledgment. His disfigurement was further physical proof of the failure of the Smoke Jaguars.

Inanna handed him a green bottle of what warriors called "Flush," a sweet-tasting drink packed with electrolytes and vitamins. He sat across from her, taking a long drink. Some of the fluid missed his reconstructed lower lip and dripped down onto his sweat-soaked chest.

Two more warriors sat on the bench seats, one next to him, one next to Inanna. They both had short black hair, apparently of the same genetic stock, though one of the men was old, even older than Trent. He recalled that Khan Leroux was older than him as well, and it struck him as odd. *The Smoke Jaguars spurn age; they treat it as a disease, a weakness. It was one of the reasons they discarded me. Here, things are different.*

"You are Trent, the former Smoke Jaguar, *quiaff*?" the younger of the pair asked.

Trent eyed him for a moment, then nodded. "*Aff.*" He wondered if an insult would be forthcoming; he expected one. So far, none of the Nova Cats except Inanna had engaged him in conversation other than simple greetings.

"I am Star Captain Clifford Keating," he said, extending his hand. Trent shook it with his bionic appendage. "This is Antony Oberg. We serve in the Keshik." Oberg nodded. "We saw you working with the *Supernova*. They can be tricky to handle at speed. Even trickier on landings when you fire up the jump jets," Keating said.

"*Aff*," Trent replied, relaxing slightly. "I practiced for an hour with the jets yesterday. Some of my landings were less than spectacular." While he had not fallen upon landing, he found the *Supernova* to be an ungainly 'Mech in the air.

"You will be fighting in my Binary," Star Captain Keating said. "We will need to incorporate you into our exercises. Our tactics are no doubt different than what you were used to in the Jaguars."

Inanna piped up. "He needs more practice, but he is ready for you, Star Captain." Trent looked across the table at her, and she allowed her deep green eyes to drift to him as she spoke.

"We should begin this afternoon, then," Keating replied. "Trent, have you ever fought Ice Hellions before?"

"*Neg.* I am familiar with their preferences in combat, but I have no experience against them."

"That is too bad," Oberg said. "Only two of our warriors have experience battling them."

"Khan Leroux has devised a plan for our trial," the Star Captain said. "One that will require us to turn their style of combat against them. I have been given a specific role in that battle, one I believe you can assist in."

"What is the plan?" Trent pressed.

The Star Captain leaned slightly toward him. "The Ice Hellions favor coordinated attacks and rely on striking with speed...a blitzkrieg. We know, from their comments during the bidding for this trial, that they despise our Clan and our leaders for our choice to support the Star League. Our Khans will be their primary objective—it is the nature of the Hellions. They will do what they can to kill them in battle."

Trent nodded as Star Captain Keating continued. "Our Khan has only bid his Keshik, a Binary, for this battle. Knowing this, they will direct the brunt of their assault at our Khans. Khan Leroux plans to draw the Ice Hellions to the far north end of the Duergar Plains along the edge of the Lyod Glacier.

"The glacier is a solid vertical wall of ice rising nearly one hundred meters. Along it are many canyons, narrow cracks that cut deep into the glacier itself. The wall will limit their maneuverability, something their tactics rely heavily on for a quick victory. We can use the walls of the glacier for cover. We shall gnaw at them one bite at time, hit them with distractions that will confuse them, and cause them to lose the cohesion that is one of their strengths."

"What if they do not drive toward the glacier?" Trent posed. "They are Ice Hellions, not ignorant bilge bores. They will realize the glacier is a trap. It is hardly something that they can ignore."

"*Aff*," Keating replied. "Khan Leroux will pilot his *Scytha* OmniFighter and will remain far enough back as to compel them to drive deep into our starting position. If need be, he will challenge Khan Asa Taney. The Hellions' hatred of Khan Leroux runs deep, and for Khan Taney, Leroux's leadership of our people is a direct personal affront. Such a challenge cannot be ignored. No matter what the risks, they will come at the Khan."

Trent understood far too well the rage a warrior could feel, and how it could nearly blind them. "Their battle will be in the skies, ours is on the ground. How do we ensure their defeat there?"

"Distraction combined with skill. While the Ice Hellions are under orders to destroy our Khans, the strength of their Clan is coordinated tactics. If any component breaks off or fails to follow the plan, their attacks become fragmented and easier to shatter. We need a distraction that would compel some of the Ice Hellions to abandon their designated plan. Something that is as great, if not greater, an affront to their honor as our Khans."

Trent felt the left side of his face blush as all eyes turned to him. *It is me. I am to be the distraction.* "You refer to me, *quiaff*?"

"*Aff*, Star Captain. You, the person who brought the Smoke Jaguars to heel. You, who are seen as a traitor to the Clan cause. You, who brought the Star League to our homeworlds. You are the perfect distraction."

"I prefer to see my role in the battle as contributing with my skill as a warrior, not merely as bait for the enemy," he replied flatly. *Is this the only way they see me as being useful,* quiaff?

This time it was Star Captain Keating who appeared embarrassed. "You misunderstand, Star Captain. Your being here can accomplish more than what Khan Leroux might be thinking. Your presence is exactly what we need to give us the edge. You will use your consummate skills in combat, as is our way. Your presence, however, will be too tempting for the Ice Hellions to ignore. Once they know you are here, their ire will boil to rage. Timed properly, spurring them into that rage could spell the difference between defeat and victory." His voice rang with respect, something Trent was still unused to.

"I am to announce myself to them, draw some of them to fight me rather than our Khans, *quiaff?*" he asked slowly, carefully, listening for subtext in their response.

"Affirmative, Star Captain. You will get the battle you seek. Some, if not all, of the Ice Hellions will be unable to resist going after you."

Trent considered the implications of what he was saying. Of course the Ice Hellions would come at him, the betrayer of not only the Smoke Jaguars, but of all of the Clans. They were now forced to fight a unified Star League for the right to conquer the Inner Sphere. That would have been impossible if he had not given the Exodus Road to ComStar. *I served up not only my own Clan to the Star League, but the whole of the Clan invasion effort.* He lowered his head slightly at the new insight that his role as traitor had such far-reaching effects.

"I mean no disrespect, Trent," the Star Captain continued. "Even you must admit that this plan of battle offers a good opportunity to confuse our foes at a critical moment."

"*Aff.* Assuming they know the role I played in matters. Other than a few Smoke Jaguars, none know who I am or what I have done." Trent's betrayal was not widely known. What was known was that the Smoke Jaguars had brought the wrath of the Star League to Clan space. How that had unfolded was something few seemed to question.

"We could let them know, in advance, that we have taken you in. We will tell them what you did. Their Watch will confirm it. Their Loremaster, Jonas Cage, has displayed little cunning in the past, but we will make it easy for him to confirm your placement and your presence in our Clan. This will further fuel their outrage. All that remains is for us to let them know you are actually on the field of battle. That is something we will surprise them with, at just the right moment—if you are agreeable."

From what he knew of the Ice Hellions' blitzkrieg approach to warfare, Trent thought the plan had merit. The thought of a Binary of warriors rushing at him gave him a pang of dread. It was never his intention to die in battle, only to fight once more. Trent's desire to be in combat again tempered that trepidation. If anything, the last few days' familiar strain on his muscles reminded him how much he loved combat.

"They will come at me for vengeance," he said coolly.

Both Nova Cat warriors nodded. "Some will," Antony Oberg said, "some will stick to their drive against our Khans. It will divide them and allow us to crush them."

"I have no desire to die, only to fight," Trent replied.

Inanna reached out and covered his left hand with her right. "Death stalks us all. It is the shadow of every true Clan warrior. You can no more shake it than you can your own shadow."

Trent turned to her, his bionically enhanced eyepiece showing her thermal readings, which made her seem to glow slightly in his gaze. "You have foreseen my death in this fight, *quiaff*?"

She said nothing for a moment, then met his eye. "The future is always unclear. I see you, the true man that you are, emerging from this fight." It was clear that she was choosing her words carefully.

"What say you, Trent?" Star Captain Keating asked. "I need to know, if I am to take this plan to our Khans."

Trent looked at Inanna then to the pair of Nova Cats. "I live to serve the true vision of Nicholas Kerensky. I am a Nova Cat, and my fate is intertwined with yours. I will fulfill the role you would have me play. Together, we shall crush the Ice Hellions."

"Well bargained and done," Keating replied, flashing a smile.

Trent rose to his feet and took a long gulp of his Flush. "I must go. I must use every hour possible to train for this task you have asked me to take as my own."

Inanna rose as well. "Go ahead, Trent, I will join you shortly."

Trent nodded once and walked off. His *Supernova* came into view, and seemed smaller to him now, more in his control. Having a role to play in the upcoming trial, and an important one, despite the risks, made him feel good. He understood that feeling: it was purpose.

As Trent walked away, Star Captain Keating turned to Inanna and his forehead immediately wrinkled. "Inanna, you did not tell him the truth."

Inanna looked back at Keating, and then at Oberg, and nodded. "How did you know?"

"Khan Leroux told me about these visions you had regarding Trent. You told the Khan that Trent was going to die at the hands of the Ice Hellions. I was there when you said it. You said that his death would be his final release, did you not, *quiaff*?"

Inanna nodded. "I did say that to the Khan, and more. He did not share with you all of what I saw in my visions."

"What are you withholding from us, from Trent?" Antony Oberg demanded. "He is one of us now, a brother warrior."

Inanna turned to the older warrior. "No one should know the details of their future. We as a Clan are just beginning to understand the ways of visions. I did not want to risk corrupting the future."

"He should know the truth," the Star Captain interjected. "If you knew my fate, *I* would want to know. It is only right—only fair."

Inanna put her fists on her hips in defiance. "These visions are mine to do with as I please. If you tell Trent what may happen to him, it will alter his path. He still has a greater role to play, even beyond death. If either of you choose to interfere, you may set things in motion that cannot be understood or controlled."

Keating shook his head. "It does not feel right to me."

"Nor to me," Inanna replied. "I feel no joy in these matters. You must trust my judgment. If you do not, we will face each other in a Circle of Equals, and I *will* win."

Star Captain Keating rose to his feet. "The path you are walking is dangerous, Inanna."

She glared back at him. "I know. The future, by its very nature, is perilous." She pivoted and walked off after Trent.

CHAPTER THREE

DUERGAR PLAINS, NEAR THE BASE OF THE LYOD GLACIER
STRANA MECHTY
THE KERENSKY CLUSTER, CLAN SPACE
23 APRIL 3060

A quarter of a kilometer behind Trent rose the Lyod Glacier—a dominating wall of ice that was cloudy at the top as the warmer season melted off the surface snow. Before him was an undulating sea of rolling hills covered in two-meter-tall green spring grasses that rippled in waves as the wind swept across them.

This was the day chosen for the Inner Sphere's Star League forces to face off against the Clans. At stake was the end of hostilities if the Clans lost. The Nova Cats had thrown in their lot with the Star League, which was nearly an act of war on its own. Trent had been surprised that in the last three days he had heard only minor griping about the decision, and those who did complain found themselves in Circles of Equals to battle for their spoken words. *As a people, they seem to have accepted the decision to face off against their former brethren for a sustained peace. They trust their leaders, which is something I can comprehend. If they fail, the Clans will come at them and devour them—purge them like the Unspoken Clan.* It added gravity to the battle that was to come for him. *Every shot counts in this fight.*

The Nova Cats had bid a Binary for the trial, the Keshik that was led by both Khans. They had been slightly underbid by the Ice Hellions. Trent had heard the rantings of Ice Hellion Khan Asa Taney. It had been filled with flowery bravado, none of which had impressed or frightened the Nova Cats.

"We, the Ice Hellions, following the true sight and path of Nicholas Kerensky, are proud to defend the honor of our people and our ultimate destiny: to rule the Inner Sphere. This false Star League is a deceptive ruse, a lie perpetrated for the sole purpose of a genocidal war against our brothers and sisters of the Smoke Jaguars.

"And whom do we face? A betrayer as sinister as Stefan Ukris Amaris, the Usurper: Clan Nova Cat. These traitors conspired with our enemies to bring about this trial. They stabbed the Smoke Jaguars in the back. Now they have in the ranks of their warriors the very snake, the Judas that sold out our people—the traitor Trent.

"We face them with honor, and will defeat them. When we are done crushing the rule of Khan Leroux and his ilk, we shall call for their annihilation. Against these forces, I bid one Star and three Points of the Seventh Attack Cluster. This shall be settled with blood and honor, in the name of the great Kerenskys. Our pack shall tear the meat from your very bones for your decision to side with this false Star League."

Trent was happy that Star Captain Keating's plan had worked thus far; the Ice Hellions knew he was in the Nova Cat force. Soon, at the right time, they would learn that he was on the field of battle, too.

Over an open frequency, Khan Leroux declined to shower his foes with prose. "Ice Hellions, we await you, if you have the intestinal fortitude to face us. We anxiously await the inevitable." There was something in the last sentence that struck Trent. *Does he know already if we are going to win or lose,* quineg?

The Nova Cat Khan switched to tactical channel two. "As we planned, Nova Cats. I shall see you in the mists of time..."

Before Trent could process what Leroux had said, Star Captain Keating's voice rang over the same channel. "Pouncer Star, per our plan, follow me."

He saw Keating's *Executioner* painted in the same colors as the waving sea of grass. Adorning the side of its cockpit was a Nova Cat emblazoned on the star of the Star League. The Khan had had each of the 'Mechs painted with the symbol, homage to the new League the Cats were fighting for. The lumbering *Executioner* led the charge to the west, and Trent followed.

There was a low roar overhead as a sleek OmniFighter raced toward where Khan Leroux circled in his *Scytha*. *If nothing else, the Ice Hellions are predictable.* The Hellion *Visigoth* left a twisting contrail in the sky over their position. He ignored the raging dogfight in the distance and focused on his own movements. *Leroux can take care of himself.*

Trent's *Supernova* tore up the sod as he followed Star Captain Keating. The rolling, grass-covered hills were deceptive. At first glance they appeared to be shallow hills and ridges, but the depressions were, in some cases, deep enough to conceal a BattleMech. They broke up the line of sight, forcing combat to be up close and personal.

Keating and the rest of his Star stopped. "Trent, proceed to Waypoint Bravo and wait there."

"*Aff*, Star Captain," Trent replied, and checked his tactical display, which mapped out the second waypoint, some three kilometers south into the rolling plains.

When he reached the designated waypoint, he stood in a depression between two massive hills that concealed him. Checking his display, he saw the red, pulsing lights marking the Ice Hellions hitting the Star commanded by the Nova Cat Khans. The aerospace fighter dogfight was only visible as contrails in the air, but the chatter on the tactical channel spoke of a vicious battle being waged.

The remainder of the Hellion assault bore down on the Khans while Star Captain Keating's Star, sans Trent, pivoted slightly, preparing to hit them in the flank. The Ice Hellions were moving fast, adhering to the straight line boring in on the glacier face where the Keshik defenses were anchored. *Their lust for vengeance makes them predictable.* That was something Trent understood. He had faced the same with his own Smoke Jaguars. Rage could cloud logic, thinking, and tactics.

"In position," Trent signaled. Watching the tactical display, he saw Khan Taney's red dot of light on the tactical display flicker off. A few seconds later the same happened to Khan Leroux's signal.

SaKhan Lucian Carns's deep, rolling voice came on the channel. "Khan Leroux has fallen. Now we shred these Hellions for supporting a false vision!"

A chorus of "*affs*" rang out on the channel, including Trent's.

Keating's voice came over the tactical channel. "Star Captain Trent, it is time. They are bleeding us here, one plate of armor at a time. Get their attention."

Trent found himself smiling as he switched to the broadband channel to transmit into the clear. "This is Star Captain Trent, formerly of Clan Smoke Jaguar. It is I who brought the Star League to your doorstep, Ice Hellions and the rest of the Clans. It is I who was the fuel on the funeral pyre of the Jaguars. It is I who gave the Exodus Road to your enemies. Come to me, if you have the courage!" He had gone over the statement several times in his head prior to the battle. As he said it, he did so with vigor and energy that he had not felt in a long time. *That should do it.*

On the tactical display, two red dots closed in on his position within a half-minute. Their reactor signatures and scans from the other Nova Cats told him what he was up against. *A Naga...they must have won it from Clan Wolf. That is their artillery support.*

The other approaching signal was a 100-ton *Dire Wolf*. Bristling with weapons, the OmniMech was a formidable foe. As a Smoke Jaguar, Trent had experienced the 'Mech up close many times. Even his *Supernova* seemed dwarfed near it.

One-on-one, these would be equals to his 'Mech. Two of them meant that he would have to be decisive in his victory. *I trained my entire life for this moment: a chance at redemption in a new Clan, one not marred by arrogance and brutality.* He hit the warmers on his six extended-range large lasers and flexed his muscles against his safety harness.

The first Ice Hellion to crest the ridge of hills was the *Naga*. It looked like a hooded cobra, with fanlike arms ending in boxy Arrow IV missile racks where its hands should be. It unleashed a pair of salvos the moment it locked onto him. The Arrow IV missiles roared through the air between them as Trent broke into a sideways run, heading perpendicular to the incoming warheads. It was to no avail; the explosions tore into his upper torso and right arm. Shards of armor fragments from the hit peppered his cockpit like hailstones.

"I am Benjamin Rood of Clan Ice Hellion. Prepare to die, defiler!" a voice broadcast on the direct channel in his neurohelmet's earpiece.

"Not yet," Trent replied, more to himself than his Bloodnamed foe. "You disappoint me, Rood. I expected better than you in response to the litany of my crimes against the Clans. Perhaps intelligence was something they forgot to mix into your iron womb."

The *Naga* paused in mid-step at his response. "You are unworthy of taunts, defiler. You are barely worth the ammunition needed to kill you."

"Words do not cut, but I will," Trent said through gritted teeth. His training brought to mind the *Naga*'s specifications. *If I'm going to take this out, I need to negate its firepower and maybe cook off its ammo.* The key was to concentrate his fire on the target 'Mech, not easy while being shot at.

He raised his right arm, bringing his targeting reticle onto the right arm of his enemy, and unleashed three of his large lasers. The searing crimson beams stabbed outward like lances, one hitting the center torso of the 'Mech, the others cutting deep, black scars in the hood and arm actuator, sending armor plates spinning off behind it.

The *Naga* sidestepped along the ridge of the line of hills, keeping its waist pivoted and locked on Trent. Trent ignored the slight rise in his 'Mech's temperature and reversed his stride as another salvo of Arrow IV missiles launched. He had timed it just right. Only one of the large missiles hit him, this time in his left leg. The explosion rocked his 'Mech while the other missiles hit the hillside behind him, sending a thundering concussion that pushed him forward as he coped with the hit to his leg. It altered his balance, and he had the presence of mind to hold his shot until he was sure he could make it count.

Raising both arms, he zoomed his targeting reticle in on the right side of the *Naga*. This time he unleashed four of his large extended-range lasers, once more favoring the right side of his target. One shot went high, just above the large hood of the *Naga*. One lanced again into the Hellion's center torso just under the cockpit. It made a crater-like hole there, shimmering red as it punched into the myomer muscles. Smoke curled out of the gouge he had burned.

The other two lasers hit the already-damaged torso and arm of the *Naga*. The impacts seemed to make the 'Mech stagger back, if only a half-step.

Trent juked his stride again, backstepping out of the shallow low ground and moving up the hillside opposite his Ice Hellion foe. The heat was now nearly impossible to ignore. *I have to manage this, give myself some time to cool.* He slowed his gait, then pivoted sideways.

The air between the two 'Mechs filled with the thin, snakelike smoke trails of Arrow IV missiles. One explosion tore up the sod behind him, raining grass and clumps of dirt on his *Supernova*, while a huge explosion tore into his right leg. The damage display chirped, and amber warnings appeared on the outline of his 'Mech's right thigh. Trent still held his fire as his 'Mech continued to vent heat.

He angled his climb along the hillside, gaining altitude as he moved. It was tempting to run, but he wanted to cool down as much as possible. He stopped suddenly, as another salvo rained down on him, one explosion rocking the left torso of his 'Mech and a blast hitting his right foot. The hit staggered him slightly, and he fought to maintain his balance. The Arrow missiles brutalized him with each impact. He checked his temperature, and a smile rose on his twisted lips.

It is time.

He switched the massive lasers in both arms to a single target-interlock circuit, allowing him to fire them all in one salvo. He knew the heat would hit a critical spike, but he ran the calculations in his mind unconsciously. Trent used the com stick to adjust the targeting reticle onto the center of the Ice Hellion 'Mech and fired.

There was a whining hum as the lasers fired and the air filled with scarlet beams stabbing out at his foe. One missed, going high into the air. The other five found their marks on the *Naga*.

The Ice Hellion's right torso erupted from within as the remaining missile ammunition cooked off from the damage. The destruction made the entire arm of the 'Mech go limp. Even with cellular ammunition storage, the explosion still did some damage to its torso.

The rest of the shots stitched into the body of the 'Mech just under the cockpit. The *Naga* seemed to shake violently—*damage to its gyro*. Trent's tactical display showed a severe heat spike in his foe's 'Mech. Either the lasers or the exploding ammunition had savaged the heart of the 'Mech, its fusion reactor. As his own cockpit became a furnace around him from the heat of the weapons fire, he stopped moving—mostly an attempt to bleed off some heat, but also some out of awe.

The vibrating *Naga* tried to step toward him, but it was as if the 'Mech itself was fighting Benjamin Rood. Its massive footpad wobbled, then locked up as the *Naga* fell. He thought it might topple over backward from the laser impacts, but instead it slumped forward, down the long slope of the hill. As it slid, it furrowed the turf with its shoulders as if they were bulldozers.

He might still stand up—still fight. Trent moved his *Supernova* forward slowly, his body wet with sweat except for where his coolant vest struggled to keep him conscious. His muscles, despite the last few days of working out, strained as he moved the 'Mech to point-blank range.

Trent's tactical display chirped a warning—the *Dire Wolf* was closing on his position. Trent switched one laser in his 'Mech's left arm to a single target-interlock trigger. He aimed it at the *Naga* as Benjamin Rood struggled to rock his crippled war machine to its side.

He fired at the rear left torso as the *Naga* finally rolled enough to get to its knees. He had to admire Rood—he was still fighting not only Trent but the laws of physics to try to kill him.

The brilliant red beam stabbed into the armor, searing a blackened hole. He aimed right at the loading hatch for the Arrow IV missiles—searing inward and setting off the remaining warheads and fuel housed there. There was a loud, semi-muffled *whump!* as the majority of the explosion blew out of the torso. The rest channeled into the already mauled internal structure of the *Naga*. Trent saw a momentary spike in his crippled foe's reactor heat, then a complete shutdown of the fusion reactor, leaving the powerless *Naga* crouched on one knee and one foot.

"Benjamin Rood, you are defeated," he said. Trying to ignore the wavering heat of his cockpit, he twisted to face the new threat. As he glanced at his tactical display, he came to the grim realization that he would not have enough time to cool down before the *Dire Wolf* was on him.

"I would rather be dead than face this indignity," Rood spat back.

Trent maneuvered his *Supernova* so the *Naga* was between him and the approaching *Dire Wolf*. He bent the knees of his 'Mech to lower its profile, using the *Naga* as cover. "Be quiet," Trent replied, "or I will make you my bondsman." It was one thing to have been beaten by Trent, quite another to be made his chattel.

The *Dire Wolf* lumbered over the crest of the hill. Looking like a forward-hunched man bristling with weapons, the 'Mech was painted in off-white and light-blue streaks, not entirely unlike lightning bolts, but somehow not quite the same. Dark-blue jagged striping, narrow and erratic, ran vertically like lightning-like camouflage, breaking up the lines of the 'Mech. Trent's tactical readout told him it was loaded out with lasers—medium pulse and extended-range large lasers like his own. The autocannons the *Dire Wolf* also carried made it even more menacing.

"Behold the defiler, cowering behind a Bloodnamed warrior. You truly have no honor in you, false Jaguar," a voice said over his broadband channel. "I am Star Captain Adam Bragg, and I am here to kill you, traitor."

Trent eyed his heat levels. *Time...I need more time.* "You call me a traitor, yet you know nothing of me. What I have faced—what I have endured. I am not a traitor to the vision of Nicholas Kerensky, I am its keeper," he said, goading Bragg into conversation rather than combat. He knew that as he spoke, Star Captain Bragg was adjusting his targeting reticle on the *Supernova*, preparing to unleash a barrage. The only thing holding him back was that he might hit his fellow Ice Hellion.

"If that were the case, you would not be hiding behind a true warrior. Benjamin Rood will not protect you. You are and will always be a coward. Step out, Trent. If you are indeed what you say, prove it in battle."

He is right; he could still hit me despite the cover. It is enough to give him pause, and that purchases time for me to cool.

His tactical channel crackled to life for a moment. "Trent, we are on our way to your position. The plan worked. Your contact is the only

Ice Hellion left standing." Star Captain Keating's voice was oddly reassuring. Trent saw on his tactical display that the Star Captain was still precious minutes away. *I have fulfilled my role, and have proven to the Nova Cats that I am still worthy of being a warrior.*

"You could fire now," he taunted Bragg.

"*Aff*, I could. My aim is exceptional. I have no desire for Benjamin Rood to suffer further insult and injury in this contest. It is enough that he was defeated by a character as low as you. Step out, and we shall end the façade that is your life. Stand tall, and I will kill you quickly."

His taunts made Trent grin. *We are a people given to bravado and poetry when it comes to battle.* He waited for a few seconds, then rose slowly to the full height of his *Supernova*. His lower torso was still protected by Rood's kneeling *Naga*, but he was standing upright, ready for battle. "You question my honor, *quiaff*?"

"*Neg.* I say you have none, now or ever. You have sold out our people to a false Star League. You have cast your own blood into the ashbin of history by stabbing them in the back. For that, you will die."

Trent watched his heat drop into the green. "So be it, Star Captain Bragg," he said, assigning three lasers to two of his target-interlock triggers. He stepped to the side of Rood's *Naga*.

Bragg opened fire as he charged down the hill with a speed that pushed the Clan OmniMech to its limits. The emerald-green pulse lasers peppered Trent's *Supernova* in several spots, while one of the large lasers came so close to its mark that it seared the camouflage paint on Trent's right arm. The pulse lasers tore into his 'Mech's hulking body, pockmarking numerous armor plates.

Trent extended his right arm and brought his targeting sight onto the looming *Dire Wolf*, unleashing three of the large lasers. The red beams lanced into the assault OmniMech, hitting it on the left side, in the leg, and carving a scar up its torso. As the heat rose, Trent stepped again, moving sideways to the charging *Dire Wolf*, trying to maintain some distance.

Bragg did not relent. He fired his four large lasers and his pair of autocannons, catching Trent as his eyes darted to his heat readout. The autocannon rounds rocked his 'Mech hard, almost toppling him to the side, and the two of the large lasers tore into his left arm while the others hit his legs. Looking out of his cockpit, he saw smoke rising from his left arm, and the yellow damage indicator on his display flashed to crimson.

Trent swung both of his arms toward the Ice Hellion and adjusted his trigger settings, firing four of his lasers. One missed, hitting near the left foot of the *Dire Wolf* and flaming the grass. Two of the beams hit the rounded left leg of the 'Mech, gnarling the armor and twisting it under the heat. The other hit the *Dire Wolf* in the cockpit just above the canopy, causing the 'Mech to jerk momentarily to one side. *That seems to have gotten Bragg's attention.*

The Ice Hellion warrior moved in beside Rood's *Naga* and fired another barrage of pulse lasers. Two hit his 'Mech's bulky body, the emerald bursts searing off small chunks of armor and sending them flying. One hit his left torso, the other hit his left arm. A warning light flared on his damage display. Two of his lasers were out of commission from the impact. Trent killed the power feed to those weapons. *At least that will help my heat buildup.*

Trent brought two of his right-arm lasers onto a trigger and fired, aiming for the *Dire Wolf*'s legs. Both hit the already-damaged left leg, one high and one low. The upper one left a nasty blackened gouge in the armor up into the crotch of the OmniMech, while the other simply burned in deep. A thin green ooze boiled out of the hole—coolant.

Star Captain Bragg fired his autocannons, both into Trent's left side. One hit his damaged arm, while the other hit his leg. His last laser on the left side was lost in the assault, as was most of the arm from the elbow actuator down. The forearm flew off in bits and pieces, leaving a bundle of dangling myomer and bits of internal structure dangling in the air.

Another pair of large lasers followed the autocannon shell impacts, slicing across his *Supernova*'s center torso just under his cockpit. Trent's body ached against his restraining straps. Damage indicators flickered from yellow to red as he staggered under the barrage. The *Supernova* fought him, and he tried to compensate for the shift in his center of gravity from losing the arm, but overdid his efforts. His 'Mech toppled, falling backward, mangling his rear armor in the process.

Trent was tossed hard against his safety harness, and despite the padding, it dug deep into his left shoulder. His coolant vest tore open and began leaking, the stench of the gel penetrating his neurohelmet. Immediately, instinctively, he extended the right arm of the 'Mech and tried to get to his feet.

Bragg did not relent as Trent struggled to stand the *Supernova*. Damage warnings flashed in Trent's heat-soaked cockpit as pulse lasers peppered his legs and torso, melting armor plating as he rocked the 'Mech to its side, then slowly got to its feet. His muscles protested every move.

As he rose to his full height, another barrage of autocannon fire blasted his right arm and center torso. Each round exploding on his Omega Heavy Stellarguard armor made the big Nova Cat 'Mech quake and rattle. There were other explosions, too, hitting everywhere—long-range missiles. Even at this range they speckled damage all over his *Supernova*. His damage display readout showed almost every part of his 'Mech was damaged, badly in some areas.

He unleashed his remaining trio of large lasers at the looming *Dire Wolf*, which seemed to walk toward him almost casually, closing the distance to a brutal point-blank range. It would be nearly impossible for Bragg to miss. Trent's scarlet lasers seared into the left torso of the Ice Hellion, punching deep. There was a low, thunderous rumble as he hit the long-range missiles stored there. While the force of the blast channeled out the rear of the 'Mech, it still tore a nasty hole and ricocheted some internal damage. Black smoke billowed out of the laser holes.

If the damage shook the Ice Hellion warrior, he did not show it. Instead, Bragg let go with another pair of large lasers, ravaging Trent's already riddled legs. His right knee actuator protested as he tried to backstep to keep some distance from the advancing *Dire Wolf*, an indication that the damage was worse than his readout was telling him.

His training and combat experience told him he was losing the fight. Between the damage from the *Naga* and what the *Dire Wolf* had poured into him, he was on the edge of complete destruction. He checked his tactical display and saw two Nova Cat 'Mechs closing on his position—but a mental calculation told him they were still too far to be there in time. His options were diminishing with each beat of his heart.

"This has come to an end, traitor," Adam Bragg's voice boomed. "I shall be written in *The Remembrance* for slaying the great Betrayer of the Clans." He closed to thirty meters and seemed to hold his fire for a few seconds, no doubt cooling down before unleashing a killing salvo of hellfire.

Trent licked his lips and tasted the salt in the corners of his mouth. Glancing down at his damage display, he saw there was still one system he had not used.

"Perhaps," Trent replied on the open channel, half hoping the other Nova Cats were listening in. His jaw locked and his teeth gritted as he managed the next words. "Perhaps not."

He fired his 'Mech's jump jets.

The thrust to lift the 'Mech into the air was considerable and the jets' range was short—but Bragg had gotten so close Trent felt he couldn't miss. Heat rippled through the scorching cockpit as his *Supernova* took off straight at the *Dire Wolf*. Trent ignored the blast of heat and concentrated on his enemy.

Star Captain Bragg seemed stunned for a moment, but regained his composure and unleashed his weapons one after the other, trying to pluck Trent from the air as he loomed up and over him. The *Dire Wolf*'s pulse lasers tore off the last bits of the *Supernova*'s leg armor and the autocannon hit Trent's right arm, taking out a laser.

Trent felt the 'Mech rock in the air and saw two of the large lasers streak into the sky near him, while the other punched a cut deep into his *Supernova*'s torso, searing a heat sink in the process. He didn't waver, though, fighting the com sticks and foot pedals with the skill that came from a lifetime of Clan training.

As he came over the *Dire Wolf*, he killed the jets, dropping down like a 90-ton pile driver on his Ice Hellion prey. He felt the jarring impact under his right footpad, and the *Supernova* toppled off to the right side. There was a tremendous grinding sound, metal and armor twisting and protesting as the two 'Mechs collided. He felt weightless, if only for a millisecond, as his entire body weight slammed into his safety harness.

The *Supernova* toppled to the ground, the grass filling his cockpit view as he went facedown. Darkness and the crimson damage display dominated his view through the hot air all around Trent.

He checked his tactical display and saw that the *Dire Wolf* was down as well, only a few meters away. He had done a great deal of damage to the Ice Hellion 'Mech, but had failed to come down on its cockpit and crush it.

Trent pushed with the stump of his 'Mech's mangled left arm to twist to the side. His right leg was slow to respond, then he saw why. The knee actuator was gone. Like his left arm, his leg had been blown away. It would make standing difficult, if not impossible. Regardless, he tried. *My entire life has been about doing the impossible.* He knew Star Captain Bragg would be attempting to stand, too.

Trent got to his knees, and daylight streamed through his fractured cockpit canopy. Twisting his torso and pushing off, this time with his right arm, he managed to shift his weight out enough to rise. He stood on one leg, with one arm, his 'Mech mangled, burned, and blown apart. What little armor he still had was random plates that looked like islands in a sea of carnage, all twisted metal and seared myomer bundles.

As the heat slowly dissipated, Trent twisted slightly to turn enough to see the *Dire Wolf*. He had come down on its right side, shearing down the torso and into the arm. It hung limp at the side of the Hellion's 'Mech, twisted and dangling off a lone myomer muscle that was sparking from electrical damage. The autocannon barrel was twisted and dragging on the ground as Bragg moved like a drunken freebirth.

Trent had two large lasers left, though he wondered how reliable they might be, given the condition of the arm. He raised his arm and fired them both, embracing the wave of heat that hit him. The shots both found their mark, hitting the already-mauled leg of the *Dire Wolf* and sending a gray cloud of smoke rising from what was left of its hip actuator. Bragg's attempt to move was in vain—the hip seized and melted into place.

"You fought well, traitor, but no one will ever know. Now, before you die, know that I will tell them that you pleaded with me in the end. That you begged for *bondsref*. I will tell your brethren that in the end, you turned on them, sold them out, told me they were followers on a misguided path of ruin. You will be remembered as a criminal, and your name will be spoken only in the same breath as the Usurper's." Bragg raised his remaining arm slightly and fired.

The autocannon rounds shattered Trent's fusion reactor. He saw it go offline and felt his *Supernova* start to topple. The cockpit exploded all around him, torn by lasers and autocannon rounds. Cool air rushed in as the 'Mech fell hard to the ground. Smoke and pain greeted him. For a moment he blacked out, almost happy to embrace the darkness. *I died a true warrior, but no one will know.* He coughed and tasted the coppery hint of blood on his gnarled lips.

In the darkness, he experienced a flashback to Tukayyid, where he had been so badly burned and injured. The feelings were nearly the same, though the pains were in different parts of his body.

He opened his human eye; his bionic one didn't respond. Blood filled half of it, oozing in his neurohelmet. He tried to wipe it away, but his arm sent a hot ripple of pain to his brain. Coughing, more blood came up. *Broken ribs–punctured lung.* From the way his head was twisted, he saw his bionic arm, now burned off just below the shoulder—probably from a pulse laser hit.

The canopy of his cockpit was gone, torn open to the sky. He saw the *Dire Wolf* still standing in the distance. Trent tried to shift his body, but the agony was too great. His vision tunneled, and a tinny sound filled his ears. *Is this death?*

There was an explosion in the distance, and a plume of fire and smoke rose from behind the Ice Hellion 'Mech. His Nova Cat brothers and sisters—they had arrived!

Trent grinned as the *Dire Wolf* fell forward, crashing some dozen meters from his broken cockpit. His last moment of consciousness before the tunnel of light collapsed on him was the sight of a Nova Cat *Timber Wolf* standing on the hill in the distance.

I am ready now to face death...

Then the darkness took him and pulled him down.

LOOKING FOR MORE HARD HITTING BATTLETECH FICTION?

WE'LL GET YOU RIGHT BACK INTO THE BATTLE!

Catalyst Game Labs brings you the very best in *BattleTech* fiction, available at most ebook retailers, including Amazon, Apple Books, Kobo, Barnes & Noble, and more!

NOVELS

1. *Decision at Thunder Rift* by William H. Keith Jr.
2. *Mercenary's Star* by William H. Keith Jr.
3. *The Price of Glory* by William H. Keith, Jr.
4. *Warrior: En Garde* by Michael A. Stackpole
5. *Warrior: Riposte* by Michael A. Stackpole
6. *Warrior: Coupé* by Michael A. Stackpole
7. Wolves on the Border by Robert N. Charrette
8. *Heir to the Dragon* by Robert N. Charrette
9. *Lethal Heritage* (The Blood of Kerensky, Volume 1) by Michael A. Stackpole
10. *Blood Legacy* (The Blood of Kerensky, Volume 2) by Michael A. Stackpole
11. *Lost Destiny* (The Blood of Kerensky, Volume 3) by Michael A. Stackpole
12. *Way of the Clans* (Legend of the Jade Phoenix, Volume 1) by Robert Thurston
13. *Bloodname* (Legend of the Jade Phoenix, Volume 2) by Robert Thurston
14. *Falcon Guard* (Legend of the Jade Phoenix, Volume 3) by Robert Thurston
15. *Wolf Pack* by Robert N. Charrette
16. *Main Event* by James D. Long
17. *Natural Selection* by Michael A. Stackpole
18. *Assumption of Risk* by Michael A. Stackpole
19. *Blood of Heroes* by Andrew Keith
20. *Close Quarters* by Victor Milán
21. *Far Country* by Peter L. Rice
22. *D.R.T.* by James D. Long
23. *Tactics of Duty* by William H. Keith
24. *Bred for War* by Michael A. Stackpole
25. *I Am Jade Falcon* by Robert Thurston
26. *Highlander Gambit* by Blaine Lee Pardoe
27. *Hearts of Chaos* by Victor Milán

NOVELLAS

1. *A Splinter of Hope* by Philip A. Lee
2. *The Anvil* by Blaine Lee Pardoe

ANTHOLOGIES

1. *Shrapnel: Fragments from the Inner Sphere*
2. *Onslaught: Tales from the Clan Invasion!*
3. *The Corps* (BattleCorps Anthology vol. 1)
4. *First Strike* (BattleCorps Anthology vol. 2)
5. *Weapons Free* (BattleCorps Anthology vol. 3)
6. *Fire for Effect* (BattleCorps Anthology vol. 4)
7. *Counterattack* (BattleCorps Anthology vol. 5)
8. *Front Lines* (BattleCorps Anthology vol. 6)
9. *BattleTech: Legacy*

www.ingramcontent.com/pod-product-compliance
Lightning Source LLC
Chambersburg PA
CBHW070825180626
46818CB00001B/402